The Real Hoodwives
of Detroit

The Real Hoodwives
of Detroit

INDIA

URBAN BOOKS

www.urbanbooks.net

Urban Books, LLC
300 Farmingdale Road, NY-Route 109
Farmingdale, NY 11735

The Real Hoodwives of Detroit

ISBN 13: 978-1-64556-158-3
ISBN 10: 1-64556-158-5

First Mass Market Printing May 2021
First Trade Paperback Printing December 2019
Printed in the United States of America

10 9 8 7 6 5 4 3 2 1

Distributed by Kensington Publishing Corp.
Submit Orders to:
Customer Service
400 Hahn Road
Westminster, MD 21157-4627
Phone: 1-800-733-3000
Fax: 1-800-659-2436

Chapter 1

Nikki (The Boss's wife)

What up, doe! I'm Nikkita, but everybody calls me Nikki. I've lived in Detroit all of my life, born and raised on West Seven Mile. I love my hood and where I'm from, but life for me was no picnic, so I had plans to get out of the city right after high school. I hustled hard by selling the expensive items that I boosted from high-end department stores. I saved my money and planned to be out the very night that I graduated; but halfway through my senior year, I met a man that I knew I would never be able to let go of or leave behind. His name was Mario, and to be honest, he had me wide open. Not only was he 6 feet 6 inches, brown-skinned, with beautiful jet-black wavy hair that hung way past his shoulders and an award-winning smile that belonged on a Colgate commercial, but he was also a sweetheart, and he treated me like a queen. See, when you come from a broken home where nobody says "I love you" or shows you any kind of affection, you want to hold on to the first person that does, and for me, that was Mario.

We dated the rest of our senior year and moved in together shortly afterward. Rio, that's what I call him, took care of me, and I went from rags to riches the day that he became my man. I had a little money saved myself, but he had stacks on top of stacks. Rio was heavy in the drug game, and it didn't faze me not one bit, because I'd been around drugs my whole life. My mother sold pills and a little ecstasy from time to time to make ends meet and keep herself fly, so I wasn't new to the game, and I knew the rules. Hell, sometimes I would even pitch in and make runs for him. That's just how down I am for the cause.

One day, to my surprise, Rio popped the question, and of course, my answer was yes. We've been married now for ten years, and it's been nothing but love. Three months ago, we had our first child, Rio Jr., and we're planning to leave this game before our lucky streak runs out. With all the shit going on in the D, hopefully our family makes it out before our time is up!

Chapter 2

Tonya (The Hater)

Hey, I'm Tonya. What's good? I see you been hanging out with Nikkita! That bitch thinks that she and her husband Mario can't be fucked with, but they will find out real soon that they shit ain't as solid as they think it is. I'm a eastside bitch, so I fights for mine, and as soon as my baby daddy, Roscoe, get out of jail, we're going to teach those muthafuckas a lesson, and you can bet on that! Me and Roscoe have three kids together—Shana, Roscoe Jr., and Ciara. As soon as he touch down, we're going to have a few more, because he wants a big family. "More soldiers for the family hustle," he jokes. I love that man's dirty drawers, and he knows it.

We met at a club downtown a few years back. We got a hotel room that night, and the rest is history. I hope that you don't think I'm easy, but if you do, I don't really give a damn. When you see that sexy chocolate thug with muscles out the ass, you'll see exactly why I love him like I do. Our relationship ain't been perfect, but I know that I don't want to let him go, and I'm willing to do whatever he asks me to just to prove to him that I can play my position.

He should be gettin' out soon, and I can't wait until the day he comes home, because it's gonna be some smoke in the city. He and Mario started the H.O.F. organization together, which stands for Hand Over Fist, and they were partners until he caught a case for the possession of narcotics and intent to distribute to an undercover officer. We think that Mario's ass set him up, because that nigga has been doing nothin' but shining while his partner's family sits over here and struggle. Roscoe has been gone for five years, and Mario has only dropped off a little money here and there in between that time, so you know we've got to get even by any means necessary.

Chapter 3

Chloe (The Protégé)

Welcome to Detroit! I'm Chloe, a real down-ass chick straight off of Schoolcraft. I've been rollin' with my man Sam for two years, and I just know that we gon' be the next Bonnie and Clyde. Right now, he works for Nikki's husband, Mario, and we're cool with that. Mario is a fair businessman, and he treats his workers good. Mario and Nikki are well respected in the Detroit dope game and, quite frankly, I'm addicted to his hustle. That shit keeps me in designer names, so I make sure that Sam is always on top of his job and never gets caught slipping. I tell him, "If we want to be the best, we've got to hang around the best." And right now, hands down, the best is Nikki and Mario.

When Sam and I first started to date, he was a damn car wash attendant, and I would've been left his minimum-wage-making ass, but he was too damn fine! He was brown-skinned, basketball-player tall, with beautiful teeth, and his swag was all the way turned up. Not to mention the fact that he was tatted up like the subway in Harlem, as my girl B put it in one of her songs. One night, he talked about how he wanted to get into the game and make money to take care of me, and of course you know that I encouraged him to take action. He made good on his word by joining the H.O.F. organization as a runner, later working his way up to Mario's right-hand man, and he has been taking care of me ever since.

I help him whenever he needs me to, just as I saw my mother do with my father years ago. My whole family was in the game. Currently, my brother is doing time behind bars. My mother died a hustler's wife, and I planned to do the same. My father died in the penitentiary, as state property, and I *refused* to let that happen to *my* man. You see, I'm not new to this. I was born into this lifestyle, so I know how this works. I help cook the product, bag it up, and sometimes I even distribute to the trap houses. I know that some people would frown on the way I live my life, but I also know if the tables were turned, they would do the same in a heartbeat. I understand that this lifestyle had its ups and downs, but no risk no rewards, right? I don't mind playing dirty if I have to, and that's a fact.

Chapter 4

Mina (The Innocent Bystander)

You're at the point of no return now. My name is Mina, and I've been in Detroit for about five years. I ended up here after following my husband, Tre', from our hometown of Cincinnati, Ohio. We relocated here to escape a very bad situation back home. Tre' got robbed one night and ended up losing a huge package that belonged to his boss, a very powerful man named Warren. Zeke, Tre's right-hand man, told us Warren wasn't trying to hear that he was robbed, so he put out a hit on Tre' and me. Needless to say, we left our home in the middle of the night and never looked back as soon as we heard that news. Our plan was to head to Canada, but we got turned around at the border because we didn't have our birth certificates. Without any other options, we decided to stay in Detroit until things blew over.

After a year of staying low key, we had gotten into the swing of things and later found out I was pregnant with our son, Tre'von. Tre' decided to go legit and open up a business with the money we had saved during his hustlin' years. We opened up a clothing boutique. Things were going good until six months after our son was born. Tre'von died in his sleep from Sudden Infant Death Syndrome (SIDS). That tore us up and really damaged our relationship. We barely talked some days. For about two years, I shopped like a maniac for therapy, while Tre' turned to drugs for comfort. So, our money dwindled down to almost nothing.

Finally, not wanting to lose the other man in my life, I snapped out of my grief-stricken trance. I fought hard to get my husband back and get him clean. So far, I'm a success, but this morning Tre' told me he wants to get back into the game and hustle. I'm scared to death that if he's around drugs, he'll relapse, but what can I do? I have no one or nowhere to turn to for help, so I guess I'll have to ride this one out.

Chapter 5

Gucci (The Boss's Best Friend)

What up? Welcome to my city. I'm Gucci, and no, that's not a fuckin' nickname. That's exactly what my mama named me, and you can believe that my name rings bells around this city. See, I ain't your average girl. I been out here hustlin' with the big boys ever since I was sixteen. Shit, all I know how to do is hustle, and no matter what the consequence, my mission is always to get it. I work with my best friend, Mario, and his wife, Nikki, by day, but by night, I dance at the Doll House. I'm single and loving it! I ain't settlin' down until I'm good and ready. The nigga that I marry must definitely have stacks on deck 'cause I can do *broke* all by myself.

I'm hated by most but confronted by none, and that's how it's always been. You ask anybody in Detroit about Gucci, and they'll tell you, "Shorty ain't to be fucked with." I'm small, but I ain't nothing nice. I live the good life and will take anybody out that threatens to put me or my people in danger, which is exactly why I can't stand that bitch Tonya! The streets is talkin' and they sayin' she's plottin' on my peoples. That shit ain't cool, and she know it. Her raggedy-ass baby daddy ain't made for this shit, and he got caught up, plain and simple. She wants to blame everybody else for her troubles instead of that punk-ass nigga Roscoe.

I'm glad Mario ain't his partner anymore, because he was nothing but a liability, and Mario is too much of a real nigga to be associated with a fuck-up like him. I speak highly of Mario because he got it like that! He was the man of my dreams, and we messed around a few times, but then he met Nikki and never looked back. It didn't faze me, because I knew she was good for him and Nikki had his back, but I've always been his bottom bitch. Until they put me in the ground, I'll continue to ride wit' him. I'm ready for whatever, whenever, and wherever.

Chapter 6

Nikki

"Hey, Rio," I answered when my cell phone rang. I knew that it was my husband because of the ring tone.

"What up, Nikki? What you doing?" he asked in his gruff tone.

"Nothing, boo. Just paying the bills as usual. What's good?" I said while putting the checks inside of the envelopes for the electric, cable, and phone companies.

"I need you to go upstairs and take four thousand from the safe to give to Gucci when she gets there."

"Why?" I asked with a bit of an attitude.

I liked Gucci, and she had never crossed me, but for some reason, I was always a little defensive when it came to her. She had been my husband's best friend since they were kids. He even told me that they messed around a few times, but he said that he never had serious feelings for her. I believed him and took him at his word because I had no reason not to, although she *was pretty and petite*. She was about 5 feet even, light-skinned, and very curvy. She always kept herself up, which made me stay on top of my shit, even though I knew I looked good my damn self. I was 5 feet 5 inches, caramel toned, and curvaceous. A lot of people have said that I remind them of the singer Alicia Keys, but I'm just a little thicker in the thighs and around the waist.

"Because, Nikki, today is the day that she goes and puts money in the commissary accounts of our team that's locked up," he said.

After returning my attention back to the phone call, I smiled because my husband always looked after his people. He made sure their accounts stayed full and their families stayed comfy. Feeling stupid, I said, "Oh, yeah. I forgot that it's been a month already. My bad, baby."

"Yeah, this month did go by quick. Hopefully, we don't lose any more of our soldiers. Nikki, Detroit is gettin' wild. Niggas is either dyin' to eat out there or gettin' locked up left and right," he added.

I thought about Li'l D, the young man whose funeral we had just paid for. He was a nineteen-year-old who was shot in the head while walking his grandmother home from her church service, which was just three doors down from her house. The shooter was still at large, but a few of the spectators and churchgoers said the killer looked to be no more than about twelve or thirteen. I shook my head at what my city had become and the type of children that we were producing. On one hand, it was unbelievable and repulsive; but on the other hand, it was almost expected in the hood for these children to step up to the plate and put food on the table. For the boys, it was either dealing or killing, and for the girls, it was stripping or tricking!

"I know, Mario. Detroit is gettin' wild, and people are going ape shit in this economy." I chimed back into the conversation.

Then, as I was speaking of how wild things are, I switched gears. "Babe, have you talked to Roscoe?" I asked, thinking about Rio's old partner. He should have been gettin' out soon, and I wanted to make sure that he and Rio were on good terms. I didn't want Rio to have any beef with the nigga because his baby mama, Tonya, made it seem like we weren't paying her the whole time that he was locked up. Hell, just because that bitch was sneaky, I'd been keeping copies of the checks that we gave her every month, which to date, totaled about two hundred thousand dollars.

"Naw, I haven't talked to him, but I am going to reach out soon. Don't worry about it." He seemed to just brush it off.

"Mario, make sure that you do, because we don't need that drama when he get out. Me and you have come too far to get messed up at the finish line." I said it, and I meant it from the bottom of my heart. I wasn't no fool. We had beaten the odds so far, and I often wondered every night as I laid my head down when our time would be up.

"Nikki, don't worry. I'm gonna handle it, but, baby, I have to go. Gucci should be by there soon. Be nice," he said, and we disconnected the call.

I went up the white semi-spiraled staircase and entered the spare bedroom that we used as our office and slid the black file cabinet over to reveal the floor safe. After carefully putting in the combination, I removed approximately four thousand in neat, crisp stacks. I slid the file cabinet back over the safe then headed into Rio Jr.'s room because I heard him wake up from his nap, letting out a huge wail.

"What's the matter with my big boy?" I asked as I entered the room. I picked him up and placed him on the changing table to dispose of the stinky diaper. I loved my son. He was beautiful, just like his father. After his diaper change, I picked him up and placed him on my shoulder as he began to coo at me. "Aw, Junior, Mommy loves you too."

Just as I made it back downstairs to retrieve the bottle that I'd prepared for Junior while doing the bills, I heard a car pull up, bumping Trey Songz as loud as possible. I didn't have to check the security camera to know that it was Gucci. Loud music was her trademark. I grabbed the bottle and headed to the door.

"Hey, come on in," I said with a forced smile on my face.

She looked fierce as always in her Seven jeans and a pink halter top that barely covered her nipples. Her coal black hair was pulled up into a tight ponytail, her eyebrows and eyelashes were perfect, not to mention the fact that her makeup was flawless. To be honest, she was almost the picture of perfection. I say *almost* because her ghetto ass was standing there chewing and smacking on her bubble gum like it was going out of style.

"What up, doe. Hey, little Mario," she said as she entered, patting Junior on his back.

We made our way into the informal living room. She took a seat on the black leather sectional, and I sat next to her to feed the baby.

"I love this house, girl." She admired the taupe room with the red accent wall. Adorning the walls were various pieces of African American art. Continuing, she said, "As soon as I find Mr. Right, I'll make sure that he gets me one, and I'll have you decorate it for me." She smiled.

"Yeah, that's no problem. Just let me know when you find him, and I will hook you up, girl. You know that's one of our side businesses, so whenever you need me, I got you," I said with more enthusiasm than I actually felt.

We talked for about five more awkward minutes before she got right to the point.

"So, you got that for me?" She looked at her pink Coach watch like she had somewhere else to be, and I was glad.

"Oh, yeah, I don't want to hold you up. Here it is," I said, pulling the money out of my back pocket and handing it over to her along with the check for Tonya.

"Cool. I guess I'll go ahead and take care of this business. Where is Mario?" she asked, looking around the house as if she didn't already know that he wasn't here.

I mean, why else would I be the one to give her the money?

"He had to step out for a bit," I said and stood with her.

She bent down to kiss Junior on his cheek and then told us bye.

I knew I was still trippin', but that girl had another side to her that had yet to be shown. I didn't want beef with my husband by dissin' his best friend, so I tolerated her but kept her at a safe enough distance. I'd seen her damage plenty of homes over Detroit and its surrounding areas, and I'd be damned if I let her ruin mines. That bitch wasn't as slick as she thought she was. I was hip to her ass, and she knew I was not the one to be fucked with!

Chapter 7

Chloe

"Damn, baby, you smell good," Sam said as he walked up to me and hugged me from behind.

"You do too, baby. Where are you going?" I quizzed because just a few moments ago, I'd left him in the bed sleeping, and now his ass was fully dressed and smelling good. Don't judge me, but my man was fine, so I had to keep tabs on him like that! I wanted to know everything: where he was going, what he was going to do while he was there, and, of course, who he was doing it with.

"Mario is on his way over here to scoop me up. We got some shit to handle," he said as he adjusted the collar on his Black Label button-up.

"What kind of business?" I wanted to know.

"Chloe, you know I can't tell you all that," he said and then went into our cramped bathroom to brush his teeth. Both of us wouldn't be able to fit in there together comfortably, so I remained in the hall and went right into my next discussion.

"Sam," I whined. "We need a bigger place. I mean, shit, only one of us can fit in there at a time." I pointed at the bathroom.

"Damn, just chill. I ain't trying to have beef with you today. Girl, we talked about this last night, and we both agreed that it's going to take some time before we can save enough money to get up out this two-bedroom apartment," he said in his usual calm manner.

He was right about that. We had talked about it last night, *but* this morning was entirely different, so I continued.

"Sam, look at this place. With the kind of money you makin' now, we can afford to move into a big ol' house or a condo. Matter of fact, I saw the most beautiful condo on Jefferson for sale in the paper," I said and then turned to go and retrieve my newspaper clipping.

Sam snatched my arm so hard that I flew backward and my back almost hit the wall.

"That's your fuckin' problem, Chloe. You want shit done when you want it done! I guess you don't give a fuck about what I'm tryin' to say, do you?" He paused and took a breath then continued, "Hell no, you don't! All I'm sayin' is that we need to save a little more money. Damn, as quick as I make a dollar, you think of ways to spend it. Just chill the fuck out! The little bit of dough that we did have saved is gone because *one of us* just had to go shopping!" he spat and then went back in the bathroom to rinse his mouth out.

I couldn't believe this nigga had just grabbed and yelled at me like that. Usually, Sam was calm and laid back, which was part of the reason that I fell for him in the first place. Lately, he had been gettin' out of hand, yelling more, staying out late, and I didn't know what his problem was. Shit, I was somebody that he'd better hold on to. With my mindset and get-'em-girl attitude, I could have another one in his place in a heartbeat. So fuckin' what, I wanted a bigger house? I was worth it! Mario's wife had a damn mega house in Bloomfield, and all I wanted was a fraction of that.

I was about to give him an earful, but that nigga was lucky that the intercom buzzed. "Yo, who dat?" Sam pressed the talk button and asked.

"It's me. I gotta piss. Buzz me up."

I heard Mario's sexy ass and I panicked. I was so embarrassed that he was coming into our small-ass apartment and had to go into that tiny bathroom. On top of that, our house was decent, but it was nothing like his and Nikki's. Most of our stuff came from Walmart, while their things were custom pieces.

I looked around the living room and tried to straighten up the magazines that I had thrown over my glass coffee table. Next, I made my way to the burnt orange sofa and loveseat, trying to fluff the pillows back up. I was on my way to check my appearance in the mirror that was hanging on the wall in the narrow hallway but was interrupted by Mario's knock on the door. I put on my best smile and swung the door open.

"What up, doe, Chloe? Where is your bathroom?" he asked, looking as fine as ever with that jet-black hair free-falling down his back. He smelled good, too—even better than Sam. He was draped up in a brown-and-tan Evisu hook-up with brown Nike socks and tan Nike flip flops. I could tell that he was high because his eyes were real tight and he smelled liked Cheech and Chong.

"Hey, Mario, right this way," I said, leading him down the hallway, silently cursing Sam out in my head.

"What up my, nigga," Mario said and nodded to Sam, who was coming from the bedroom, brushing his waves and applying his black du-rag. They dapped fists, then he entered and closed the door.

Sam didn't even look my way the whole five minutes that Mario was in the bathroom because he knew that I was beyond pissed. As if I wasn't already embarrassed enough, Mario made matters worse when he came out.

"Damn, my nigga. That muthafucka is small! I barely had room to pull my dick out," he said to Sam as he stood in the doorway, drying his hands with a paper towel, and let out a laugh.

I looked at Sam and rolled my eyes as they left the apartment. That nigga better have my damn house by the end of the month or else!

Chapter 8

Tonya

"You have a collect call from a Michigan inmate . . . *Roscoe*. Press one to accept."

I sat up in bed and followed the instructions. "Hello," I said into the receiver.

"What's up, T? What's going on in the D?" Roscoe asked, just like he did every other day when he called me collect.

"Same old same, baby. The kids are working on my last nerve as usual, and I still ain't got my money from Nikki and them, so I'm going to be late on the rent *again*," I said, reiterating to him how bad we were being played.

"Not this shit again, T, damn," he complained like some punk.

"T, damn, my ass!" I mocked him. "If you are tired of hearing about how your family is struggling, then your jailbird, inmate ass need not call home no damn more," I shouted. I was about ready to hang up when he started talking again.

"So, you being straight up with me when you say they ain't paid you shit since I been gone?" Roscoe asked with uncertainty in his voice.

"Not as much as I would've gotten if you were still here. The crumbs that I get is nothing compared to bread we had when you was here. With a few dollars here and there, I'm doing the best that I can on the rent and the car notes. It's amazing the landlord ain't put us out yet," I snapped.

"T, you know that the money they give you while I'm locked up is only to keep you comfortable, not to have you living the glamorous life," he said like he was playing for their team.

It was pissing me off, so I yelled, "Muthafucka, whose side are you on? I mean, you should want your family to live the glamorous life while you're locked up. That's what we deserve! I'm the muthafucka putting money on your books. I'm the bitch feeding your kids and running this shit by myself, so you should want me to be on top."

"Tonya, got damn, I ain't trying to argue with yo' ass. I know what you deserve, and please believe I'm going to provide for you when I get out, but right now, please just go with the flow of things. I'm going to set shit straight when I get out of here. Please believe that!" he pleaded with me.

"All right, I hear you, Roscoe, but I get so mad thinking about them over there in that big-ass house with money to blow, and we over here trying to make ends meet." I was getting madder by the second.

"Look, I got'chu and my kids as soon as I get out, but right now, I don't need to be making waves with a nigga like Mario. No more crazy talk in the hood from you about them, because If he think that we got problems, he can make it to where my ass won't never make it home, if you get my drift! Keep yo' head up, boo, and kiss the kids for me. One!" he said, and we ended the call.

I got up from the couch and headed into the kitchen to grab a cup of Kool-Aid. Still charged up from my conversation with Roscoe, I decided to fire up a blunt. I grabbed the swishers from the top of the refrigerator and began to break it down. As soon as I began to sprinkle the weed onto the paper, my doorbell rang.

"Shit!" I went to my side window and looked out to see a pink Dodge Charger with chrome wheels and tinted windows in my driveway. I rolled my eyes because I knew it was Gucci, especially bumping that loud-ass music. I didn't say nothing, just opened the door and looked at her.

"Hoe, what the fuck is your problem?" that bitch had the nerve to ask.

"Excuse me?" I asked for clarification because I knew that I couldn't have heard that heffa right.

"Tonya, I ain't here to play games. Here go yo' funky-ass check, bitch," Gucci said and basically threw my check into the door.

We both watched it fall to the ground. Without saying a word, I reached down and picked it up then slammed my door shut. I couldn't stand her ass, and she knew it. She thought her shit didn't stank, and it irritated the hell out of me. That bitch was a wannabe. She wanted to be Mario's wife so bad that she could taste it.

I finished rolling my blunt and smoked it on the way to the mall. I was in a great mood. I was high, the kids were in school, and I had $5,000 to blow.

Chapter 9

Mina

"Aye, Mina, come here, baby." I heard Tre' call from downstairs.

"What's up?" I asked as I entered the basement where he was entertaining two guys, one with long black hair and a cute younger guy.

"Baby, can you grab us a few beers?"

I know he didn't just call me down here from way upstairs when he could've walked up there and got them his damn self.

I must've had a certain look of disbelief on my face, because the younger interjected, "You don't have to go out of your way, ma'am. I'm cool."

Did he just call me ma'am? I'm probably only five years older than him.

"Yeah, we're cool," the long-haired guy added.

Just to be polite, I asked them if they were sure, and they both said yes. As I walked back upstairs, I couldn't help but check out the young guy again. His ass was fine!

I played around in the kitchen, pulling things out for dinner, when the younger guy came upstairs and startled me, causing me to drop a few potatoes that I had in my arms.

"My bad, ma'am," he apologized.

"How old are you?" I asked him, about to shut this *ma'am* business down.

"Twenty-two," he said, looking up with a boyish grin on his smooth baby face.

"I'm only twenty-seven, so you can stop calling me ma'am," I said, and we both laughed.

"My bad. I didn't mean to offend you, I swear," he said while placing my potatoes on the counter.

"It's cool. What's your name?" I openly flirted, much to my own surprise. It was so unlike me, especially with my husband so close.

"I'm Sam, and you are?" He extended a tattoo-covered arm my way.

"Sam, I'm Mina. Nice to meet you," I said as the hairs on my back stood up from his electrifying touch.

"Please believe the pleasure was all mine." He winked. "Um, Mina, where is your bathroom at?" he asked as if finally remembering why he had come upstairs in the first place.

After I showed him the way, I stood there and watched his fine ass walk down the hallway to the guest bath. He was 6 feet, light-skinned, kind of thin, but had a swag about himself that was sexy than a mutha. Ol' boy was all the way turned up, and I was all the way turned on! Once he retreated back to the basement with Tre' and the other guy, I tried to shake him off of my mind, but it was useless.

It had been several hours since Tre's company left, and even though I sat at the dinner table with my husband, I couldn't help but think about Sam. I couldn't figure out why this young boy had me gone, but he did, and that was a fact.

"Baby, that nigga that was here earlier is going to make us rich," Tre' said, taking a mouth full of steak and then a bite of the loaded potato.

"Oh, yeah," I said more for his amusement because obviously, my mind was elsewhere.

"Yeah. Right now, he is the one doing big thangs in the D. He got the best product on the streets, and niggas respect his gangsta." Tre' praised the stranger, and I rolled my eyes.

"So, where do you fit into that?" I asked, hoping that he wasn't going to tell me that he had gotten involved with these guys and their drugs.

"Well, since I'm new with them, I gotta start at the bottom and work my way up, baby, but that won't take no time. You know how I roll," he said, patting my hand like that was what I wanted to hear.

"Tre', are you sure that you can handle being around drugs again?" I asked.

He looked up with rage in his eyes, and I instantly regretted my last question.

"What the fuck kind of question is that, Amina?" he said, calling me by my government name. He stood up from the wooden dinette table.

"Baby, sit back down. I'm just asking because— " was all I could get out of my mouth before he back-handed me and knocked me across the room like I was a flimsy rag doll. As soon as my ass hit the floor, I was thankful that I was bottom heavy for the cushion that it provided.

"Dang, you didn't have to hit me," I said, madder than a mutha, but I wasn't stupid enough to fight back. I was 5 feet 7 inches, 178 pounds. and Tre' was 5 feet 11 inches, 235 pounds of solid muscle. I knew he could whoop me with one hand behind his back, so I just stayed on the floor, cowering in fear.

"You shouldn't be asking stupid-ass questions then, Mina. You are my wife, and you should support me in whatever I choose to do," he said, tapping at his chest like he was King Kong.

Reluctantly, I got up off the floor and cleaned up the mess that was knocked over when I fell. I went into the kitchen and put some ice in a Ziploc bag then applied it to my face. This wasn't my first time being hit, but I swore on my deceased son this was the last time.

Chapter 10

Gucci

"Put your hands together for the one and only Gucci Doll," DJ Black announced as I got up on stage. I wiped the shiny gold pole down to clean it free of the juices that were left behind from the person before me, all while winding my hips. Next, I bent over and made my ass clap. Then, when I was sure that I had everyone's attention, I started bouncing my ass up and down to the Soulja Boy song "She Got a Donk." I jumped up on the pole, flipped upside down, and hung there for a minute while a customer slipped a twenty in between my thong. Then I did a quick spin and slid down, giving the men in the audience a money shot, and the crowd went wild. Even a few female customers threw a couple of dollars my way. I blew them kisses, and they threw more money. I wasn't a dyke, but some nights, the lesbians were my best tippers, and I was never going to stop my cash flow, so I gave them what they'd come to see.

After a few more tricks and three songs later, I stepped down from the stage and went over to the VIP area, where I had spotted Mario and Sam. The club was packed, standing room only, and I expected nothing less in Detroit on a Saturday. The Doll House was one of the most elite clubs in or around the city. Most of the customers were ball players, hustlers, or businessmen just looking for a good time. The first two drinks were on the house because the admission to get inside was one hundred per person. Some people were outraged and refused to pay that kind of money to see some ass and tits, but that's how the owner weeded out the broke niggas from the ballers.

"Aye, what's up, Gucci? Let me get a dance," a customer asked, slapping me on my ass.

"That's gon' cost you," I said, pointing and smiling at the regular, who was a sweetheart.

"Don't be like that, baby," he said, pretending to be offended.

I smiled and then entered the intimate but comfortable space that was elevated off the main floor. There were three VIP areas that rented for fifteen hundred. This one was by far the largest and most luxurious. It was plush with red carpet, black walls, two large white sofas, its own speaker system, and five poles that came equipped with dancers. In addition to your choice of two top shelf bottles of alcohol, each VIP section had a private bar with a bartender, as well as two private rooms in case you required a little personal time with a dancer. This muthafucka rented for five thousand dollars, and Mario has been renting it for years.

They had already gotten the party started with the drinks and the weed, so I made myself at home. I rolled my eyes at the extra dancers. Instead of the five that came with the room, I counted about six more of those stank bitches in there.

"What up, doe?" I addressed Mario, Sam, and the rest of the crew that were scattered throughout the room, doing their own thing.

"What up, Gucci," Sam replied, and Mario nodded his head. I took a seat right next to Mario, damn near bumping this Asian chick on the floor. I didn't like her ugly ass anyway.

"What up, bestie?" I asked then poured myself a drink of Cîroc and lemonade.

"Just chillin', my nigga." He played with his smart phone. "Aye, did you handle that business for me?" he asked in his relaxed tone. Mario was a quiet guy, and he believed that men shouldn't constantly run their mouths because to him, that was a woman's job.

I looked at him and gave him the once over. He was laid back like a boss in his Armani Exchange attire, platinum pinky ring, bezeled-out wedding band, and some earrings that looked like diamond-encrusted ice chips. I smiled as I remembered the night he told me he was going to be rich one day and run the world. We were some little young-ass teens then with no destination on our GPS of life; we just handled things as they happened. He was a go-getter, and I was his soldier. We'd ended up in a few tight spots, and things may not have always worked out the way we planned them, but Mario always kept his word. He sure did become rich, and although he may not run the world, he sure did have Detroit on lock!

"Girl, did you hear me?" He nudged me, snapping me back into the conversation.

"You know I did, Mario. I got everybody straight. Even that damn Tonya," I said to answer his question about handling business.

"For sho, girl. Thanks for having a nigga's back." He put his arm around me and gave me a tight hug.

"'Til death do me," I said, using our childhood term to let each other know that we would be down 'til death did us part. We bumped knuckles and went back to socializing with the others.

We partied into the night, and they stayed until the club closed. Sam even got loose with a few chicks, so things at home with Chloe must not have been peaches and cream. I had only met her a few times, but I knew she came on too strong. She wanted Sam to be Mario so bad it was breaking them apart. I wanted to put her young butt on game and tell her to chill, but I didn't know her like that, and it wasn't none of my business.

Before I knew it, the clock hit three, and it was time for us to bounce.

"Aye, Gucci, when you gon' leave the Doll House, girl? I mean, damn, yo' ass make more than enough money working for me to buy this bitch and still have a big stash left over," Mario pointed out as we walked to our cars in the parking lot.

I smiled and looked back at him as I opened my car door to get in. "I guess old habits die hard!" I said and skidded out of the parking lot.

Chapter 11

Chloe

It was around four o'clock by the time Sam finally came through the door. I pretended to be asleep while I watched him go from the closet to the bathroom. Then finally lay down next to me, but facing the other way! I didn't know what his problem was lately, but I was sick of it. Normally, he came in and we made crazy love after he left the strip club because he was turned on.

I sat up in bed, cut on the light, and asked him what was the matter. He tried to brush me off at first, but I was persistent. "If it's somebody else, please tell me," I said, letting my concern spill out.

"Chloe, it ain't nobody, baby," he said with a reassuring tone.

"Then why have you been playing me to the left?" I wanted to know.

"Baby, sometimes you do too much, or say too much, and after a hard day, I don't want to hear that shit. I just want to come home to my girl and chill," he said while rubbing his temples.

"What you mean, I say or do too much? I bet Mario don't talk to Nikki like that," I cut in.

"That's another thing, I want you to be happy with Sam and Chloe. Stop being so concerned with making us Mario and Nikki. He's been hustlin' for years, and I just really got started, baby, so be patient . . . please."

He turned to look up at me with those puppy dog eyes, and I had no choice but to give in, so I decided to back down until the opportunity presented itself again. I was going to make Sam into Tony Montana if it killed me.

"Baby, can I ask you a question?" Sam asked, pulling at a burgundy curl on the end of my wet and wavy styled hair.

"What's up?"

"How come every time we argue, you always think I'm cheating?"

I looked down at Sam's handsome face and told the truth. "Because you're fine, and I'm a little jealous. Baby, I see how other women look at you when we're out together, and sometimes it makes me feel a little insecure." I was being one hundred percent truthful. I was very insecure and a tad bit jealous.

"Damn," he said, giving my words some thought. "All this time I thought the women were checking you out when we're out together." He laughed and winked at me.

I laughed too, because he always knew exactly what to say to make me feel special. I wasn't ugly by far, but I wasn't a beauty queen either, and I knew it. Sometimes, I felt my dark skin made me less attractive, and the fact that my birthmark was right on my forehead didn't make it any better. Growing up, I was teased, so almost my whole life I'd a had a complex about it. However, Sam always reminded me that to him, I looked like Kelly Rowland, who just happened to be his favorite celebrity crush. He also told me that he loved my birthmark because it gave me character, but he did remind me that I could always cover it up with makeup.

We made love for about thirty minutes, which was unusual, because Sam could definitely put in work. This time, he didn't even look down at me or kiss my lips like he usually did. Instead, he leaned down and buried his face in the pillow. I could definitely tell that something or someone else was on his mind.

Chapter 12

Nikki

I woke up from my power nap just in time to see my husband walk into our room carrying a huge bouquet of pink carnations, which he knew were my favorite flowers. He also had a small box in his hands that piqued my interest as well.

"Eww, for me?" I squealed like a schoolgirl.

"Of course it's for you, baby. I just wanted to thank you for not only riding wit' me for all these years, but being by my side no matter what! I not only respect you as my wife, but I respect you as a woman who's 'bout it, 'bout it. You my gangsta boo, girl!" he said and nudged me.

I smiled on the inside as well as on the outside. Not only had he made me the happiest woman in the world when he proposed, but he continually outdid himself almost every other day with flowers, jewelry, cars, and money. But nothing was better than the handwritten love notes, because I only got those on rare occasions. Some may beg to differ, but honestly, I was not a material girl at the end of the day. All I wanted was to be loved and respected. Some women in this game threw themselves at anybody they thought may have money just for a taste of the good life. Over the years, I'd seen it all: groupies sleeping with the whole crew just to please the head guy, and of course, he didn't even want them after that. I'd watched women lose their souls in this game, trying to prove how much they loved these ballers. Shit, if Mario didn't respect me, then I would bounce flat out. I didn't marry the money, I married the man, and I'd rather be broke and happy versus rich and miserable any day!

"Baby, did you hear me? I said you my gangsta boo," Mario said, snapping me away from my thoughts.

"Yeah, you know I'm your bottom chick," I said and stood up from the bed, kissed his cheek, and placed the flowers on the end table right under the window.

"What you got up for today?" he asked.

"Nothing much, but what's up?" I asked as I rearranged the flowers.

"I wanted to have you plan a li'l get together with everybody for a few weeks from now. Just to show them that I appreciate all of the work they been puttin' in on them blocks. In the last few months, we been clockin' hella dollars, and I don't need them niggas thinking we over here being selfish and shit. I love my niggas, and I know that they know it, but sometimes it just needs to be reiterated." Mario laid back in the bed and stretched out, almost looking too tall for the California king-sized mattress.

"That would be nice, Rio. What type of party should this be, and where do you want to have it? You know we can't have all of them up in here," I said as I sat on the beige chaise, which was on the side of the bed.

"I was thinking that maybe we can do a bowling party or something different for them hood niggas. They need to get out of grind mode and just relax a li'l. I ain't feelin' no clubs, 'cause you know I don't like places where I can't be strapped up. Most of these clubs now don't have regular security anymore. They have cops, and I'm trying to avoid the law at all costs." He laughed and made himself more comfortable on the bed. "Anyway, baby, I don't know, but I'm sure you'll think of something." He shrugged his shoulders.

"Yeah, I got you. Hey, where is Junior?" I asked because I left him with Rio so that I could take my power nap earlier.

"Gucci got him. She came over while you were asleep; said she wanted to take him shopping. They should be back soon," he said, reaching for the remote to the 60-inch plasma mounted on the wall.

He must've seen the look on my face, 'cause I know my expression turned from sweet to sour instantly. "Nikkita, don't start trippin'. That's her godson, and she got a right to spend time with him."

Not wanting to argue, I just threw my hands up and walked away. "I bet she wished he was her son," I mumbled under my breath and left the room.

Chapter 13

Gucci

"This parenting shit is for the birds," I said in frustration as Mario Jr. had just shitted for the third time in five hours. I wrapped the dirty diaper up, carefully trying not to let it touch my nails, and carried it over to the trash. I must have let the cold air hit his little wee-wee, because just as I got ready to put the fresh diaper on, his little ass peed straight in the air. I ducked under the changing table for cover.

Satin, a friend of mine that I danced with, ran over from the sink where she was applying more makeup and placed the diaper between his legs to stop the action.

"Damn, girl, yo' ass definitely don't need no kids," she blurted out.

"Bitch, yo' ass got two damn kids, so of course you know what to do," I hissed as we walked out of the restroom back into the mall. I was not motherly at all. I had no motherly instincts, and I prayed to never have children. I knew that I wasn't cut out to be a mother, because I myself never had one. Her name was Nia, and she was murdered when I was a baby, so growing up, I lived with my dad, Leo. He was an alcoholic with no money because he drank it all up on payday from GM. I pretty much had to fend for myself, put food on the table and clothes on my back.

Starting at the age of ten, I hustled with the big boys on the corner, and by the age of thirteen, I was stealing cars and had even robbed a few people. At sixteen, I eventually ended up dancing at the Doll House, which was where I'd been ever since. For some reason, I found security there. It was almost like a family, the way we protected and looked out for one another. Not to mention the fact that the money was good, and it sure beat watching my back in the streets every day.

"Hello." Satin waved an acrylic nail in my face. "Did you hear me, girl? I said being a mom ain't all that bad."

"Well, it may not be bad, but it ain't for me. Shit, I'm not even sure that I would know how to love a kid properly, 'cause my ass is screwed up and I know it. With no mama and basically no father, I would need to take a class first or something." I laughed to hide the pain that had just hit me in the heart. I was over it and had been for a while now, but the hurt still showed up from time to time and caught me slippin'.

"Aww, Gucci." She tossed a sympathetic glance my way. "You don't need a class to learn how to love a child. It just comes natural to most people. Mines mean the world to me, and kids are special because they love you even after the world has wrote you off, so stop trippin'," Satin said as we took our seats in a booth at the food court.

As I looked at my cute god baby who was now out like a light, I thought about giving motherhood a try. I smiled at how nice it would've been if he was me and Mario's, but I quickly shook it off because I'd missed that boat a long time ago. I'd been pregnant twice by him, which was my little secret. Nobody knew about the abortions, not even Mario, and nobody ever would. I had gotten pregnant back-to-back during our little rendezvous back in the day. I knew a baby would slow us down and stop our shine, so I put it on the back burner. I figured he would eventually ask me to be his woman; we would settle down and have children later, but Nikki slipped her ass in, and I gracefully bowed out.

"Yeah, you're right. Being a mother might not be so bad." I jumped back into the conversation. "Especially now that he's sleeping. He does look like an angel. His little ass did all that shitting, and now he's laid out like a grown man." We both laughed at my joke.

"What's up with Nikki? Is she cool with you watching her son?" Satin had completely changed the subject, catching me off guard. She stared at me intently while waiting on a reply.

"I guess. Shit, she has no choice but to be cool with it, because I'm his godmother and you know Mario ain't gon' have no shit about that," I stated matter-of-factly.

"I'm just saying, she is one hell of a woman, because if it were me, let's just say you wouldn't be my man's bf!" she teased, and I waved her off because I knew Nikki could probably care less about little ol' me.

"She's the one with the ring, the dick, the house, the whips, and the baby, so why would she trip over me?" I counted on my fingers for emphasis about the number of things that she had and I didn't.

"Because your ass has the mistress role on lock. You're pretty, you got a nice shape, and you're with her man a little too damn much if you ask me." She looked all serious, and I laughed again, then continued.

"Me and Mario work good together. We make money, and that's how it's always been, straight up! He brings home the bacon, I fry that shit up and then serve it to her ass on a platinum platter. I bet her ass ain't complaining when she spends the money I helped him make!" I slapped the table to stress my point.

"I'm just saying she better stay on her game, 'cause if she don't, I bet yo' ass won't mind stepping up to the plate." Satin mimicked my action and slapped the table too.

She always kept it one hundred. I knew she wanted to get a rise out of me, but I didn't respond, because she was right. I didn't want anything to happen to Nikki and Mario, but if it did, I would pick up the pieces and keep it moving. Bottom line!

Chapter 14

Tonya

I was at the mall and about to grab some Chinese food to go when I spotted Gucci and some other chick sitting in the food court. I quickly turned on my heels and headed out the door. I didn't want her to see me with the nine bags I was carrying and go back reporting it to Nikki. See, when Roscoe first went to prison, he asked me to save most of the money that Mario was giving me. When he got out, he wanted to be able to go independent rather than partnering up. By purchasing his own packages, he could receive all of the profit. To be honest, I thought it was some bullshit that I had to save money for his ass. For five long years, instead of living the good life that I deserved, I was living off of those small-ass checks every month. Had he not been locked up, I would've been getting way more. I mean, damn, a bitch can't go from Red Bottoms to Rainbow! So, like a real boss bitch, I decided to do things my way. I'd been blowing money since day one, telling myself that I'd have time to replace it before he got out of jail.

Now, his five-year bid would be up in a month, and I knew I couldn't replace that money. So last year, I started telling Roscoe that Nikki quit sending checks over and they didn't care about us or our children. I told

him I had to borrow money from my family to feed our
kids because whenever I did receive a check, I used it to
pay the mortgage and back taxes on our house. I knew
that I might've exaggerated a bit, but I needed to get
my point across and take the heat off me. So, I pointed
the finger right at their asses. Better they deal with the
repercussions than me.

Just as I made my way to the parking lot, located my
truck, and put the bags in my Durango, I heard my cell go
off. "Hello?" I answered, knowing it was my damn kids.

"Hey, Ma, can you bring us a pizza home? Ain't no
food up in here," Roscoe Jr. asked.

"Damn, R.J., I ain't got no money, and I know it's
something there you can eat! What about that cereal I
just bought two days ago?" I yelled into my BlackBerry.
I swear, these damn kids worked my nerve. They always
needed something, and I was just flat out tired. I only had
five hundred dollars left, and I needed that to get my hair
and nails done the next day.

"Ciara had the last bowl, and me and Shana haven't
eaten at all today," he said, and I rolled my eyes.

*Got dammit, if it ain't one thing, it's definitely another.
These little niggas must think money grow on trees or
something.*

"Call Grandma and ask her to get y'all a pizza," I said,
frustrated.

"Didn't that lady just bring you some money yesterday? I heard you tell your friend that on the phone last
night!" R.J. had the nerve to say.

*No, this little muthafucka didn't just question me about
mines.* He was thirteen going on thirty, and I couldn't
wait 'til he and his sisters was old enough to get out. Shit,
they were only good for one thing, and that was taxes!

"Boy, don't ever question me like that. Do you under-stand me? Now, call your grandma and—"

His little bad ass had hung up on me. I started the car and pulled off, leaving smoke behind. I was going to whip ass if it was the last thing I did!

I pulled up to my modest brick house on Mendota and gritted my teeth because my mother was standing on my porch with her arms folded. I knew she was about to go hard on me.

"Hey, Mama," I said with a smile plastered on my face. I purposely left my bags in the car so she wouldn't call me out on it.

"Hey, Mama, my ass! LeTonya, why haven't my grandkids eaten today?" She was pissed, and I knew she was mad, because she had called me by my government name.

"Ma, you know they ate today, but I guess they just wanted a pizza, and I told them to call you because I don't have no extras right now," I said, running my sob story.

"Girl, bye! I been upstairs in your closet, and every-thing up there is brand new, so I know you've been shopping! Haven't you?" she asked but already knew the answer.

"I got a few new things, but—" I was cut off when she walked down off the porch and got into my face.

"Girl, I know you know better than this. Look at you . . . and then look at your kids! They look poor, and you look ghetto fabulous. You always talking about how you never have money, but you keep the note up on that Durango that you're driving. You keep your hair nice, but the kids are in dirty, wrinkled clothes. Come on! This isn't right, and God don't like ugly. LeTonya, these children didn't ask to be here, and now that they here, they're yours, and you've got to take care of them. Your behind has the nerve to want more kids, and you can't even take care of the three you got. You're selfish, and I'm sick of it. These kids are coming with me until you get it together. Is that understood?" she chastised me like a child, and I just stared at her.

She just didn't know it yet, but she was actually doing me a favor. If the kids were out of my hair, I could do me and not have to look in their faces every day. I mean, don't get me wrong. I loved my kids, but I only really had them to keep and please Roscoe. Now that he was gone, it wasn't no need for them to cramp my style. Hell, I was entitled to a vacation. I would get them back before he came home, and then everything would go back to normal.

"Mama, please stop trippin'. I ain't selfish. You just have them spoiled!"

"Girl, please, you need Jesus." She dismissed me with a wave of her hand and then turned back toward the house to retrieve my kids.

I sat down on the porch and pulled out a Newport. Just as I put it to my mouth, the front door opened, and out came my mother ranting and raving *again!*

"Your behind is trifling. I can't even find them nothing clean to wear, so now I have to go buy new stuff. This is horrible."

"Why don't you just take the dirty stuff home and wash it?" I asked like she was stupid.

"Because I saw some roaches in there on the floor, so I know they're all up in the clothes, and I'm not taking nothing like that home with me." She rolled her eyes.

I looked at her and rolled my eyes back. She was always making a mountain from a mole hill. I stood and went into the house to get out of her space before I got disrespectful.

I must admit the house did sorta look a mess. Clothes and shoes were everywhere, old dishes on the dining room table, my trash was overflowing, and I could smell a slight odor.

"Little Roscoe, bring yo' nappy-headed ass in here now!" I stood with my arms folded.

He walked into the living room with a Detroit hat turned backward and a wife beater with some basketball shorts on.

"What?" he had the nerve to say.

Oh, no he didn't just say "what" to me.

"What you mean, what? That's not how you should ever address your mother. Anyway, boy, why was the trash not taken out? Why do my table have dirty-ass dishes on it? You were supposed to be in charge and make sure this shit was clean before I came home." I was about two seconds off of him, not just for his mouth, but for leaving this mess and embarrassing me in front of my mother, who was cleaner than Mr. Clean himself.

"Man, I'm tired of cleaning up behind you and your trifling-ass friends!"

I can't believe that he is talking to me like this.

"You and them tired-ass hoes don't do shit but smoke all day, eat, and then leave this shit for me to clean up," he said while squaring up to me.

Without hesitation, I snatched his ass up by the strap on his wife beater. "Muthafucka, I'm your mama, and as long as you live, you bet' not ever disrespect me like that." I was so angry that I almost forgot that my mother was in the room.

"R.J., that's enough, baby. Now, go and get your sisters so we can go," my mother said as she walked over to the commotion.

I let him go, and he did as he was told. Moments later, he and his sisters walked right past me toward my mother, and nobody even looked back or said bye except for my baby girl, Ciara. She was eight, and at times, I thought she had more sense than the other two.

I watched my mom pull off with the kids. Then I closed the door, pulled out my phone, and called a few people to see what we could get into that night. I was about to party! I was kid-free, carefree, and as Li'l Wayne would say it, I was single for the night.

Chapter 15

Mina

I awoke to the sound of bath water running and the smell of breakfast, so I knew this was Tre's way of apologizing, but I wasn't in the mood. I got up from the queen-sized pillow-top and made the bed. Choosing to ignore the hunger pangs in my stomach, I went to the closet, put on my sweats and my Nikes, grabbed my iPod off the dresser, and walked right out the door of our condo, letting that bitch slam right behind me.

I needed to clear my head, so the plan was to do what I did every time I was in deep thought, which was to run. I always ran from our condo on Chene near Mt. Elliot all the way down to Jefferson, near IHOP and back. I did a few quick stretches on the porch, then put my ear buds inside my ear and pushed play. "Irreplaceable" began to play just as Tre' made his way outside. I was about to run like I didn't see him, but he grabbed my shoulder, so I had no choice but to acknowledge his presence.

"Yeah," I said, removing the ear buds while continuing to jog in place.

"Where you going, baby? I made you breakfast, and I even ran you a bubble bath," he said with a Colgate smile.

"I'm not hungry," I lied. "And I'll take the bath when I get back, but thanks anyway." I shut him down as gently as possible.

His look turned cold and icy, so I knew he was pissed. he grabbed my face and gritted his teeth. "Bitch, get your monkey ass in the house now, before I—"

I cut him off. I was sick of this shit, and it was about to end. "Before you what? Hit me? Well, go ahead. I'm ready!" I turned my jaw toward him, daring him to take his best shot, but he didn't, just like I knew he wouldn't on a main street in broad daylight.

"Tre', you got me so numb that it don't even hurt no more," I said and turned back to him. He looked at me in confusion and didn't know what to do, so I continued. "Look, if you ain't gon' do shit, then get the fuck out of my way!"

He clenched his jaw, then stepped aside.

I placed my ear buds back in and ran off into the distance, leaving him and his bullshit standing on the sidewalk.

My husband was a beautiful nightmare, and I was ready to wake up and shake him off. The good years for us were over, and I knew it, but a small part of me never wanted to let him go. He was handsome and charming, the man of my dreams in the beginning, but after our son died, he became someone else, and I was tired of it.

We'd been together since forever. We met in eighth grade, and it was love at first sight! He was tall, medium build, copper skinned, red hair, and had the most gorgeous hazel eyes that I'd ever seen on anybody. My grandmother used to say, "Men with red hair and funny-colored eyes have the devil in them." I remember laughing then, but I wanted to cry now. I'd given up so many things to be with him, and it hadn't been worth it all.

About an hour and a half later, I returned home and was glad to see that Tre's Escalade was not in the parking lot. I walked into the house, removed my sweatshirt and gym shoes, went to the refrigerator, and removed a bottle of water. I was about to head upstairs to take a bath but was stopped by a knock at the door. I opened the door and was shocked to see Sam.

"Hey, what's up?" I asked while immediately covering my breasts because I'd forgotten I only had on a sports bra.

"Hey, Mina, is Tre' home?" he asked while trying hard not to stare at my sweat-drenched C-cups.

"Nope. I think he stepped out for a while. I just came back from a run." I pointed down to my attire. He looked me over seductively, and I felt the juices begin to flow, and it wasn't perspiration either.

"A'ight cool then. Well, tell him he's on, and everything he needs is right here." He handed me a large black duffle bag.

"Okay," I said reluctantly because I wanted to give it back to him and tell him Tre' wasn't ready for this, but I knew better than to put myself into their dealings.

"A'ight, Mina, you have a good day," Sam said and then hustled over to his black-and-green Ninja bike.

I closed the door and placed the bag on the couch. I didn't care to see what was in it, so I continued with my plan to get clean, but I opted for a shower instead of a bath. As I entered the hot, steamy water, I placed my fingers between my legs without hesitation and fantasized about Sam's fine ass. I imagined him coming into the shower with me, kissing me from my neck to thighs, and of course, giving extra attention to my vagina.

"Damn, Mina, that kat is juicy, baby."

"I know, daddy, and it's all for you," I whispered.

"Is that right? Well, let daddy taste it," he said as I imagined him getting on his knees and spreading my legs. The scene was extra sexy as the water poured down on top of him, covering all of his tattoos and waving up his hair.

I let out a moan just as I was about to cum, but the shower curtain was snatched back so hard that it tore from the rings that were holding it on the curtain rod.

"Who the fuck is in there, Amina?" Tre' spat.

Looking at him like he was crazy, I didn't say a thing, partly because he had just scared the piss out of me, literally. I looked down as the yellow fluid mixed in with water and went down the drain.

"Why are you in here moaning and shit?" he asked, looking like the Incredible Hulk with veins popping out of his head and arms.

"Because the water feels good against my aching muscles," I lied, thinking quick and trying to conceal my pounding heart because I was sure it was making my chest jump erratically.

He looked me over from head to toe. "Open up. Let me smell your coochie!"

"What?" I asked.

"I want to see if you been fuckin' while I was gone. I smelled cologne when I walked in, so I know another nigga been up in here." He stood with his arms crossed.

"Tre', ain't nobody been fuckin'. You know I always take a shower or bath after my runs, and the only reason you could smell cologne is because that young guy stopped by and left you a package. He never made it past the front door, though."

"Oh, shit. I forgot that nigga Sam was stoppin' by. Where the package at?" he asked, completely changing his mood.

"Downstairs on the couch," I said, relieved he had calmed down.

I watched as Tre' walked away without another word. I continued to shower with the shower curtain hanging down to the floor.

Chapter 16

Chloe

I'd just come back from the mall and was trying to hide my purchases before Sam came home. I didn't see his bike outside, so I was relieved. I opened the door and flew into our bedroom and stuffed the bags under the bed. I would come back later and hang them up, remove the tags, and take the bags down to the garbage chute. Sam and I hadn't argued in two weeks, and I wanted to keep it that way. Just as I stood up from under the bed, I heard the door open.

"Chloe, I'm here," he said as he went into the kitchen.

"Hey, baby, how was your day?" I said as I lay across the sofa.

He leaned down and kissed me on the forehead. "Any day that I can make money and not end up in handcuffs is a good day," he said, and I nodded my head in agreement to the statement he had just made.

"So, what did you do today? Anything exciting?" I asked, knowing he wouldn't tell me much, if anything at all.

"You know, the usual, a little bit of this and a little bit of that." He took a seat behind me at the dining room table to break down a cigarillo, getting it ready for the weed he was about to place inside of it. "We're giving this new guy a try, so I went downtown to drop off his package. Mario is testing him. Hopefully he passes, or that's his ass!"

"Dang, I hope he passes too, because Mario don't play at all. Remember what happened to Scoot?" Scoot was a guy that called himself dropping dime to the narcs about Mario and his operation. Mario had half the department on payroll, so he was put on game way before the informant got to the people who really wanted to hear what he had to say. A hit was put on Scoot, and needless to say, we never saw or heard from him again.

"Yeah, I know, but at least Scoot was solo. This guy has a wife, and I would hate for her to get caught up because he fucked up."

I nodded, but that's the risk you take when you get with someone in this game, so I didn't have anything for this chick. She had just better hope that her man handled his business, or it would be lights out for both of them.

I had enough of talking and was ready to get a quick sex session in before Sam had to leave and make rounds with Mario again. So, I stood up and pulled him toward the bedroom with me. I removed his shirt and got turned on looking at his tattooed body. I pulled his pants down, and his erect nine inches told me he was just as ready as I was. He removed my dress, then my bra and panties in a hurry and laid me down across the bed.

As he bit on my nipples, I felt the tip of his penis touching my clit, and it felt awesome. My juices flowed as I spread my legs even farther apart. He placed himself in the right position, then glided it inside of me.

"Oh, baby, it feels so good!" I moaned.

"Damn, baby, you're so wet," he said as he glided in and out of me in a rhythmic motion. He flipped me over, and then we made love doggy style. He grabbed my ass so hard he left handprints on it. I watched him work it through the mirror on the dresser and got even wetter as the erotic scene played out.

"Daddy, you feel so good. Oh my god. Sammmmmmm," I screamed, and he hit it even harder. "Baby, say my name when you come. Say my name," I yelled.

"Girl I'm 'bout to come. Oh, shit! Oh, shit Mina, I'm comin'!" he yelled, and I instantly froze.

"What did you just call me?" I turned around to face him.

He knew he was busted because the look on his face told it all.

"Chloe, baby." He reached for me as I got up and ran into the bathroom. I couldn't believe he had just confirmed my suspicions that he was fucking around.

Chapter 17

Nikki

Tonight was the night of the Off the Block Bowling Party, and it was going to be huge. It had been three weeks since Mario asked me to plan the event, and I was glad that it was finally here. I rented out Lexmark's bowling alley and had been busy planning everything to a tee. I wanted this to be nice because our team really did deserve it. We bought the bar out, so all of the drinks were free. We had food catered from one of the most exquisite restaurants in the Renaissance building. A picture booth was in place, and of course, some local Detroit artists came through for the music and entertainment. We even had Demar, a local Detroit clothing designer who specialized in customizing clothes with Swarovski crystals, put pieces from his Luxury clothing line inside of the goodie bags that would be handed out at the end of the party along with other goodies like jewelry, iPods, gift cards, etc.

"Baby, you ready?" Mario called out to me from downstairs.

"Here I come, baby," I said as I gave myself the once over in the mirror. I was wearing a custom-made dress that I had ordered straight from Mrs. Knowles. It was a gold minidress that fit to the tee. I had on the matching

Jimmy Choo heels, and my hair was spiral curled and pinned up off my back so that my diamond necklace could be seen.

I grabbed my clutch and headed down the stairs to see my fine-ass husband decked out in a tailor-made Armani suit that was the perfect complement to my dress. His hair was crisply braided down his back, and he smelled like the fragrance Jean Paul. He reached up to help me down the last five stairs, and the shine from his pinky ring reflecting off of the chandelier damn near blinded me. I knew he was feeling good, because Mario very seldom wore his jewelry unless it was a special occasion.

"Um, um, um," he said while twirling me around while I blushed.

"You look good yourself, and I love the Cartier glasses," I said, pointing to the glasses that he'd just picked up from the jewelry store. He paid to have his glasses blinged up with a few diamonds on the nose piece, as well as the wiring around the lenses. They definitely gave him the boss appeal hands down.

"Thank you, baby. Let's roll!"

We walked out the door, and I looked at the Maybach sitting in our circular driveway all shined up.

"Wow, we get to ride in the Maybach. About time we get some use out of this five hundred thousand dollar car."

Mario had purchased the Maybach about six months ago, and we had only ridden in it twice. The first time was just a test drive from the dealership, and the second time was when we drove it home from the car lot. I didn't understand why he had to have it but still continued to drive his Range Rover.

Mario looked at me. "Nikki, we look like money, so we got to ride in style." He laughed as we drove off into the night air.

We pulled up to the bowling alley, and it was packed. A line was formed outside. I assumed that it was for the people that weren't invited, like the groupies and the wannabes. We got out at the front door, and the valet ran over to grab the keys to park the car.

"Naw, blood, leave mines right here at the door and don't let nobody lean on it, look at it, take a picture of it, or nothing, you understand?"

The young boy nodded furiously.

"Baby, I'm glad you got valet parking, because everybody brought the sweet whips out tonight," he said as we admired the parking lot. I had never seen so many expensive cars in one place in my whole life. I wondered if this was how the parking lots looked at some of those celebrity parties in Miami, Beverly Hills, or the Hamptons. Whoever said Detroit was broke must've never been to a party like this one.

"Yeah, I kind of figured that would happen, so valet was a must. I also paid for extra security," I said as we walked inside the building. There was a cameraman right at the door, and he instructed us to come over to his photo station to take a few pictures. The backdrop had the words *Made in tha D* at the top, the Detroit skyline in the middle, and the Joe Louis fist in the front, holding some money. The bottom read: GETTING MONEY H.O.F. (HAND OVER FIST), which was the name of Mario's crew.

"What up, boy?" we heard from the crowd by the bar. Recognizing the voice, Rio went over and dapped up someone, and then I noticed that it was Sam. He looked fresh to def in his Evisu hookup, and his girl Chloe looked good as well in her royal blue strapless Luxury dress. I could tell that she was bothered by something, but tonight it just wasn't my problem. I looked at her like a little sister and tried to steer her in the right direction with her relationship from time to time because they reminded me of Mario and me a few years ago. However, tonight I was going to enjoy the fruits of my labor and call her tomorrow.

"Hey, Nikki." Sam hugged me.

"Hey, guys. How long you been here?" I asked as Mario walked away and went to the bar to get us some drinks.

"About an hour. This party is dope! You did a really good job. I heard the radio stations are up in here," Sam said, looking around the place.

"Yeah, I saw the station's promo van out in the parking lot. I'm glad everyone is having a good time," I said in a loud tone because the music was definitely on full blast.

Sam excused himself and walked away into the crowd to greet another person. So, there I was, left alone with Chloe and with no choice but to acknowledge her sadness.

"What's up, boo?" I asked her. She looked like she was about to cry, and it broke my heart.

"Girl, I can't tell you now, but can I come over tomorrow and talk to you about a few things?"

"Yeah, of course. You know I'm always here for you," I said, and Mario walked back up, handing me a Nuvo bottle. I smiled because that was my drink, and I loved the bottle because of its perfume design.

"Baby, did you put a VIP area up in here for us?" he asked, taking a sip from his cup.

"Yeah, it's this way," I replied as he and Chloe followed me.

We walked past the dance floor, and they were getting down in true Detroit fashion. Right in the midst of the action was Gucci, sporting a GiGi Hunter dress and popping ass up and down like she was at work.

"Go, Gucci! Go, Gucci!" the crowed sang to hype her up even more.

As we made our way past her, she must've spotted us, because she stopped dancing and caught up with us.

"What up, doe?" She fanned herself and finger-swept her hair to put it back into place.

"Hey, Gucci," we replied in unison.

We all took seats in the VIP area that overlooked the entire bowling alley. I looked at the crowd in amazement. There had to be at least five hundred people in attendance, and it appeared that everyone was enjoying themselves. I was thankful because I wanted the night to be drama free.

Chapter 18

Mina

I didn't want to go to the Off the Block party when we first got the invitation two weeks ago, but I knew Sam would be there, so I quickly changed my mind. I put on a red parachute dress and had my hair professionally done that morning into a cute short bob with red highlights. We pulled up to the party and valet parked the car. As we approached the man at the door, I looked at the crowd lined up, then back at the Maybach, and knew there were definitely some big names inside.

"What's the name, sir?" the man asked, looking down at his clipboard.

"Tre' and Mina," Tre' answered. The guy flipped a few pages, then let us pass. We were ushered over to take a picture, and I asked Tre' what did H.O.F. mean.

"Hand Over Fist, because that's how we gettin' it!" he answered. I nodded, and then we got in line at the bar.

"What up, Mina and Tre'?" I heard Sam say and smiled because he looked finer than ever.

"What up, my nigga." Tre' dapped him up.

"Hi, Sam," I said like a nervous schoolgirl.

"You look nice," he whispered in my ear as he hugged me.

"Where is the boss man?" Tre' asked as the bartender handed him our drinks.

"I left him right here, but If I know him, he and his wife are up there in the VIP area. Even though this is family, that nigga don't like crowds," he said, scanning the club for an easy route to get up to the VIP, I assumed.

I instantly got nervous again because this was the first meeting I would have with the boss's wife. In the car, Tre' warned me to not fuck anything up. I was also nervous because it had just hit me that Sam had probably brought a date. The thought of him having a woman had never crossed my mind, and I didn't know why. He probably had chicks in line just waiting for a chance to talk to him.

I knew I had no right to be jealous, but nevertheless, I was, and it was hard not to show it. We followed Sam through the crowd, then up about fifteen steps into a nice semi-crowded area with reserved tables. Then we stopped at a table with so much liquor on it that you could barely see the white tablecloth. There were bottles of Patrón, Don Julio, and Moët, so I knew this was where we were stopping.

"Hey, boss," Tre' said and pounded Mario. "This is my wife, Mina. Mina, you know Mario. This is his wife, Nikki, and I'm sorry, what's your name again?" he asked some chick in a half-naked GiGi H. dress. I wondered if that was Sam's girl.

"What up? I'm Gucci," she said and tipped her champagne glass my way.

"Hello," I replied.

"And this is Sam's lady, Chloe," he said, but she didn't say anything. She just looked at me and rolled her eyes. I didn't speak either. I just nodded because the feeling was mutual.

We sat down, and everyone engaged in small talk. Gucci complimented my hair, and we chatted about other things, but I couldn't help but notice how Chloe never took her eyes off me.

"Girl, that young girl is something else, and she think everybody want her man. Don't let her get to you," Gucci whispered in my ear.

If she only knew, I thought.

Chapter 19

Chloe

Ain't this a bitch! I bet the Mina who Sam called out is the one sitting right across from me right now. Where in the fuck did she come from anyway with that simple-ass dress and hairstyle? That bitch can't be from here, looking all lame and shit in that red dress. I rolled my eyes as she pretended not to notice me looking at her and Gucci whispering.

"Aye, baby, you okay?" Sam asked, sitting down beside me.

I smacked my lips because he knew he was still in the doghouse for calling me Mina. I hadn't said anything to him ever since that happened unless it was absolutely necessary. He'd been bringing me gifts home every day, and he swore that he had never cheated on me, but my momma didn't raise no fool.

"Well, thanks for inviting us, Mario," Mina's husband said, interrupting my thoughts.

He was an attractive older man, but for some reason, he stood out like a sore thumb, and something about him wasn't right at all. For one thing, his ass was a tad too nervous if you ask me. The others may not have been paying attention because they were engaged in conversation, but when you're quiet and observant, you notice a whole lot.

"You part of the team now, so it's nothing, homie. This is how we do it," Mario said back.

"Let's all raise our glasses for a toast to the man in charge of H.O.F. If it wasn't for you, Mario, we wouldn't be enjoying the good life!" Gucci said as she raised a bottle of Moët and we all did the same with our drinks.

"Yeah, bro. H.O.F forever," Sam added, and everyone repeated.

As if on cue, someone handed Mario a microphone. He stood and loosened his tie. The music went off, and a spotlight hit our table.

"First of all, I want to thank all of you for coming, because if it wasn't for y'all, there would be no H.O.F. We been gettin' money hand over fist for years, but this has been our best year thus far, and I just wanted to show you my appreciation. I also want to thank my beautiful wife, Nikki, for sticking by a nigga's side through the good and the bad times. I want to thank my best friend, Gucci, for being down with me since H.O.F. was just a thought. From the bottom of a nigga's heart, I'm really thankful for my squad. It's been wonderful, but as you know, all good things must come to an end so that better things can happen, and unfortunately, my time is up."

The crowd gasped. There were whispers between the partygoers. One man even shouted out, "Mario, man, you can't leave! Without you, there ain't no H.O.F."

"Yeah, man, where you going? Ain't nowhere like the D, so you must be facing a bid or something," another man hollered out, and everyone laughed.

"You right, Jay. Ain't nowhere like the D, but ain't nothing like my family, and I'm retiring on New Year's Eve. I wanted all of y'all to hear from the horse's mouth that I'm passing the throne to my youngin', Sam. I been training this nigga for two years. He's shown me a lot and has proven himself. I hope that you all respect my decision and give him the same respect you've given me. I still got six months left before I retire, so let's go out with a bang H.O.F. fo' life!" he screamed, and the crowd cheered back.

I should've been happy that Sam was going to be the king, but how could I? Sam got up from the table, gave Mario a pound, and I smiled a somber smile. I excused myself from the moment, whispered in Nikki's ear that I would see her the next day, and headed toward the door.

As I stood outside in line to retrieve the car from valet parking, Sam came up behind me.

"Why you leaving, Chloe?"

"Nigga, you ain't stupid. You know why!" I folded my arms.

"What, Chloe? Damn. Ain't this what you wanted? You about to be the first lady, and this is how you act?" He shook his head.

I turned toward him and stared him straight in his face. "Is that her?"

"Who?" He played dumb.

"Mina. Is that the one you fucking?" He didn't say shit, so I asked again. "Is that the one?" I screamed as my Dodge Avenger pulled up to the curb.

"Baby, I ain't fucking her," was all he said.

"Whatever. Get a ride home, 'cause I'm out!" I walked away, and much to my surprise, he didn't come behind me. When I was inside the car, I looked back to see him re-enter the party.

Chapter 20

Gucci

"Now, that was a party!" I told Satin on the phone the next day. She hadn't been able to make it because her daughter was sick. Therefore, I filled her in on all the details from those in attendance, including the drama between Mina and Chloe. I didn't know why Chloe thought that everybody wanted her man, but I guess she had good reason. After she left the party, I noticed Sam was all in Mina's face, and her husband didn't even seem to pay attention, because he was too far up Mario's ass.

I liked Mina, because she wasn't trying to be seen. She just sat back and played her position, unlike Chloe. Hell, quiet as it's kept, if Mina and Sam did fuck around, I wouldn't say nothing, because I thought Mina was better for him anyway. With his new position next year, he needed a chick that could work from behind the scenes.

"All right, girl, I'll hit you up later," I said and ended the call with Satin. I rolled over and placed the phone back on the cradle, then stood up from the bed and headed into the bathroom to run some bath water.

Just as I slipped my panties and bra off, I heard my doorbell ring. "Damn," I cursed then grabbed my hot pink robe from behind the bathroom door. "Hold on.

I'm coming!" I yelled as I ran down the stairs. I peeked through the peephole, and to my surprise, it was Mario.

"What up, doe," I said, swinging the door open.

"What up, G." he said, then closed the door behind him. He walked over to my living room and took a seat on the green chair. Then he looked up at me with a huge grin on his face.

"What you smiling for?" I smiled back because it was contagious.

"Because I just got the call of a lifetime. Gucci, this shit right here is 'bout to make us rich. We gonna retire way sooner than we thought."

I sat down on the foot ottoman in front of him, eager to hear the good news. I said, "Okay, keep going."

"I got a call from Zion about a large package of heroin and cocaine in Miami that needs to be delivered back here to him in two weeks. The nigga that got it is afraid to bring it this far because of the risk. I was about to tell him that I wasn't gonna take the risk either, but he cut me off. He told me the package was worth ten million dollars, and if I got it back to him safe and untouched, I could keep half of it."

I couldn't believe my ears. We were about to be rich. I knew Mario had money saved from his younger days, but he probably never made that much at one time—ever.

"Oh my God, nigga! When do we leave for Miami?" I asked, cracking up.

"See, that's why I keep you around. I knew if nobody else would be down, you would!" He squeezed me tight.

"Hell yeah, I'm down. Just tell me what the plan is and when to be ready," I said.

I listened intently as he ran down how we would fly to Miami and get the package back to Zion. As he continued to talk, I had begun to dream of all the new things that I would buy. I knew Mario was breaking me off a big chunk of change, so I didn't have to ask.

As he stood to leave, I reached to give him a hug, and my robe opened, completely exposing my bare ass. "Oh, my bad." I fastened my robe and felt a little ashamed.

"Girl, it's nothing that I've never seen. I'll call you later," he said and closed the door.

Chapter 21

Nikki

"Can you believe he did that, Nikki? And I bet it was that bitch from last night." Chloe went on and on as she told me about her drama with Sam.

I felt bad for her, because I knew what it felt like to be jealous. However, I never had my suspicions confirmed by being called someone else, so I didn't know exactly what she was going through.

"Do you really think it's the red-headed chick from last night, though?" I asked, because her husband had only been down with the team for a hot second. Therefore, I wondered where Sam could've possibly met her, talked to her, and become so infatuated with her that he would call Chloe by her name.

She looked up at me and gave the *hell yeah* face, and I laughed.

"It ain't funny. I'ma kick her ass!" she stressed.

I pulled a strawberry from the fruit dish that was on the table and placed it in my wine. "Chloe, you're tak-ing the wrong approach. You need more evidence, and until you get it, just make him pay for his mistake. See, a guilty man always tells on himself, and if he did some-thing wrong, please believe that his actions will show it." Hell, my mama didn't raise no fool, and I didn't have this house for nothing. Mario never cheated on me as far I knew, but I didn't put nothing past him.

"How will his actions show it?" She looked as dumb-founded as a deer caught in headlights.

Poor girl. "Well, you've been asking for a new house, right?"

She nodded, and I continued, "Well, ask him again and see what he says. If he still says no, then his ass is innocent. If he says yes all of a sudden, then his ass is guilty."

We slapped fives just as Mario walked in through the side door.

"Aye, we need to have a meeting," he said, pointing to the office right off the kitchen to the right.

"Me and you, or all of us?" I said, referring to Chloe.

"All of us. Sam should be right behind me. He was parking his bike in the driveway."

We looked at each other, then followed Mario into the office. Just as I took a seat in one of the recliners, Sam walked in and closed the door behind him. The office was sound-proof and had a metal detector inside the door jamb. This was the only room in our house that Mario would ever talk business in.

I watched my husband pace back and forth in his red Dickie pants, wife beater exposing his tattoos, and red Detroit hat with a huge grin on his face. Even though he was smiling, a small part of me was nervous.

"What, baby?" I asked, growing impatient.

"We're going to Miami!" he exclaimed.

"What?"

"I got some business to handle, so we are taking a trip down to Miami," he repeated and then proceeded to provide us with all the details.

After hearing the basics, I must admit that I was leery at first. Nonetheless, I soon shook it off, because my husband knew what he was doing, and I trusted him.

"So, how exactly are we going to get all that shit back here?" Sam asked out loud as I was silently wondering the same thing.

"Me and Gucci was talking. We think the best way is to get an eighteen-wheeler truck and load it up with boxes of baby formula. I'm talkin' baby logos on the side of the truck and all. Hell, we can put decals all over the truck so that it looks real legit, ya feel me?"

I heard the excitement in his voice, but I was still asking myself, *Did he say him and Gucci?*

"Who's driving the truck, though? Those eighteen-wheelers are some big muthafuckas," Sam exclaimed.

"Probably me. Though both me and Nikki have a commercial driver's license that we've been keeping up just in case we needed. I'm glad we did. We got two weeks to get the truck back. I was thinking we should head down there in a few days just to get the shit in order. We can party and vacation the first few days, then come back and deliver that package. Once it's been delivered, I'm retiring, my nigga, and the throne is all yours," he said, dapping Sam.

Hearing that he was retiring in two weeks instead of next year totally changed my mood from pissed to pleased in a matter of seconds. Hell, after he retired, we could leave Detroit and Gucci behind. So, for that reason alone, I was down with the plan. I decided not to question him about why she knew about it before me.

"Ewww, girl, I'm going to pack." Chloe jumped up, grabbed her purse, hugged me, and ran from the room with excitement.

Sam pumped his fist in the air, jumped up and down a few times, thanked Rio again, then leaned down to hug me. While we were in the embrace, I told him to make things right with Chloe. Being in his new position, he would need a down-ass chick by his side.

"Yes, ma'am, Nikki. I'm 'bout to fix it right now!" He grabbed his helmet and went to catch up with his girl.

I looked at my husband and gave him a big smile. "What you smiling for, baby?" he asked.

"Because you're about to retire, and I never, ever thought this day would come. Hell, I've been waiting on you to get out of the game from the beginning, back when you were making a few thousand here and there." I laughed at the thought of where we'd come from.

Sitting down on the floor next to my recliner, he began to rub my feet. "Nikki, we have been through some shit for real, girl, but look at us. We made it!"

I played with his curly ponytail and reminisced about the time he went to jail for six months, and the time he got shot and the doctors didn't think he was going to make it, but my boo was a soldier, and he had proved everybody wrong.

I also remembered the day that I was abducted at gun-point from the apartment complex that we lived in at the time. Rio had just made a major deal with the top guy on the street, a guy named Chino, and we were living it up—shopping sprees, jewelry, and cars. Some members of Chino's organization were pissed that Chino chose to upgrade Rio and not one of them, so they planned an attack on us.

One night, just as I got out of the car, a masked gunman placed a nine-millimeter handgun to my head. He took my cell phone out of my hand and told me to get inside the trunk. I was scared shitless, to say the least, but I did as I was told. Moments later, like a bat out of hell, we flew out into the night. About an hour and a half later, they opened up the trunk and took me into what looked like a shed. It was so dark that I couldn't make out anything familiar.

"Tie her mouth and hands up, then blindfold that bitch," the taller of the two men said. The shorter guy did as he was instructed. I cried because I knew that my life was over and I would never see Mario again.

I listened as the men walked in and out of the shed as if they were waiting on something.

"Damn, girl, where in the fuck is yo' man at? I called his bitch ass 'bout two hours ago," one of the men said aloud.

"Please don't kill me if you want money. I can get that for you." I begged for my life, although they probably couldn't make out what I was trying to say with the gag in my mouth. That's when I heard the phone ring.

"'Bout damn time. I was 'bout to pop her, cuz," the guy said.

"Nigga, who the fuck is this?" Mario snapped. The man must've had him on speaker phone, because I could hear him as clear as day.

"It's the nigga that got a nine to yo' bitch's dome, so the question is . . . what you gon' do about it?"

"What the fuck!" Mario said while registering what ol' boy had just told him. "Nikkita, are you okay, baby?" he yelled, panic evident in his voice.

"She a little tied up at the moment, but listen closely, 'cause I ain't repeating myself. I need you to drop off fifty stacks inside of the dumpster behind the Church's Chicken off of Jefferson and . . ."

As he continued, I had become somewhat pissed, because this asshole was about to kill my black ass for a measly fifty grand. Shit, I had that much in my personal safe at home for petty cash.

"Do you know who you're fuckin' wit'?" Mario asked.

"I do know who I'm fucking wit,' but you don't! I'm the crazy nigga with the gun, so don't keep testing my gangsta with these dumb-ass questions!" the man yelled. "Aye, watch that broad. I'm 'bout to take this call outside."

I prayed silently the entire time that the man was wrong; that somehow, I would make it out alive.

"What did he say?" the other guy asked as the head guy returned.

"He said that he'll be there in fifteen minutes, so I'ma go over there and post up. Once he makes the drop and the money is in my possession, I'll hit you up and tell you where to meet me."

"Well, what about her?"

"Put two in that bitch's head! Somebody will find her eventually, but we'll be long gone."

I cried out again at the sound of that. I began to pray again. This time, I recited the Lord's Prayer and asked that he forgive me for my sins. I heard the door slam; then everything went quiet.

About twenty-five minutes later, the door opened, and I heard the voice of the shorter man say, "Listen, li'l mama, I'm gonna shoot off two rounds. I don't want you to come out until ten minutes after you hear my car pull off, okay?" he said, and I vigorously nodded my head. Then he removed my blindfold and untied my mouth and hands. "Listen, sweetie, you're on Belle Island in a storage shelter. When you come out, turn left, and that will point you in the direction of the bridge, all right?"

He looked back with an apologetic expression and vanished into the night air.

A few weeks later, we got word on who it was. Let's just say neither of those guys made it, not even the one that had saved my life, because Mario wasn't having it.

The sound of the doorbell snapped me back into reality. Collecting my thoughts and storing them deep in my memory, I got up from my chair and kissed his forehead. "Thank God this will soon be over and we can live like simple folk!"

Chapter 22

Tonya

"Please take a seat at that table, and he will be in shortly," a prison guard instructed me.

I sat there in my Apple Bottom dress, waiting patiently for my man. It was visiting day, and I couldn't wait to lay eyes on my Roscoe. While I waited, I looked around the room and took note of all the ladies that came out to show their men some love. Most of them were accompanied by children. Some of them were scantily dressed, and a few of them were old, looking as if they were the ones behind bars. I snapped my head toward a corner where some young girl was screaming and making a commotion, causing guards to rush over there.

"Fuck you, Tony! I been the one holding it down for you, and that's how you do me?" she spat.

"Man, Brandy, go 'head on wit' that bullshit. You know better than to come at me like that!" the guy that I assumed was Tony snapped back.

Just as the girl was being pulled away, kicking and screaming, Roscoe walked up in his gray jumpsuit. "What's up, ma?"

Damn, my baby was gorgeous. Even in prison attire he still made my pussy wet!

"What's up, baby? You looking good," I said with a smile.

"You do too, ma, for real." He grabbed his dick, and I squirmed in my seat.

"How you holding up, baby? When do you get out?" I flooded him with questions.

"I'm one hundred. You know this ain't nothing to a real nigga. How are my kids? I miss they asses like crazy. I should be getting out in about three months, so it'll be no time before I'm back up in that pussy, baby. It's still, mine right?" he said in a demanding tone.

"Of course it's yours, and it always has been! The kids are cool, just working my last nerve." I didn't mention that my mom had them, because that would really piss him off as well as mess up our visit. I wasn't trying to do either of the two, so I just sat there looking pretty.

"So, what's going on with Mario and them?" he asked.

You know me, I got right down to the nitty gritty and went right into my exaggerated truth. "Baby, they ain't gave me nothing! No money, no support, no visits just to see how me and the kids are doing . . . nothing! Plus, the word on the street is that Mario set you up with those undercovers."

Roscoe rubbed his goatee while looking straight at me, and I didn't even blink.

"Well, I guess I'ma have to put some heat to that nigga to get what's mine then."

"Baby, can you believe that they had a big party last week to celebrate the success they had this year, and I didn't even get a got-damned invitation?" I damn near shouted because I was pissed. To me, that was a real low blow.

"Straight up, Tee, dat shit ain't right, and please believe I'ma handle that shit. Keep your ears open and report back to me on what you hear, no matter how small it is. I'm 'bout to develop a plan to catch that pretty boy slippin'." Roscoe frowned.

The guard announced that visiting time was over. We said our goodbyes, and I headed for the door, laughing all the way to my car, because I knew victory was closer than I had thought it was.

Chapter 23

Mina

I laid in the bed and pretended to be asleep while Tre' felt all over me. I wished he would just lose the urge or get a phone call or something. My prayers were answered when his cell phone vibrated on the nightstand. I peeked through one eye as he fumbled with his phone, then scrambled to his feet.

"Hey, Mario, what's up? . . . Unh-huh . . . okay, fo' sho. I'm on my way." He hung up, went into the closet, got dressed, grabbed his keys, and hurried down the steps.

I sat up as soon as I heard his truck leave the driveway and grabbed my new book, *Dope, Death, and Deception* by India. I continued to read from where I'd left off earlier.

It was something about a good story. Quiet time had me so relaxed and in the zone that I hadn't even realized it was going on two hours later. I was almost finished with the book when I was interrupted by the house phone ringing.

"Hello?" I asked as I looked at the caller ID, trying to figure out who was calling at four in the morning.

"Hey, Mina, sorry to wake you, but we have a problem. Have you seen Tre'?" he asked in an irritated tone.

Closing the book, I stood up with knots in my stomach. "Um, no, what happened? All I know is that he got a call from Mario, then he left. He's been gone for at least two hours now." I started to pace back and forth.

"Well, he was supposed to make a pickup, drop it off, get the cash, then meet me. I just called around. He made the pickup but never made the drop. He got us on the line here, and I'm wondering if everything is okay."

Oh my God. He did it again, I thought as tears began to fall. I knew then and there that we were dead!

"As soon as he get here, I'll make sure that he calls you. Okay?"

"Yeah, a'ight!" he yelled and hung up.

I immediately called Tre,' but he didn't answer. After the fifth call, I texted him: What the fuck happened? Call me!

Twenty minutes had passed, and there was still no word on Tre'. Feeling alone and knowing the only one that was going to save me was me, I went downstairs and sat by the door with my .22, waiting on someone to bust it down because of his dumb-ass mistake. I should've just gotten in the car and driven away from there, but where would I go? I hadn't spoken to my family in years, and I really didn't have any money, so I wouldn't get far. I rocked back and forth, jumping every time I heard a sound from outside.

I must've dozed off. The sun shining in my face, as well as the sounds of chirping birds, woke me up. I looked up at the clock on my cable box. It read 8:15 a.m.

"What the hell?" I picked up the phone and called Tre' several more times. I still didn't get an answer. I was about to try again, but the phone rang. I answered it instantly.

"Tre'?" There was a pause, then Mario coldly replied.

"I don't mean no disrespect, Mina, but where in the fuck is your husband with my shit?"

"Mario, I don't know what to say, but he ain't been home all night, and I'm worried," I said, because I honestly was scared that he might be hurt or something.

"For your sake, he better be hurt, because if he ain't, then he gon' be a lot worse when I find him."

"Please, Mario. Please give me a minute to find him. I'm sure whatever he did can be sorted out," I pleaded.

"Look, I'm going out of town later tonight, but when I get back, I want my shit or my muthafuckin' money!"

"Just out of curiosity, how much was the package worth?" I couldn't believe I had just asked that question, but I had to know what I was dealing with. I held my breath, waiting for the amount.

"Twenty thousand dollars," he answered. Then the phone went dead, signaling to me that Mario had hung up. I began to cry again, because I damn sure didn't have that kind of money.

Chapter 24

Nikki

"If I don't get my shit, that nigga and his wife is dead!" Rio slammed his cell phone down, then sat on the edge of the bed, causing me to jump up.

"What happened?"

"My nigga Rob got knocked by the hook last night. We needed a package to be picked up from his spot then dropped off over at Tiger's spot, where he would get the cash and meet up with Sam. We put that nigga Tre' on tonight in place of Rob. Now that nigga done went missing, and my gut is telling me that I got played! My fuckin' heart told me that I shouldn't let that nigga in my circle, but we was low on manpower. Besides, a few niggas in the hood vouched for him, saying he was that nigga in Ohio. Man, shit!" He punched the bed, barely missing my foot.

"Baby, calm down. We gon' get it back! What did his wife say?"

"She ain't heard from him, talking 'bout he might be hurt. I ain't hearing that, because ain't nobody in Detroit stupid enough to fuck wit' my shit, so I know for a fact that he wasn't robbed or no shit like that."

I got up from the bed and sat beside him. He was so mad he was shaking his leg rapidly. "Rio, what if he had a car accident or something? His wife knows her husband, and she's probably worried out of her mind," I said, thinking of Mina, because I'd been in her shoes a few times, waiting for Rio to come home for days.

"That nigga was ridin' with twenty thousand dollars' worth of heroin, Nikki. If he had an accident, they would've found that shit in the car. You can bet some shit like that would've been all over the news by now."

He had a point, so I decided to drop the issue, because the more we talked about it, the more pissed off he would get, and I wasn't in the mood for one of his bitch fits. I kissed his cheek, then walked into the bathroom to brush my teeth and take a shower. I would've told Rio to join me for some top-of-the-morning sex, but I knew he was not in the mood.

I dressed in a yellow sundress with gold accessories and my new Coach sandals. I heard Junior crying, so I headed across the hall into his room. I smiled to see that Rio had already picked him up and was rocking him back and forth.

"Stop crying, Daddy's li'l man," Rio said then made the *shhh* sound.

"Aww, you guys look too cute. Well, don't let me interrupt your father-son time." I kissed both of them on the forehead and told Rio I would be back. He nodded, and I headed out the door.

I pulled my Range Rover up to the front of Chloe's building. She came right out, waving and smiling. "What up, doe?"

"Girl, I'm too geeked about the trip. I can't wait. Shit, I'm already finished packing!" she exclaimed as she snapped her seatbelt.

"So why are we going to the mall?" I quizzed, because she was the one that called me last night, begging me to go shopping with her.

"A girl can never have too many things for Miami, and we will be there for two weeks. Girl, please." She waved me off like I was the rookie and she was schooling me.

"Well, darling, you can shop all you want here in Detroit. A real boss like me will do all my shopping when I get there. I want to pop tags on everything, all the way down to my panties." We both laughed at my joke as I merged onto the Southfield Freeway.

About thirty minutes later, we were inside of Fairlane Mall. We'd decided to stop at the nail shop for pedicures first. As soon as we walked in, I noticed Tonya in the waiting area, reading a magazine, and I smacked my lips.

"What up, Nikki? What's wrong?" Chloe asked.

"Nothing, boo. I ain't trippin'. I ain't sweatin' that bitch . . . at all!" I was about to sign my name on the list when Amy, the owner who did my nails from time to time when I wasn't at my main salon, waved me and Chloe toward two pedicure chairs in the back. This made the ladies who were in the waiting area really angry, but I was used to it.

"Oh, hell no, Amy. Are you serious? I been here for a damn hour and a half already," I heard Tonya say, and I smiled even harder.

"These are priority customers. I will be right with you," she said to Tonya as well as the small crowd while she continued to run our water. I slipped my sandals off and placed my feet into the hot water. It felt great. Chloe took the seat to my right and did the same, while Amy's husband, John, cleaned the seat to my left.

"Nikki, would you and your friend like something to drink?" Amy asked.

"Sure. May we have some white wine, please?" I replied, and Chloe looked at me with an impressed look. Whenever I was here, Amy rolled out the red carpet for me. I assumed it was because I always tipped $100 or more. I mean, don't get me wrong. This wasn't the lifestyle of the rich and famous with Dom P. and champagne-filled pedicure baths, but this was VIP treatment for my hood-fabulous ass, and I loved it.

I grabbed a magazine off the rack and thumbed through a few pages while Chloe talked on her phone. I was so deep into the story on Tiny and T.I. that I didn't even notice Tonya sit down in the chair next to me.

"Living the good life, huh? Must be nice."

I looked up to see her all in my face. I placed the magazine on my lap and shifted to face her. "Tonya, don't get on my shit list, okay? I'm not in the mood."

"It would be nice to hear from Mario every now and again. Hell, he could even pay a visit or two to his ex-partner. I mean, his ass is doin' a bid for the team!" she said just a tad too loud for my taste. I wanted to smack the shit out of her, but I was too ladylike for that.

"Roscoe fucked his own self up, so the bid he's doing is not for the team at all!" I snapped, and before I knew it, she was out of her chair and in my face.

"Bitch, please! Don't act like you got the only real nigga in the D. Roscoe is a thoroughbred, so don't get it twisted."

"More like a pony!" I laughed.

"Yeah, bitch, keep laughing. Yo' ass won't be laughing soon, and you can bet on that!" she spat as the nail salon owner, John, handed her the shoes that she had placed on the floor. "Miss, please leave. You are disturbing my customers."

"Is that a threat?" I wanted to know. I was a nice girl, but even nice girls go gangsta when their life is threatened.

"Nikki, it's whatever you want it to be," she yelled over John's shoulder as he forced her toward the door.

"Yeah, okay, bitch. You better leave while you can still walk on your own."

Chapter 25

Gucci

The limo that Mario ordered had just arrived at my house. I locked up while the driver retrieved my bag from the porch. As I opened the door, I heard laughter and loud talking from the inside.

"Gucci, get yo' ass in here and sip somethin', my nigga!" Mario said as he handed me a shot of what smelled like Don Julio.

"Miami, here we come," I said as we all tipped our shots up.

We talked shit and took shots all the way to Metro Airport. As we waited in the terminal, Mario filled me in on what happened with Tre,' and I was shocked.

"Damn, are you serious? Do you think he cut like that?"

"Gucci, I'm from Detroit. I don't put shit past no nigga or female," was his response, and he was right. But I just didn't get that vibe from them, especially not his wife.

I brushed it off, and before I knew it, our zones were being called to board the plane. Chloe was so excited, because she had never been on a plane. Sam was all bug-eyed, looking like a bitch, hyperventilating in his seat. I was laughing my ass off, and I'm sure the liquor played a part in that.

It was about three hours later when we finally touched down in Miami. I couldn't have been more excited. We grabbed our luggage, then waited at the curb for our ride to arrive.

"Damn, y'all famous or something?" some pimpled-face teenage boy asked as he entered the airport carrying a torn-up duffle bag that had definitely seen better days.

I quickly replied, "Detroit's finest, baby."

"I wonder why he asked if we were famous," Nikki asked, looking back at the guy.

"Shit, it's probably all of this LV luggage that Chloe just had to have," Sam answered, wiping the sweat from his forehead.

"Or it could be all the jewels we're all flossing," Chloe added, pointing around the crowd to our necks, wrists, fingers, and ears.

"All of y'all are wrong! That youngsta think we famous because of that right there," Mario chimed in, turning our attention to the fleet of luxury vehicles parked right in front of us. There was a yellow Lamborghini, a red-and-black Bugati, and a white-and-silver Ducati sports bike. I jumped up and down, almost breaking the heel on my sandal.

"Oh my God, you rented this for us?"

"Hell yeah. You know we gotta show out. You and Chloe take the Lambo. We'll take the Bugati, and Sam, you know what it is."

We all headed off to our vehicles. I was glad none of us had packed a lot of shit. At least Chloe, who had packed the whole house, had the great idea to mail most of her stuff to the hotel. It was a good thing, because there was definitely no room for massive luggage in those tiny cars.

I jumped behind the wheel and followed Mario, even though I didn't have to, because there was a GPS in the car. We pulled up at the Royal Palms and were greeted by a man in a suit made with shorts instead of pants.

"Welcome to the Palms. I'm Georgio, your concierge."

"What up, doe," we replied and walked inside like we owned the joint. This was going to be the best two weeks, and I was about to make the most of it.

We made our way across the marble floor to the check-in desk and were presented with our keys.

"Hey, let's hit the bar before we go up to our rooms." I pointed over to the bar, which was neatly tucked to the right of the lobby. Everyone followed me over there.

"What can I get for you, ma'am?" the bartender asked.

"Let me get two tequila sunrises with Patrón, one Miami Vice, and two shots of Don Julio," Mario said, cutting me off. I didn't make a fuss, because he knew exactly what I wanted, so I moved aside and let him handle his business. The lady was back in a few minutes, handing out drinks. We all held them up in the air.

"Here's to big things and real niggas!" We clinked glasses and tossed our drinks back, even Nikkita with her prissy ass.

"Dang, baby, this is so good and flavorful. How do you know about this drink?" she asked Rio as she bit the cherry off of the toothpick.

"They sell those everywhere, baby, and I know you like colorful drinks, so I figured you'd like it," Mario replied, shrugging his shoulders.

"Oh, and what do you have, Gucci? Yours is pretty too."

"This is a Miami Vice. It's piña colada and strawberry daiquiri mixed. Girl, you should definitely try it. These taste so good, but they do sneak up on you," I said, grabbing my head to soothe the brain freeze that I felt coming.

"Yeah, Gucci, you remember last time we were here. Yo' ass was tore up off those things, so yo' ass better chill out," Mario said, and I could tell that he didn't mean to let that slip. I looked at him, and he looked at Nikki, who was now red in the face, and it wasn't because she was blushing.

"Okay, y'all, let's meet back here in three hours for dinner," Sam said, trying to take the attention off of what he knew was sure to be a situation. Everyone agreed and headed to the elevators in silence.

Chapter 26

Tonya

I stood up from the couch and paused my *Bad Girls* show. It had been four days since my visit with Roscoe, and I was glad that he gave me the heads up about him not coming home for another three months, because that gave me more time to get my shit together. Next month, I would begin fixing the house up and work on bringing the kids home. But for now, I was about to continue enjoying the single life.

I walked into the kitchen to see what leftover food I could find in the refrigerator, but immediately slammed the door closed after smelling what must've been some old greens or something.

"Damn, I gotta remember to throw that shit away later," I said to myself, then grabbed a bunch of menus off the counter. As I reached for the phone to place an order with Panda Palace Chinese restaurant, Adonis called out to me from the living room.

Adonis was my plaything from back in the day. His fine ass was six foot even with a dark chocolate complexion. He had a damn eight pack with pearly white teeth, so it was only fitting that his name be Adonis, which was actually his stripper name. He worked at a popular male strip club called The Lion's Den. We hooked up from time to time. Shit, don't judge me. My man been locked up, and a girl has to get hers.

"Yeah," I answered back just as the Chinese lady on the phone answered.

"Yo' man is walking down the street. What'chu want me to do?" Adonis asked.

"What man?" I called out to him as I turned my attention back to the lady on the phone. "Um, yes, can I place a delivery order for General Tso's chicken and—"

"That nigga Roscoe. Why you ain't tell me that nigga was out?"

I dropped the phone to the ground and ran into the living room, where Adonis was standing, peeking through the blinds. Sure enough, Roscoe was making his way toward the house. I almost died right there on the spot. Not only was I about to be busted alone with Adonis in my house, but he was also butt-ass naked.

"Oh, shit! Get your shit on and hit the back door," I screamed, picking up his clothes, which were scattered across the living room floor.

"What? I thought you quit that nigga?" he asked, still standing there like a fool.

"You thought wrong, and if you don't move your ass, he's gonna fuck both of us up," I said as I saw Roscoe crossing the street into my driveway.

"Ain't no nigga gon' fuck me up. I'm Adonis!" he said, pointing to his chest.

"Look, nigga, get yo' ass out the back door before he gets up in here, please? If you do, I'll make sure that I swing by the club tonight and drop off a big tip for your troubles." At the mention of money, his ass booked up like bullets were behind him. "Typical male dancer," I said, smacking my lips.

Just as Roscoe banged on the front door, I heard my back door slam. I sighed a huge breath of relief. "Here I come, baby," I said as I scanned the room for anything unusual. Then I swung the door open with a big grin on my face, although I was pissed!

Chapter 27

Mina

As I watched Tre' walk into the house like everything was good, I almost lost it. I jumped up from the chair that I'd been sitting in for almost a week and slapped the shit out of him.

"What the fuck, Mina?" he asked me like I was the one trippin'.

"Where you been, and where is the fucking package?" I spat and tried to slap him again, but he blocked it. I looked up at him, and for the first time since he walked through the door, I noticed the glaze in his eyes, and I knew that he was high.

"Baby, I was holding that shit for Mario. It's all good." He flopped down on the couch.

"What do you mean, you was holding it? Where is it?"

"I may have tasted a little bit, but I'ma get that back no problem, Mina."

I burst into tears, because I knew that all of it was gone. I knew that we were dead. I couldn't believe he had placed me in this situation yet again. The other day, déjà vu occurred when Tre' went missing with the drugs. This felt so much like what had happened in Ohio that it was scary. The only difference was that I now knew for sure that he was on drugs, and back then, I didn't.

"Mina, calm down. I got'chu, girl. Don't I always?" he said, then got up from the couch, attempting to make it up the stairs.

I cried silently as I watched him stagger and stumble. It killed me to see him like that.

As I got myself together, I decided to take control of this situation and call Sam. My first thought was to run away again, but how long could I keep up that game? Eventually, someone would find us, or Tre' would just keep doing this to me over and over again.

I reached into my pocket and pulled out my cell phone. I dialed Sam. To my surprise, he answered on the first ring.

"Yeah?"

"Sam, it's Mina. Can you talk?" I asked nervously. I really didn't know what I expected him to do, but I knew that if anybody was going to help me, it would be him.

"Yeah, what's up, Mina? Where's your boy, and where is Mario's shit?" he asked in a hushed tone.

"He said he tasted some of it, but knowing him, it's all gone. He just came home, and I know he's on that shit again," I blurted out. There was a noticeable pause.

"He is a fucking dope fiend? Aw, shit. Are you fucking serious? I knew something wasn't right with him. Damn! We gave a dope fiend twenty thousand dollars in dope. Mina, you should've said something that day we were at your house in the kitchen," Sam damn near barked.

"I know, but he was clean then, and—" I was cut off.

"Once a junkie, always a junkie. Believe that!"

"Please just tell me how to fix this, Sam. I need your help. Please," I begged, and again there was silence.

"Look, Mina, I don't know what to tell you. Yo' man is gonna fuck around and get murked. You know that, right?"

I didn't say anything, so he continued. "Damn I can't believe this. But I'll talk to Mario and get back with you later, a'ight?" he said, then we hung up.

Part of me wanted to blow Tre's brains out for doing this to me, to us, but part of me wanted to figure how I could spare our lives. So, I got on the computer and pulled up our bank accounts to see what we had left that could be used to pay Mario. I almost died again when I noticed that both of my bank accounts were negative— the one I shared with Tre' and the one I had by myself. He had spent over twelve thousand dollars in less than one week. I couldn't move. I was numb, and I was hurt.

Chapter 28

Nikki

"Baby, it's been a whole week, and you still got an attitude?" Rio questioned.

"I don't have an attitude. All week I've been noticing the inside jokes that you and Gucci share, and it's making me sick!"

"Like what?" He threw his hands up and walked into the living room of our hotel suite, and I followed suit.

"Like last night at the restaurant, when you took the liberty of ordering me what you and Gucci had the last time y'all was there. Or the other day, when we were on the beach, and I said I wanted to go Jet-Skiing. You told the story about when you and Gucci went out, and she fell off hers. No matter what you think, I don't want to hear that shit!" I said and grabbed my purse off the couch. I felt myself getting angrier by the second, so I decided the best thing that I could do was to leave. Just as I reached the door, my husband grabbed my shoulders.

"Nik, don't go, baby. I'm so sorry. I didn't know that it bothered you like that. Gucci is my best friend, and we came here years ago on business. It was me, her, Roscoe, and another nigga."

"Whatever, Rio. I don't even care, so forget it. Just don't let it continue to happen." I dropped my purse down on the television stand and decided to drop the issue.

"Okay, baby, I'm sorry. I love you and you only, baby. I know you don't want to hear this, but If I wanted Gucci, I would have her."

I looked away, and he turned my face back toward him then continued. "But you're the one that I chose to marry and, baby, you had my seed. Ain't nobody gon' ever take your place. You hear me!" he said, then slid his finger inside of the orange wraparound skirt that I had on and began to massage my clit.

"Ooh," I moaned.

Then he pulled me into the bedroom and laid me across the bed. "Let me taste you, baby. I want that pussy to drip in my mouth," he said as he put his face under my skirt and began to lick and suck with a vengeance. In a matter of moments, I came all over his face, leaving a sticky residue over his goatee.

Rio stood and wiped his mouth with a devious grin. "Later tonight, there is more where that came from."

I watched him walk into the spacious bathroom. I followed behind him, removing my clothes. "What do you mean, later? What about right now?"

He looked up at me from the sink where he was washing his face. "Me and Sam got a meeting today in about . . . twenty minutes." He looked down at his big-face Cartier watch, which I had just purchased for him while shopping at the huge outdoor mall in South Beach where he had taken me last night. It was a long strip in alphabetical order, starting with the cheap stores and ending with the costliest stores.

"When will you be back?" I asked as I stepped into the garden shower.

"You'll probably be asleep when I get back, baby. I'll leave some money on the dresser in case you want to go shopping . . . *again*." He smiled, and I blew a kiss through the glass shower door.

After washing up, I stepped from the shower and walked into the bedroom to retrieve my cell phone. I punched redial, and there was only one ring before I heard a voice.

"Girl, would you stop calling here? This boy is fine," Ms. Claudia teased, and I giggled. I loved her to death. She was my mother-in-law, and she always had my back. She was baby-sitting Rio Jr. while we were on vacation. Although she was very trustworthy, I was beginning to miss him terribly, which was why I called her every few hours or so just to check in on them.

"I know, Mom, but I'm baby sick. What are you guys doing?" I put the phone on speaker and began to dry off.

"Well, we've been taking it easy, just watching our soap operas and taking naps. I think my grandson is a true *Young and the Restless* fan just like his Granny."

I laughed as I pictured the two of them sitting in the rocking chair, trying to see what was happening on the soaps, but dozing off at the same time.

"Well, I didn't want anything. I was just bored."

"Bored? Girl, you're in Miami with your husband. Get off the phone with me and go enjoy yourself," she lectured.

"I'm trying to enjoy myself, but this vacation would be a lot better without Gucci!" I reached into the top drawer and pulled out a matching set of lime green Victoria's Secret bra and panties.

"Chile, that Gucci works my last nerve! I just wish she would find a man and go on 'bout her business," she confessed.

"I didn't know you had a bad taste for her," I said in utter shock. "I thought y'all were cool, Mom. Damn, this is news to me." I smiled as I pulled on a D&G lime green jumpsuit with gold trim and matching accessories.

"Girl, please! I only put up with her to please my son, the same as you, darling. They've been close for years, and I learned a long time ago that there is nothing that anybody can do to stop that."

I let out a sigh and rolled my eyes because she was right.

"Nikki, even though they're close, you've got to remember you're his wife, honey, and the mother of my precious grandbaby, not her! Don't let her steal your happiness. No matter what it looks like, remember that he chose you to spend the rest of his life with. She's just along for the ride."

She made all the sense in the world. I was actually beginning to feel better. I ended the call and dialed Chloe to meet me in the lobby. I grabbed the four large stacks of money from the dresser, placed them in my purse, grabbed the room key, and headed to the elevator.

Chapter 29

Tonya

"So, what the fuck is up? You happy to see a nigga or what?" Roscoe asked as he stepped into my living room wearing the same clothes he had on that fateful night he was arrested five years ago.

"Come on, Roscoe. You know I am, baby." I faked happiness and hoped he couldn't sense it. Don't get me wrong. I was extremely happy he was home, but I was pissed that he had caught me off guard like that. My house was a mess, the kids weren't home, and to top it off, I was praying that this nigga wasn't trying to fuck right now, because I was still smelling like sex with Adonis.

"Where my kids at?" he said as he walked to the back of the house where their rooms were.

"Um, they been at my mother's house for a few days. She wanted to see them, and they wanted to see her, so it worked out for me to get a li'l me time." I tried to grab a few of the dirty dishes off the coffee table.

"Damn, Tee, yo' ass really been on vacation and shit. Look at this house! Now that I'm home, I want this shit straightened up, a'ight?" he said, and it was something in his tone that turned me on.

"Yeah, baby, I got you. Why don't you go upstairs and run a nice hot bath and relax while I take care of this mess? I can also order us some lunch or something," I said while flashing him a smile.

He accepted my proposal and ascended up the stairway to our bedroom. After I heard the water come on, I grabbed my cell phone and instantly called my mother.

"It's about time you called and checked on your kids, Tonya," she answered.

I rolled my eyes because now was not the time. "Ma, don't start. Look, I wanted to come by and get the kids today. I have a surprise for them. Roscoe's home!"

"Wow! So, let me get this straight. The only reason you want your kids is because their daddy is home. You are sorry, you know that! Girl, come on and get them then. Hell, the only reason that I'm letting you get 'em is because I know their dad is good to them. He loves them so much. I wouldn't make him suffer just to spite you."

"Whatever, Ma. I'll be there in a few hours. Don't tell them that Roscoe is home. I wanna surprise them," I said and closed my phone. I looked around the house but didn't know where to begin. I turned up my stereo and blasted 97.9, the local radio station. They always played the jams that I cleaned to whenever I did clean, and today would be no different. I grabbed the broom, mop, and a few trash bags, then got to it.

About an hour and a half later, with everything complete, the living and dining room were back in order. I even cleaned my kitchen up, refrigerator and all.

"Now, this is what I'm talking about, Tee," Roscoe said, coming up behind me, kissing me on the neck.

"You look good, and you smell good, too," I said when I swung around to face him. He was rocking an all black

True Religion fit. He must've shaved, too, because his face was as smooth as a baby's bottom, and his bald head was shining like new money.

"Yeah, Tee, a nigga had to go and get fresh. I'll be back in a few. I need to link up wit' my niggas in the hood real quick."

I gave him another once over and finally noticed that he had his car keys in his hand. "Okay, don't be long, baby. I'm going to get the kids in a minute, so you know they'll wanna see you."

"Yeah, no doubt. When I get back here, we need to talk about that Mario thing, too." He kissed my cheek then went out the side door.

I watched him pull out of the driveway in his black and blue Marauder, bumping Notorious BIG's CD, *Ready to Die*. My thoughts were instantly consumed with what was up with him. Although I had prayed that he didn't want any booty, I was very much in shock that he actually didn't. For as long as I'd been with him, whenever he was away from me for a while, sex was always the first thing on his mind, but today it wasn't. To be honest, I didn't like it.

I told myself that maybe he had a lot on his mind about Mario or gettin' back into the game. I shrugged it off because I knew that real soon, we would be on top and things would change.

Chapter 30

Gucci

"Damn, baby, are you really gon' do a nigga like that?" the stranger that I had woken up with that morning asked as I was throwing him out of my hotel suite.

"Nigga, I don't know you. You played your part, and it was fun. Now get the fuck on!" I yelled as I tossed the wedding ring that he had left on the nightstand back at him.

I met him the night before at the Liquid Club. He was a sexy-ass Jamaican, chocolate skin, beautiful dreads, and the perfect smile. He brought me several drinks. I could tell by the bulge in his pocket that he either had a big wallet or a big dick, so either way, I couldn't lose. I invited him back to my suite, and he took me for the ride of my life. He was working with a nine-inch curved piece, and I ain't lyin' when I say he fucked me into submission.

"So, me only good for da fuck." He stood in the hallway, pulling up his pants, and I folded my arms like, *so what*?

"All right, all right, me leavin', you crazy bumbaclot!" He continued to curse me out on his way down the hall toward the elevator.

When I was tired of laughing at his ass, I slammed my door and went over to the phone to order room service. I had decided to stay in today because, to be frank, I was sick of running behind Mario and his wife. Nikki hadn't done shit but complain and whine this entire trip, and I, for one, was tired of it. She was cool people, but she was too damn emotional. I knew she felt threatened by me and Mario's friendship, but she needed to woman-up and get over it. If I wanted her man, I would have had him, and that's that!

Mario told me about how she was trippin'. Then he asked me to fall back last night, which was how I ended up meeting the Jamaican dude at the club that I went to by myself. Nikki didn't know how lucky she was to have a nigga love her the way Mario did.

I was snapped away from my trance when my cell phone rang.

"Wassup, girl?" I looked on the caller ID, and it was my girl, Satin.

"Hey, Gucci, how is life in Miami treating you?"

"Girl, I actually miss Detroit. I'm ready to come home, real talk." I flipped through the channels on the television.

"What? Girl, bye!" She smacked her lips. "Anyway, girl, Roscoe was released from the pen. I saw him ridin' through the hood last night."

I sat straight up in the bed and muted the sound on the television. "What? When did he get out?" I wanted to know. "Did he mention anything about Mario?" I rambled on, barely giving Satin the chance to reply.

"Yeah, he got out early for good behavior, I guess, but I'm not sure exactly what day. Girl, niggas is saying he's plotting on Mario big time. They say Mario wasn't giving his bitch money for the kids and shit while he was locked up or something like that."

I smacked my lips and thought of that dirty bitch Tonya. "That's a lie! Mario always take care of his people no matter how small of a position they have. You know damn well he looked after his ex-partner's family. Hell, I personally delivered the checks myself to that gut-bucket bitch. I can't wait to get back in the D so I can bust that bitch right in her mouth." I stood from the bed, now pacing back and forth. "Aye, let me hit you back. I gotta call Mario and put him up on game."

"Okay, girl. If I hear about anything else, I'll call you. Bye," she said.

I immediately hung up, calling Mario, whose phone went straight to voicemail.

"You know who you reached, so leave a message." *Beep.*

"Yo, my nigga, hit me back. Word from back home is that Roscoe out, and he lookin' for you. We gotta put a handle on this A.S.A.P."

Chapter 31

Chloe

After meeting Nikki in the lobby of the hotel, we headed out for a day of sightseeing. We took a boat tour to view Oprah's penthouse, Shaq's old house, Diddy's famous mansion, and many others. Of course, we did some shopping. Now we were dining at Bubba Gump Shrimp.

"So, is everything okay with you and Sam?" she asked while sipping from a strawberry margarita.

"Well, he is trying to make up to me, so he's been hella nice, spending money like it ain't nothing, so you know I'm milking this shit." We slapped fives.

"I know that's right, girl. I ain't mad at'cha, and even though I'm feeling this much-needed vacation, I must admit that I can't wait to get home."

I looked up from my coconut shrimp and then smacked my MAC-covered lips. "Why? Ain't nothing in Detroit but trouble. Girl, please. I'm enjoying this warm weather, five-star hotel, and shopping sprees."

"I ain't really in a rush to see Detroit like that. I'm just saying I can't wait for this trip to be over, because once we get home and get this stuff delivered, we're free. He can retire, and we can blow that popsicle stand."

She laughed, but I felt kind of sad. She was a really good friend to me, and although I hated to lose her, I did understand. She had been in this game far longer than me, and I knew she couldn't wait to start her new life.

"Why you looking so sad? At least you know your man is getting the throne, and you'll be able to get that house you been dying for, not to mention all the other things you want." She tried to make light of the situation.

"Yeah, you're right, but I'm going to miss you, though. Not to mention the fear of Sam changing up on me. More money, more power. More power . . . more pussy!" I said flatly, and Nikki just nodded her head in understanding.

"Chloe, he loves you, so you will be okay. As far as me, you know I'll always have your back. You're like my little sister, boo." Nikki looked away, and I could've sworn she was dabbing at a small tear in the corner of her eye.

"Aw, thanks, girl. So, what are your plans after Mario retires?" I bit some more shrimp and watched her play with her food.

"To be honest, I'm nervous as hell! I feel like everything is going too smooth. Something bad is lurking in the shadows, just waiting to attack as soon as we let our guard down."

"Nikki, don't trip. Y'all beat the odds already, so count your blessings. This will all be over in a week, and you'll be home free. Until then, just sit back and think about what you want to do and the places you want to go." I laughed.

"You're absolutely right, girl. You ready?" she asked, and I nodded. We paid the bill, leaving a forty-dollar tip, and then we zoomed back over to the hotel.

Chapter 32

Tonya

Roscoe had been home for three days, and he still hadn't tried to have sex with me. I was pissed, to say the least.

"Who the fuck is she?"

"Who the fuck is who?" he asked from the bathroom as I laid on the bed and watched him brush his teeth.

"Who you been fuckin', Roscoe? Because it damn sho' ain't been me," I snapped.

He walked out of the bathroom toward me. "Lower your fucking voice before my kids hear that bullshit you talking. I ain't been fucking nobody," he whispered.

"You been locked up for how long? And you ain't tried to hit this? Don't tell me that you playin' for the other team now," I half joked.

He lunged across the bed and choked me so hard I couldn't speak. "Bitch, if I ever hear that dumb shit come out your fucking mouth again, I will kill yo' ass."

I couldn't believe this nigga had put his hands on me, and on top of that, he had threatened to kill me.

As he loosened his grip on my neck, he ripped my panties off and slid his dick in forcefully. "Is this what you want? Huh, you want a nigga to fuck you like this?" He pumped fast and hard. It felt good, but it hurt at the same time.

"Roscoe, stop," I begged because after a second or two, the pleasure was all gone and pain was the only thing lingering. He pumped harder and harder until I swore he was touching my cervix.

"No, that's how you want it, right? Tell me this, though," he said while staring down into my eyes. "Why you let that nigga get my pussy?" I froze just as he pulled out and came all over my stomach. "Yeah, Tonya, I saw that nigga leave here the other day. Then when you opened the door, you were naked, and the crib was smelling like pussy! I didn't fuck you because I was mad as hell that you gave my shit away. All you had to do was keep it real with me and I would've understood! Everybody have needs, and I wasn't here to meet yours, so I swear on my life that I would've understood, Tee, but it's cool. No hard feelings. I'm over it," he said, getting off the bed, holding his dick in his hand as he headed for the bathroom.

"Who got you over it?" was all that I could say, because I read well between them lines.

He turned and looked back at me with a smirk on his face and closed the door. He came out a few minutes later and tossed a towel at me to wipe the cum.

"So, down to business. I'm hearing that Mario got a big drop going down in two days that's supposed to get him out of this game for good, and I'm snatching that shit!"

"How you gon' do that?" I asked after standing from the bed.

"I heard that he coming through in an eighteen-wheeler and is supposed to make the drop at four a.m. at an abandoned warehouse near the Eastern Market. Rumor has it that somebody is going to pick it up an hour later. I'm going to be there waiting on that busta, and word to my mama, I'ma show him that he fucked with the wrong one. I'ma leave his ass stankin' then I'm taking that truck," he said with greed in his eyes.

"How you find all of this out?" I said in a skeptical tone.

"Let's just say I have a very reliable source."

Chapter 33

Nikki

I could've kissed the pilot as we landed at Metro Airport. I practically ran from the plane with Chloe and Gucci in tow. We made our way straight to the front door, bypassing the luggage pickup because we had already mailed our stuff home. I searched for my mother-in-law and then pulled out my cell to call Mario.

"Hey, baby, y'all made it home?" he asked.

"Yeah, we here. How are things with y'all?" I questioned just as my mother-in-law's oversized silver Escalade pulled up to the curb. We jumped in. I let Gucci take the front so I could get in the back with the baby, who was strapped into his car seat. Chloe got in the back too.

"Yeah, we got here about twenty minutes ago, so I'll see you when you get to the house," he said, and we hung up. I kissed all over my baby, and he smiled at me.

"Dang, they're here already?" Chloe asked.

"Yeah, they got here twenty minutes ago. I guess it was a good thing they left when they did since it was a twenty-four-hour drive."

"Did you girls have fun?" Ms. Claudia asked.

"You know I did, Ms. Claudia. You know how me and Mario get down in Miami," Gucci hollered.

I rolled my eyes.

"Yeah, all the times y'all went was on business, so maybe next time he go, it will be a family trip with just his wife and son." Claudia cut her up with that one, and I smiled.

"Ms. Claudia, next time we have to do a girls trip, and you have to go with us," Chloe added.

"Well, you know Ms. Claudia don't fly, darling. So, if you can drive me there, then we're good to go." We all let out a chuckle.

"Hey, little man. Mommy missed you. Did you miss me?" I played with my son as he cooed and grinned.

I was glad we were hours away from leaving this place, putting Detroit in our rearview. A lot of people fantasize about this life. They think about the money and power but tend to dismiss the risk factors, like going to jail, the threats on your life, and not to mention the frenemies that smile in your face knowing damn well they ain't happy for you. If life was different and I felt as though I had any other opportunities, I would've been thrown all of this away in a New York minute, because to me, this wasn't really living. My man was gone from sun up to sun down most days. I lived in fear of my door being kicked in by the police and the hood niggas, not to mention all the false admirers. Yeah, okay, we could take trips whenever and buy whatever we wanted, but we had to do it looking over our shoulders the entire time. So, to reiterate, this to me wasn't really living.

I knew the minute my son was born that we needed to make a change. Now that the time had come, I was more scared than ever. Something kept telling me we wouldn't make it to the finish line, at least not together.

Chapter 34

Gucci

"Thanks, Ms. Claudia. Are you coming in?" I asked as we pulled up in front of Mario's house.

"No, sugar, my bingo game starts in an hour." She smiled, looking at her brown Burberry watch.

"Ms. C, you're rich. You don't need to go to bingo." Chloe laughed, and so did I. Even though Ms. Claudia was living the good life, she faithfully attended bingo as well as played the lottery, and for the life of me, I couldn't understand why.

"Chile, I know what I have, and I appreciate what my son does for me, but I like the game. Whether I win or lose, it gives this old woman something to do. How you young folks say it? Ya feel me? Plus, it never hurts to have your own."

We all exploded with laughter. On that note, we collected our things and exited the car.

"That lady is a trip for real," Nikki said, and I nodded my agreement.

On the way inside of the house, I took note of the large eighteen-wheeler, which was parked partially in the driveway and partially on the beautiful lawn. I guess Nikki had noticed it, too, because she hit the ceiling as we walked inside.

"Marioooo! Why in the hell is that thing even here? I don't play that! You know I always tell you I'm against that bringing business home bull, and you know it. Furthermore, why in the hell did you park it on my lawn? Did you see the tire tracks you left?"

Mario came out of the kitchen with a cigar in one hand and the cigar box in the other.

"Baby, don't trip. The truck is here because I don't trust it being nowhere else, and fuck that lawn. After I drop that shit off, we out of this bitch anyway. Let the nigga that buy this bitch from us worry about that bullshit." He laughed and handed me a cigar.

Sam came behind him with two bottles of Cristal, both of which were freshly popped, and three champagne glasses. The champagne was dripping all over the beautiful, cocaine-white carpet.

"Fuck that. I ain't worried about the lawn. It's nothing!" Sam said as he and Mario laughed at some sort of inside joke while the rest of us looked confused.

"What are you talking about, Sam?" Chloe asked, looking from him to Mario.

He walked up to her and tongued her down. "Well, baby, you always wanted a big house just like this one. So, now that I'ma be the boss in less than twenty-four hours, I decided it was time you got that house. What better choice than this one?" He kissed her again; then she turned beet red, although she was dark complexioned.

"Oh my God, are you serious?" She beamed with excitement.

"Yeah, it's all uphill from here, baby. Me and Mario was just about to toast to the good life. Here, baby, take a glass." He handed each of the ladies a glass, keeping one bottle for himself and passing the other one to Mario.

"This is to H.O.F. and the life that it has given me. This is to my beautiful wife, who stuck by a nigga through the good, the bad, and the ugly; who continues to love me in spite of everything that I represent. This is to my seed. May God make him a thoroughbred like his old man. This is to Chloe and my main man Sam. You both remind me so much of me and my wife when we were your age. I pray that you have as much success in the game as I did. I hope you groom the next rookie just as I groomed you, so that our legacy will continue. I hope you know when it's time to fold and not fuck it up by being greedy." He laughed and then continued. "This is for my mama, who raised me the best way she knew how and still loved me when I chose to take a different path. Last, but certainly not least, this is for my sister, my friend, and literally my partner in crime, Gucci. Girl, words can't even explain the bond that we have. You had my back when I was just a dingy-ass teenager telling you about all my plans and dreams to be rich. You told me, no matter what, you was ridin' wit' me, and I truly appreciate you for taking this journey with me. Salut!"

We all raised our glasses for the toast and clicked them together. The ladies sipped, and the men took their bottles to the head.

It really hit me hard that Mario was leaving, so I took a minute and stepped out on the back porch to clear my mind. Me and him had been through it all, and now it was over. We accomplished everything that we set out to do, and after that night, our union would be no more. I couldn't believe that I had put so much on hold just to be on Mario's team. In my mind, it was always me and him against the world. I was so blinded by that notion that I was just now coming to the realization that he had moved on in life. Shit, he was retiring with a wife and a son, and I was just simply retiring. I had no one, just my money to keep me warm at night. That had me fucked up. My emotions were all over the place. I needed to get them in check. Therefore, I wiped the tears that were streaming from my eyes.

Just as I turned to go into the house, I was stopped in my tracks. Mario had stepped out the back door and was extending a blunt to me.

"What's poppin', ma? You good?"

I wiped my face again. "Yeah, I'm good, my nigga. Just trippin' that after tonight you gone! We been a team for fifteen years, and now it's over." I hit the blunt and passed it back. Mario hit the blunt and wiped an ash off of his grey Dickie pants.

"G, you know that I got you. If you want to relocate, just tell me where, and you out of here first thing in the morning. Plus, I was gone wait 'til tonight to give you this at the going away party that Sam put together, but fuck it."

He handed me a small manila envelope. Inside was a folded piece of paper and a check. I opened it, and my mouth dropped to the floor. It was a check for two million dollars and the deed to the Doll House!

Chapter 35

Mina

"Hello?" I sat up straight in my seat on the couch where I was relaxing in my robe and reading a book when I saw Sam's number on the caller ID. I knew they would be back in town that day, and I was scared as hell, because I didn't have that money.

"Mina, did you get that?" he asked, getting straight to the point.

"No, I couldn't. I . . . I . . ." I began to cry.

"Listen, is Tre' there?" he asked.

"No, he's been gone for two days now. He doesn't give a fuck about the situation that he put me in. He's gonna get me killed, Sam." I continued to sob and sniff.

"Look, I'm pulling up now. Open the door."

I hesitated, because I didn't know what the deal was. I was unsure if I could trust Sam with my life and let him into my house. I heard a knock, then he spoke into the phone.

"Open the door, Mina. I think I can help you."

Fuck it. If he's going to kill me, then I guess it's just my time, I said to myself as I swung the door open.

"It's cool, ma. You safe with me. I promise."

I looked into his beautiful eyes. I believed him, so I moved aside and let him inside. Immediately, I began to cry on his shoulder, and he wrapped his arms around me.

"I'm so sorry, Sam. I swear I didn't know."

He patted my head, and we moved to the couch. "Mina, as of first thing in the morning, I'm the boss."

At first, I looked at him in confusion, but then my eyes lit up. I knew he was telling me this because he would give me a break.

"Hold on. Don't get too excited. I will be the boss, but I can't forgive the debt. If I do it for Tre', then everybody will be asking me to cut them some slack. However, I will give you time to get it."

I was relieved. "Thank you, Sam. I swear I'm going to get you every dime of it back. Even if it takes me a decade." I said it, and I meant every word of it.

"I know you will. But on the real, Mina, you need to leave that nigga alone. He ain't no good for you. I know you love him, but the man you used to love is gone. Now you just stuck wit' a bitch-ass nigga."

"You're right, Sam. He has been in and out of the house more and more lately. I called his job, which he doesn't have anymore because he hasn't shown up to work for days. To top it all off, he's becoming more abusive, and I swear, as soon as I pay you off, I'm outta here," I confessed, letting all of my burdens spill out.

"Abusive?" Sam looked puzzled. "That nigga be hittin' you?" he asked, and I nodded. "Then leaving is definitely a good idea, ma." He stood and walked toward my door. "I gotta get ready for this party, so I'll be in touch. A'ight, shorty."

I didn't want him to leave. In fact, I silently wished he could stay forever, but I knew better. I closed the door behind him and sniffed the air, which was still smelling of his Aqua Di Gio cologne. I don't know if it was me, but Sam definitely had more swag about himself.

I went upstairs to take a bubble bath and to put a plan together for getting Sam's money. It was as if the thought hit me all at once. I pulled out my cell phone and called Gucci.

"Hello?"

"Hey, girl. Do you think you could use your clout and get me a job?" I asked with a smile on my face, knowing she was the woman for the job.

"A job where, girl?"

"The Doll House where you work. I need money fast to pay off a debt. Other than slinging crack, dancing is the only thing I can think of to make fast money." I held my breath and didn't know how to take her hardy laugh on the other end of the phone.

"Girl, can you dance?"

"Yeah, I'm decent," I replied, a little offended that she had asked me that, and I didn't know why, because it was a legitimate question.

"Okay. Come by the club tomorrow night at seven. The owner will be there to greet you. Bring a performance outfit, some heels, and your moves for an audition."

"Okay, but can you come, too, just for support?" I said as I went into the closet and began flipping through my lingerie collection.

"Oh, yeah, I'll be there, Mina. I own that bitch!"

Chapter 36

Tonya

"Yo, Tee, it's going down tonight, baby, and I can't wait."

I watched as Roscoe paced back and forth in the living room. "Yeah, baby, I can't wait. What you need me to do?" I asked, always willing to play my position.

"Yo, you good, ma. I got this one. Just get the kids ready. After this go down, we gotta get the fuck out of dodge for a while."

Roscoe Jr. walked into the room and joined the conversation. "You gon' dead them niggas, huh, Pop?"

I smiled at my li'l soldier, but Roscoe was furious.

"Nigga, you betta watch your mouth, li'l nigga. This here don't concern you, so stay in a child's place."

"Damn, Roscoe, he just happy to see his daddy in action, that's all." I defended my son. Hell, Junior was only thirteen, but I knew when he grew up, he wasn't gon' be nothing to play wit'.

"This shit ain't a game! This is real life. I don't want my son to idolize this bullshit. Look at what it did to me—sent me to prison!" He shook his head in disgust.

"Yeah, you went to jail, but you stood tall for your family, and that's all that matters," I said.

He stood up, then walked away from me, but I didn't understand why. I felt like he was bitchin' up. Nonetheless, I dismissed the thought as I envisioned all the money we would be spending in a few days. I had plans to live it up. I'd be damned if I let anybody steal my joy, not even Roscoe.

"Where you going?" I asked him as he walked into the living room, fully dressed in a canary yellow Polo top, white T-shirt underneath, dark denim Polo jeans, Gucci belt, matching loafers, and his signature rose gold eighteen-inch chain with the matching charm that read: *I'm so hood*.

"Out!" was all he said as he walked past me into the kitchen.

"Out where?"

"I need to meet up with a few people tonight that wanna purchase the product from the truck. I'll be back later, a'ight. Just chill." And with that, he left out the door.

Chapter 37

Nikki

"Nikki, I really wish you was coming out with me tonight," Mario said as he slipped on his Prada shoes.

"I'm still a little tired from Miami, baby. Plus, I want to spend some time with my little man. We've been apart for too long."

"Girl, after tonight, we'll have all the time in the world to spend with him. Trust me." He sprayed on his Jean Paul cologne then put on his bezeled-out chain with the matching cross.

"Baby, I feel like you should stay here tonight. My gut is telling me something ain't right," I admitted.

"Nikki, I got to get out there with my people. Hell, they made me, so it's only right that I party with them one last time. Nik, trust me. Ain't nothin' gonna happen. But in the event that it do, baby, I want you to make sure you get that truck to the spot and collect our money. Only you, baby. I trust nobody else!" He tucked his wife beater inside his slacks and slid on his Armani button-up, pulling his chain over his collar. He looked so handsome with his hair freely hanging down his back like he was a Hawaiian. His diamonds were almost blinding. His swagger was on full blast. You couldn't tell him nothing that night.

"Why would you say that if you didn't think something would happen? Please stay here with me. Please, Rio," I begged to no avail.

He leaned down and kissed my forehead. "Nik, I can't stay, but I will come home early. Deal?"

I didn't respond, so he kissed me again and grabbed his cell phone and keys.

I wanted to fuss and plead with him to stay, but I knew it was no use. Instead, I busied myself with packing up a few things, watching some of my favorite recorded television shows, and catching up on some much-needed sleep in my own Memory Foam bed.

It was going on 3:20 a.m. when the sound of Rio Jr.'s crying woke me up. I stretched, looked at the clock, and got up from the bed to calm my crying son.

"It's okay, baby. Don't cry. What's the matter? Did you have a bad dream, little man?"

The minute I picked him up, he got quiet. I went downstairs to fix a bottle. I subconsciously peeked out of the blinds to see if the truck was gone. I thought Rio may have come home early but didn't want to wake me. I frowned when I saw the truck was still there. I grabbed the cordless phone to see where he was, since the drop needed to be made in forty minutes.

"I bet his ass is drunk or something," I said to myself just as the doorbell rang. I placed the phone back on the cradle and walked toward the door. I swung it open, thinking it was Rio, because nobody else had the code to make it past our gate. To my surprise, it was Gucci, looking all disheveled.

"Nikki, Mario got locked up about an hour ago. He gave Sam instructions and told me to come get you.

He wants you to make the drop for him. He said the key to the truck is on here." She waved the key ring in my face, snapping me away from my thoughts.

"What? Locked up for what?" I questioned while backing up and letting her into the house.

Chapter 38

Gucci

I stepped into the house and began to recount the night's events. I told Nikki that we had gotten to club Vibe at about eleven o'clock, and it was in full force. People came from everywhere to show my nigga love. He was really enjoying the moment.

"Oh, shit! My nigga Mario done stepped up in this bitch!" the DJ announced. "The hood love you, my nigga, fo' real, and we really gon' miss you, my dude."

Mario threw his fists in the air, and the crowd went crazy like he was a rap star or something. At that very moment, waitresses came from the back of the club with bottles of Moët on ice with sparklers sticking out of them.

"No homo, my nigga, but thanks for all you did for the hood!" one guy said and dapped him up. I guess he was referring to all the years that the H.O.F. crew had passed out meals for the hungry, purchased brand new coats for children in the winter, as well as putting needy families in brand new or newly renovated homes throughout the years. Mario nodded back at the man, and we kept it moving to the back toward the VIP.

"Yo, Mario, I just want to let you know that it's been a pleasure working for you," a young boy named Kade came up and said as we passed by him and a small crowd.

"Fo'sho." Mario nodded.

"This is the life, my nigga! Are you sure you wanna throw this away?" I asked while taking a swig from the Moët bottle that I had taken from one of the waitresses. That night, there was no room for drinking all pretty and shit. My ass was gettin' white-boy wasted!

"Yeah, ma, I'm thirty years old, and I'm a fuckin' multi-millionaire. Why wouldn't I want to throw this away? Most niggas in my position never ever get to enjoy the fruits of their labor. Niggas hustle day in and day out, waiting for this moment, the time when they can sit back and spend all the money they done stacked over the years. Too often, when that moment comes, niggas let it pass them by, because they too damn scared to do anything else but hustle. When we started H.O.F., it was me, you, Blink, Dame, and Roscoe. Now look around." He waved his hand to gesture at the empty table that we were sitting at. *"Who do you see?"* He looked at me for a second to let it sink in; then he continued. *"All you see, G, is me and you. Blink died on his eighteenth birthday."* He poured out some liquor on the floor for the fallen homie. *"Dame is doing two life sentences, and Roscoe—"*

He was cut off as someone approached our table.

"Roscoe right here." We both turned around to see Roscoe lurking in the shadows like some goon. Mario stood and dapped him up. At the same time, I was reaching for my gun, which was inside of my pink clutch. Mario must've sensed my movement. More than likely, he felt the heat coming from my side of the table, because he turned back toward me rapidly. He put his hand over my hand to let me know it was cool.

"What up, my nigga," Roscoe said after Mario broke the embrace.

"*Slow motion, my nigga. What's crackin'?*"

"*Shit, just coming to holla at'chu 'bout something right quick.*" He took a seat next to me. "*What up, Gucci? Still looking good, girl.*"

"*Wish I could say the same about you, jail bird. What is your bitch ass doing here?*" I hissed and scooted over.

"*Okay, Gucci it's like that? Thought we was family? Guess you was frontin' back then, huh?*"

"*Ain't no future in frontin', so you got me twisted!*" I was just about to get with him some more when Mario slammed his fist down on the table like a judge with his gavel.

"*Speak on it, Roscoe! What's on your dome? You look like you got some shit on your chest.*" Mario took a sip from his bottle.

"*My girl been telling me you ain't hold my family down while I was locked up, and for the life of me, I just can't understand why. I was your partner, man, so if you lookin' out for the hardheaded corner boys and lookouts, why not my family?*" He lit a blunt that he had pulled from his pocket.

"*B, I think ya girl got it twisted. My wife sent her a check every month. Just the other day, she told me Tonya has received about fifty thousand so far. I know it ain't much, but it's a fair wage considering that we knew she wasn't doing much of what she was supposed to with the money anyway.*"

"*Yeah, nigga, your bitch is lyin'. I hand-delivered every check myself,*" I added.

Roscoe scratched his chin and looked to be deep in thought. "*Are you sure 'bout this? On your word, you being straight up?*" Roscoe choked a bit on the blunt, then got it together.

"On my word, my nigga, square biz!" Rio sipped again from the bottle just as cool as a cucumber.

"Ya bitch is dirty, Roscoe, for real. Ever since you got locked up, she been on this bitch fit. Talking 'bout somebody set you up, and you know just like I do, you wasn't cut out for this. Be honest and admit it. You're trying to be something that you're not." I snatched the blunt from him and hit it, inhaling hard through my mouth while slowly blowing it out through my nostrils.

"You know what, G? You right! I ain't cut out for this, and that mess with the undercovers was entirely my fault," he said with a straight face while Mario and I looked on. "During the time I was locked up, I did a lot of thinking. I made up my mind that I would hustle just a li'l bit longer and stack just enough bread to get my kids out of here. Tonya been on some other stuff lately, and I ain't feeling her. I can't believe she been lying all this time."

I passed the blunt back to him.

"Damn, I should've known better," he said regretfully.

"I tried to tell you that the night you met her at the club that she was a busta, but you wasn't hearing me. That trick had your nose wide open, and she still do." I laughed, and he flipped me the bird. I smiled because it was just like old times, just me and the fellas kicking back and talking smack.

"You ain't got to hustle, my nigga. I got you," Mario said, taking the conversation to another level. "You know I can never forget where I came from or who I started with. I was holding something for you. I happen to have it on me right now, because I was hoping you showed up," he said, reaching into his pocket to retrieve a small envelope that he gave to Roscoe.

Roscoe opened it and pulled out a check. "Mario, this is a check for three hundred and fifty thousand dollars and the deed to a house in Georgia." With a confused look on his face, he described the contents of the packet to Mario like he didn't already know what was in it.

"Yeah, when we were younger, you said if you ever got enough paper, you was gonna move to Georgia. So, there you go. The check is to get you started." Mario took another sip, and Roscoe shook his head in disbelief. "Don't worry. It's legit," Mario replied with a laugh. "I have the money in a special bank account from Jamaica, so when you cash it, it won't be traceable to you or me. I gave you one, Gucci one, and earlier I had someone drop off checks at Blink's mom's house, and one over to Dame's wife's house for her and the kids."

"Thanks, fam. It's greatly appreciated." Roscoe finally broke his silence. He looked genuinely touched by the amazing gesture.

"Should you ever need anything, you can hit me up, my man. Sam, who's taking over the biz, will handle whatever it is."

At the mention of his name, Sam walked up with Chloe at his side.

"What up, fam. This is my man Roscoe. Roscoe, Sam."

They pounded fists, then sat down in the booth with us.

"Gucci, can you please get to the point?" My recap was cut off by an impatient Nikki, standing there with her arms folded. "Get to the point! How did he go to jail?" she snapped again.

"Well, damn. My bad!" I said back to her, continuing on with the story. "A few hours later, after Chloe left, me,

Mario, Sam, and Roscoe were standing outside, waiting on our cars. This guy walked up, talking reckless to me."

"Bitch, yo' ass fuck with all kind of niggas, don't you, you hoe?"

At first, I paid him no mind, but then he called me out. "Gucci, don't act like you don't fucking see me. Whose dick you hoppin' on tonight, you cunt?"

I remembered seeing him at the Doll House a few times, so I walked over to him, not wanting to cause a scene. "Look, you need to take your drunk ass home! I ain't got no beef with you yet, so you better get gone before I find a reason to fuck you up." I tried to walk away, but he grabbed my arm.

"You think you hot shit, don't you? But you ain't shit but a trick-ass bitch. You wanna be so high class, but you give your pussy away for free."

"Nigga, you just mad that your broke ass still can't afford this free pussy! Now, let my fucking arm go before I shoot your bitch ass."

Shit, his ass had the audacity to punch me right in the nose. Then all hell broke loose. Mario and Sam pulled their guns out, along with a few other people in the crowd. Several shots were fired, dropping the guy who attacked me right there on the sidewalk.

People scattered, running away to their cars. However, bullets continued ripping through the night air. That's when I noticed four more bodies had been laid out as well. I couldn't tell if I recognized any of them, because I was too busy trying not to be one of them my damn self.

About seven long minutes later, the gunfire ceased. We tried to make sense of the whole situation but were distracted by blaring sirens in the distance. We all knew the cops were within five minutes of where we were.

"Shit!" Mario screamed. "Valet definitely ain't bringing nobody's car now," he announced.

"Damn, man, we 'bout to be stuck up in this muthafucka!" I noted with panic evident in my voice.

"They only brought somebody's motorcycle up here," Sam stated.

I looked at the white Ninja bike he was referring to. Then I roamed the parking lot with my eyes to find at least one of our rides.

"A'ight, Sam, the key should be in that bike, so you hop on that bitch and take Gucci and the guns and get the fuck out of dodge! I'll stay behind and take the heat, 'cause they can't keep me with no weapon and no witnesses." He tossed his gun and a set of keys to me. "Give these to Nikki and tell her to make the drop. Only her!" he yelled as we jumped on the bike, leaving nothing but smoke behind us. Just then, the police approached from the other end of the huge parking lot.

Chapter 39

Tonya

I looked at the clock, which read 3:39 a.m. I was pissed, to say the least. Roscoe still wasn't home, and he knew he had to be at that drop-off at four. I picked up the phone and hit redial, calling him for the thousandth time.

"Please leave your message after the tone," the computer said as I hung up.

"Got damn his ass makes me sick!" I said to no one in particular. I got up from the bed, went into my closet, and pulled out a black Aeropostale jogging suit.

No matter what, this job is going to get done, is what I thought to myself. While putting on a pair of black Nike running shoes, I grabbed Roscoe's gun and headed down the stairs. I tried to call one more time before I left the house, but still, I didn't get an answer. I checked in on the kids, who were sound asleep, and I quietly left out of the side door.

I pulled out in Roscoe's Marauder, since he had driven the F350 when he left earlier. My Durango was stalling and acting up, so I knew there was no way I could take that SUV to do this job.

I got on I-75 and headed south toward the warehouse by the Eastern Market. "Good thing he told me where it would be," I said aloud just as breaking news came onto the radio.

"What up, Detroit? This is ya man, Mr. Goody Two Shoes. I hope you been enjoying the cool breeze silent storm on this very early Saturday morning. We'll get back to the oldies but goodies right after this announcement: Sources tell me there was a shoot-out on Detroit's west side about an hour ago at Club Vibe. I'm getting reports that there are at least three dead and one wounded. Street boss Mario Wallace was in the midst of the partying crowd tonight. At this time, it's unknown if he was involved as a suspect or as a victim. If you have any family members that were there tonight, please get on your phone and check in with your people."

I cut the radio off, silently praying that Mario would still be making the drop. Pulling up to the vacant warehouse, I took a spot behind a huge dumpster that concealed me but also gave me full view of the entire parking lot surrounding the warehouse. As I looked at the time, I saw that I was right on schedule. It was 3:55 a.m., so I had a few minutes to spare.

Chapter 40

Nikki

I knew something was going to happen tonight! I just felt it in my soul, but the good thing was, at least my husband wasn't hurt. I called our lawyer, Tim J. Parks, Esq. on my way out of the house, and he said he would have Rio home by breakfast. He also assured me it would be a breeze, especially since they had no evidence to charge him with.

I had no choice but to leave Rio Jr. with Gucci. I told her to call Ms. Claudia, because I knew damn well she wasn't the motherly type. Sam was still waiting outside on the motorcycle, which he had obviously stolen from the club. He said he was going to follow me there, and after I parked the truck, he was going to bring me back home. It sounded so quick and to the point that I didn't even bother getting dressed. I figured the whole thing would only take about thirty minutes or so. I slipped a black leather jacket on top of my pink silk pajamas and a pair of flip flops.

After starting up the truck, I put it in gear and flew toward my destination with one mission in mind, and that was to get this over and done with. I needed to get back to my son, but most importantly, I needed to get to my man. I knew Rio would be okay, but in the back of my mind, I

still worried. On one hand, I kept replaying what the lawyer had said to me, reassuring me of his release. On the
other hand, my mind kept telling me he was an ex-con
and was not a favorite among the good ol' boys in blue.
If he was locked up, how would I be able to handle it?
I'd ridden out bids with him before, but it was for drug
trafficking and such things. This shit was much different.
This was murder!

As I pulled up toward the Eastern Market, I looked in
the rear, instantly becoming concerned because I didn't
see Sam.

I must've been driving too fast, I thought. I was ready
to get this over with, having sped most of the way there
and accidentally blowing a few traffic lights. Not only
was that stupid on my behalf because of the drugs that
were in the cab of the truck, but I also knew Sam couldn't
speed on the bike because it was stolen.

I put on my blinker, turned left, then right, and then up
into the parking lot. All was quiet. I didn't see anything
odd or out of place. For that reason, I cut the truck off,
then pulled out my cell phone to call Sam and tell him
exactly where I was.

"Hey, Nikki, I'm coming. Just sit tight for a minute,
shorty. The cops is on my ass. They ain't pulled me
over yet, but they clocking these plates and following
me tough. I don't want to bring them straight to you, so
give me a few minutes to lose these fools," he said, and I
heard the wind whipping through his bluetooth.

I let out a sigh, but what could I do? "All right," I
mumbled and closed my phone, nervously shifting in my
seat. To say the least, I was scared as hell. Not knowing
what bum or rodent could be lurking in the shadows
had me real jittery. Let's not even mention that I had *ten*

million dollars' worth of dope in the back of a truck that I just happened to be sitting in like everything was legit and I had every right to be there.

I cut the radio on to calm my nerves. That was a bad judgment call, because it was at that moment when a masked gunman walked right up to my door.

"Ahhh!" I screamed in agony as I felt each bullet piercing several parts of my body. My arm, my thigh, my chest, and my head were hit. As I fell forward toward the steering wheel, I caught a glimpse of my assassin as she removed her mask. I couldn't believe it was Tonya!

As I felt the blood drip from my mouth and the life began to escape my body, I thought about my son and what would become of him. If I could just rewind the clock to about an hour ago, I would've said the hell with this drop and left this muthafucking truck right there on the damn lawn. If only I had one more opportunity to kiss my baby or see my husband, I would give anything. Consequently, I made my decision the moment I handed my son to Gucci and started up this truck. I wasn't into blaming anyone for my actions. Ultimately, nobody forced me to do anything. I was a willing participant to this bullshit.

I was paying the cost of being the boss, or the boss's wife, at least. As women, we need to learn that even though it's our men out there polluting our city with drugs and pulling the triggers that are killing our people, in some way, we are also responsible. We choose to turn the other cheek and look the other way because we like the lifestyle that it provides. We like spending the money that comes with it, no matter whose blood is on it.

As I lay there dying, knowing my fate was inevitable, I began to make peace with my maker.

Father, forgive me.

Chapter 41

Gucci

"Oh my God, nooooooooo!" I yelled into my BlackBerry after Sam called and informed me he found Nikki's body all shot up inside the truck. He said he saw a blue-and-black Marauder speeding away from the scene. Nevertheless, he didn't want to leave Nikki to go after it. Fearful she might die, he let it go.

"Shit, Gucci, I had to pull her out of the truck and carry her over to the bike, man." He sniffed loudly.

"You put her on the bike . . . why?" I questioned.

"To get her to the hospital, G!" he snapped. "I put her in the driver's seat then turned her backward to face me. I put her arms over my shoulders and wrapped her legs around my waist so that I could hold her up while I drove to the hospital." He sniffed again and then blew his nose loudly into the phone.

"Fuck!" I cursed aloud and stomped my foot on the beige Persian rug.

"Man, it looks bad. Real bad! I don't think she's gon' make it, Gucci. You need to go and pick up Mario."

I couldn't take any more. Without saying another word, I closed my phone. My heart raced, and my head pounded as I tried to think of ways to make sense of the matter at hand. I knew this was a horrific situation. When

Mario found out what happened to his wife, he was gonna be out for blood.

"Gucci, chile, what is going on?" Ms. Claudia raced into the living room where I was. She must've heard me screaming.

"Nikki was shot, and they don't think she gon' make it." I cried hysterically.

"Oh, Lord, say it ain't so, Father." Ms. Claudia immediately started to cry herself. "Lord, please be with my daughter-in-law wherever she may be, Father. Bring her home to her family, Lord Jesus!"

She continued praying while I wiped my eyes, took a deep breath, calculated my next move. She was still praying long after I had put on my shoes and was on my way out the door. I had to get to Mario before he heard about this tragedy from anyone else.

I ran out of the house and hit the remote access for the garage. I was without my car and needed to use one of Mario's cars in order to pick him up. I chose the triple-black Hummer. I grabbed the key from the key-holder that was mounted to the wall and pulled out on two wheels.

I pulled up to the precinct, prepared to say whatever I had to in order to get my homie out of custody. However, I thought my mind was playing tricks on me. I had to do a double-take, because Mario was walking down the stairs, right up to the truck.

"Perfect timing, G! Girl, you never disappoint me," he said as he opened the door and slid onto the peanut-butter leather seat. "Hurry up and get me the fuck up out of this mofo." He clasped his hands together audibly.

I didn't say anything as I pulled away from the brown, dingy building. He rambled on and on about something that I couldn't make out because my mind was elsewhere. He looked at my face and immediately began to grill me.

"G, what up? What the fuck happened? I ain't seen you cry since eleventh grade, so what the fuck is up?"

I hadn't even realized I was sobbing until he pointed it out. I inhaled and exhaled slowly as I tried to think of the best way to break the news to him. I floated toward the hospital that Sam told me they were at. Lucky for me, it was two freeway exits up.

"G, you gotta fuckin' say something, dog. What happened? Did Nik get the package there in time? Man, *what*!" He slammed his open palm on the dashboard, causing a loud thud.

"They fuckin' shot her, Mario!" I blurted out. "Somebody shot your wife, and they don't think she gon' make it! I'm so sorry!" I said, finally turning to look at him.

"Not my wife," he said, vigorously shaking his head. I matched his shake with a firm nod of my own head, at the same time offering an apologetic glance. "Naw, Gucci, you must've got some bad information from somebody. My wife can't be dying, G. We got plans!" he screamed as the tears poured down his face.

I was distracted by my cell phone ringing. "Hello." I sniffed.

"Yeah, man, did you get Mario yet?" Sam asked.

"Yeah, I'm in the car with him now. I'll put you on speaker." I pressed speaker phone then handed my phone over to Mario.

"Sam, what the fuck went wrong?" Mario yelled as he wiped at a few tears with the back of his hand.

"Mario, man, I was following her on the motorcycle down to the warehouse just like we planned. I was right behind her at first, but she was speeding. I noticed the police behind me, so I had to slow down. Remember, I took the bike from the party." He tried to jar Mario's memory.

"Anyway, they was on my tail, running the plates and shit, so when she came up off the freeway, I had no choice but to keep going down a few more exits. I didn't want to lead them to her, because that wouldn't have been cool for nobody. She called me. I told her to sit tight for a minute while I lost them. I swear on my word, I pulled up about six or seven minutes after we got off the phone. I saw a blue-and-black Marauder scurdin' off right past me. I knew something was wrong, so I didn't chase the car. I hopped off the bike and saw Nikki slumped over the steering wheel." Sam took a loud breath. I could tell it was hard for him to relay this story. "I couldn't call the police, you know, so I pulled her out of the truck and put her on the bike. We made it to the hospital about ten minutes later. She's been in surgery for about an hour and a half now."

"So, on your word, my nigga . . . what type of situation is my wife in right now? Is Nikki gon' make it, Sam?" Mario asked with his eyes closed and head laying on the headrest.

"Man, real talk on my word . . ." Sam hesitated. "From what I saw, Mario, it ain't looking too good. She was shot in her head, man."

Silence filled the air. Suddenly, without warning, Mario slammed my phone several times against the dashboard. The battery popped out, the screen shattered, and a few buttons fell out too. Finally acknowledging that he could do no more damage, he then tossed the phone into the back seat. He was full of rage, anger, hurt, and frustration. It would only be a matter of time before he blew up.

I knew this was the calm before the storm. Mario hadn't cried since his father walked out on him and his mom when he was fourteen. After his tears dried up, he became the man that he was today, not backing down and taking no shit. I knew once Mario got himself together, it would be some serious bloodshed behind this. Somebody had fucked with the wrong one.

I pulled up to the hospital and gave the keys to the valet. Mario was walking so fast that I was barely able to keep up with him as we made our way through the lobby.

"Yes, can I help you?" asked a middle-aged woman from behind a white desk.

"We need to know what floor Nikkita Wallace is on please," I said when Mario said nothing. I watched as she typed, searched the computer monitor with her manicured index finger, then looked back up at me with concern in her eyes.

"Uh, Mrs. Wallace is still in surgery. You can wait in the lobby until they place her in a recovery room, okay."

She pointed to the chairs behind us, and that was when I noticed Sam. He was in a corner all by himself, with his head buried in his lap. His hands were covered in blood, and so were his clothes, for that matter. Mario noticed him too. He hustled over to him and sat down in an empty chair.

"Mario, dog, I tried, man, I tried!" Sam was beginning to get hysterical.

Seeing his emotion really got the best of me, so I began to silently cry again. Now, I'd be the first to admit that I was not always a Nikki fan, but she didn't deserve this. My mind raced as I thought about her and how she could've possibly felt as those bullets pierced her body. Did she scream? Did she cry out for someone to help? Did she think about her baby?

"Code blue! Code blue! Code blue! Code blue!" We all looked up as a team of doctors ran toward the stairs, responding to the code blue alarm sounding over the loudspeakers. Some must've been coming from the cafeteria, because they were tossing food in the trash can left and right.

I looked at Mario. He jumped up from his seat, and I pulled him back down.

"G, let me go, man. That's my wife they talking about," he hollered.

"No, Mario, it's not. This a hospital, and that code sounds off all day, okay. They aren't talking about Nikki. Please calm down," I begged.

"Yeah, G, they are talking about her. I can feel it in my spirit that she just left me, y'all." He plopped back down in the seat. Then the flood gates opened. "Nikki just died. I can feel it in my heart. She gone, and she ain't coming back! So, it don't even matter if those doctors tell me she made it out of surgery. I know in my heart that my wife is gone!"

Chapter 42

Chloe

I woke up in the morning and knew something wasn't right. I had left the club early the night before because I had come on my period and I needed to get home to my tampons. I didn't even attempt to wait up for Sam. I knew it would be a long night for him. I had to get used to it. I knew going forward, this was just the beginning of late nights. I looked at the clock on the nightstand and saw that it was noon.

"Damn, that's what I call sleeping in." I stretched and turned over, expecting to see Sam, but to my surprise, he wasn't there. I stood from the bed and searched my apartment, hoping to find him asleep on the couch, but again, he wasn't there.

I reached for my phone and noticed I had almost twenty missed calls and a boatload of text messages. One said, Baby, call me. The other said, We had an emergency and we're at the hospital. The last one simply said, Baby, I need you!

I pulled on my gray-and-pink Reebok running suit while simultaneously dialing Sam.

"Hello?"

"Baby, are you okay? What happened?" I put on my Reebok running shoes and was walking down the stairs before he had even answered my question.

"Nikki got shot last night."

I stopped, and my heart hit the bottom of my stomach, then flew up into my throat. "What? Where?" By this time, I had begun to descend the steps, taking them two at a time as he recalled the night's events. I couldn't understand why this had happened to her. As I got into my car, I couldn't believe that there had also been a shootout at the club.

"Okay, baby, I'm on my way." I closed my phone, said a small prayer for those that lost their lives last night, and that Nikki would come home safely.

When I arrived in the hospital lobby nearly thirty minutes later, I felt sick to my stomach. There were too many somber or grieving faces of those that were waiting to see their loved ones. The hospital always reminded me of death. It was where I lost my mother to cancer years ago.

As I approached the group in the small corner, so did an older Caucasian man. He was dressed in royal blue scrubs and a lab coat. I knew he must've been the doctor.

"Mr. Wallace," he called out, and everyone stood to greet him. "I'm Dr. Meridian." He introduced himself.

I thought Mario was about to pass out as the color drained from his face, but he regained his composure and kept it together. "Yes, I'm Mr. Wallace. Doctor, is my wife okay?"

I held my breath, praying for the best but also bracing myself for the worst.

"To be frank with you, Mr. Wallace, your wife is in a coma and hanging on by a thread. She made it out of surgery, but the next few days will be critical. To be candid, life-threatening. Nikkita has lost a lot of blood from the injuries she sustained. She had to have an emergency blood transfusion. The gunshot to her arm caused it to break. The gunshot wound to her thigh shattered her pelvic bone, and we had to reconstruct it. If she comes out of this, she might have a very noticeable limp. The gunshot wound to her chest barely missed her heart by less than an inch. The gunshot wound to her head only grazed her temple. We're extremely thankful for that miracle, but she is not out of the woods yet. There is still some swelling on her brain. We will give it a day or so to go down and perform further testing on her brain activity. This will determine if she is brain dead."

"When can I see her, doctor?" Mario asked with bloodshot eyes.

The doctor hesitated for a second, then looked around the group. "For today, you're the only one that can see her," he said sternly. "We have to make it a short visit, probably no more than five or ten minutes. Like I said, this is a crucial time, Mr. Wallace. I know you want to stay here with Nikkita, but she needs all the rest she can get. The best thing you can do for her is to go home." He turned away from us, then quickly turned back like he had forgotten something. "Also, because this looks like a professional job, we put security on her room just in case someone tries to finish what they started," he added in a hushed tone.

Mario nodded his understanding, then he walked away with the doctor, leaving the rest of us silent but grateful that Nikki was at least still alive.

"Did you hear that shit? A fucking professional! It's going to be some smoke in Detroit behind this! Mario ain't letting this go. Hell, I ain't letting this go. Muthafuckas know better than to fuck with family." Gucci started pacing the floor.

"Naw, man, this was personal," Sam added, causing both of us to look in his direction.

"What you mean, youngin'?" She stopped right in front of him.

"When I pulled up, I saw the blue-and-black Marauder speeding off, so I figured that whoever did it must've known we would be there. Maybe they thought Mario was the driver of that truck. No professional would've been that sloppy. They would've been on the rooftop or hidden in the warehouse or some shit like that!" Sam scratched his head.

"Black-and-blue Marauder, huh?" Gucci damn near yelled, and Sam nodded. She grabbed her purse and bolted for the door.

"What's wrong?" I asked, damn near yelling myself, causing people to look in our direction. A few of them had even made the *shhh* sound.

"Roscoe drives a blue-and-black Marauder!" she yelled over her shoulder. Therefore, I knew exactly where Gucci was headed.

Chapter 43

Tonya

"Oh my God! Oh my God!" I repeated to myself all the way back home. I couldn't believe that Nikki was in that truck and not Mario. Furthermore, I also couldn't believe that someone had shot her ass *fa real*! Before you start pointing fingers this way, let me explain.

As I was walking up to the truck with my gun out and pointed at my target, I was honestly beginning to have second thoughts. Like, maybe this wasn't the right thing to do after all. Shoot, even if I was successful with killing Mario, I wouldn't be able to take that big-ass truck and hide it nowhere in the city. Then I thought about just stealing a little dope from the back of the truck, but how could I ride all the way back home with it in my car? I wasn't made for jail time, so that was out of the plans.

"This shit is too fucking hot, and I should've just let Roscoe handle it," I said to myself. I was about to turn around when I heard movement above my head.

I was about to look up there to see what was going on when bullets began to rip through the truck, stopping me dead in my tracks. Instantly, I froze. Trying not to get shot, I ducked down so fast that I fell on my ass. I rolled over on top of the hard gravel to lay on my stomach, then closed my eyes and covered my ears. That shit sounded like fireworks. With my eyes still closed, I stood up shortly after the gunfire ceased.

I heard a muffled scream. It sounded too feminine to be Mario, so I snatched my mask off to find out what the deal was. I thought that it might've been Gucci. I turned on my heels to get out of dodge. That bitch was on my shit list, so helping her stuck-up ass was not on my to-do list.

"Help me, please," I heard, as well as a faint knocking sound coming from the cab of the truck. Knowing that whomever was inside had to be in real bad shape, and against my better judgment, I went and turned around. My hands were already gloved, so I reached up for the door and peeked inside. I almost threw up right then and there when I saw Nikki's eyes staring back at me with no visible signs of life in them.

"Help," she said again, and I almost pissed on myself. She was a dead woman talking.

"Nikki, hold on, okay," I said as I contemplated what step to take next. Calling the police wasn't a good decision because surely, she would become state property if and when she made it out of this predicament *alive*. Not knowing what to do, I told her I would be back. She tried to say something, but I hopped down off the truck and ran like my life depended on it. I didn't really want to leave her hangin' like that, but a bitch had to watch her own neck, ya feel me. For all I knew, the shooter could still be lurking around on top of that building, waiting to snipe my ass. Nikki was on her deathbed anyway. She would be out of her misery in a minute or two, but I wasn't trying to join her.

I ran to my car as fast as I could and pulled off, passing a guy coming into the parking lot on a motorcycle. I tried to cover my face. I hoped like hell he didn't see me. The last thing I needed was to be a murder witness and next on the chopping block.

I raced into the house, locked my doors, then called Roscoe like about one hundred times. It was just going straight to his voicemail. I went into the bathroom and threw cold water on my face as I dry heaved in the sink.

My cell phone rang.

"Where are you?" I asked, assuming it was my man.

"Bitch! I'm on my way to kick your fuckin' ass, that's where I'm at! Now, where you at so I can make sure I go to the right place?" Gucci barked so loud into my phone that it startled me and I almost dropped it. My nerves were already shot to hell, so it took all I had to sound normal.

"What, bitch?" I dried my face off with the burgundy hand towel hanging in my bathroom.

"Bitch, I know Roscoe's Marauder was seen leaving the place where Nikki was shot this morning. And since I'm sure that his bitch ass is running, I'll be there to put his ass whooping down on you! I got my nine, too, bitch, so you better do like Antoine Dodson and *hide your kids*. You came for my people, so I might come for one of yours. Yo' mama still live on Littlefield in that corner house, right?"

I looked at the phone in disbelief then hung it up, knowing that shit was about to get even realer than it already was. I called my mother to tell her to come and get the kids and stay in a hotel.

She answered on the second ring. "Ma, thank God you answered. Please come get the kids for me. I'm going to give you some money to stay in a hotel, okay?" I said with a shaky voice as I held my stomach.

"Girl, are you on dope?" she asked.

"Ma, look, now ain't the time for this. Just please come and get them," I whined, almost in tears.

"Chile, I came and got your kids this morning when they woke up to find your behind missing. You need to get it together, LeTonya, because—"

I cut her off. "Ma, please go to a hotel for the night. I will pay for it, but please just go," I said with urgency.

"What have you gotten us into?" I could tell that she was more nervous than she was mad.

I heard a bang on the door, and my heart began to pound so loud that I could hear it in my ears.

"I can't explain now. Just please trust me, Ma. I swear on my life that I will never let anything happen to y'all. Please just listen to me and get out of that house and tell my kids that I love them."

I hung up and approached the door just as Gucci shot the locks off. I jumped back from the wood panel flying everywhere and almost peed my pants for the second time that day as I stared down the barrel of her shotgun, which was pointed right at my head.

"Bitch, start talking."

"Look, you got this all wrong." I began to think of the lie that I knew I had to tell. I couldn't admit to being there, of course. I would look guilty as hell, not even if it meant that I could tell her that someone else pulled the trigger. For now, until things were straightened out, I had to plead the Fifth and hope like hell she bought it.

"Don't fuckin' lie to me! My boy saw the fuckin' car leaving the scene, the same fuckin' car that is in your driveway now! Where the fuck is your baby daddy?" Gucci snapped. She looked like she was about to go ape shit on my ass.

I knew I needed a miracle to get out of this. Over the years, we'd had our beef, and I'd seen Gucci go ham at least a dozen times, but nothing like this. It was almost like she had transformed into someone or something else. Saliva gathered in the corners of her lips, a vein popped out in the center of her forehead, and she was beet red.

"For real, Gucci, I don't know. He ain't been here since yesterday afternoon. I swear."

She popped me right in the nose with the back of the shotgun. Blood began to fall everywhere. I desperately tried to cover my nose and stop the blood, but it was no use. That shit was spilling out of my face like Forty going north.

"Now, I'm going to ask your ghetto ass one last time, and you better have an answer before I get to three." She pushed her gun into my stomach so hard that it touched my spine.

"I swear on my kids."

"One."

"Gucci, please don't do this. I'm begging you," I whispered with tears coming down my face.

"Two," she said through clenched teeth.

"Ms. Carter, you home? It's Detective Hudson and my partner Detective Swift," I heard from the front door, causing both of us to look in that direction. I saw two men examining the door that was slightly open.

Gucci stuffed the shotgun under my couch just as they took it upon themselves to step inside with their guns drawn.

"Ms. Carter, are you okay?" they asked, moving into the foyer.

"Yes, I'm just having a nosebleed. Come in." I held my head back and pinched my nose, which was in excruciating pain.

They flashed their badges, put away their guns, and then asked me and Gucci to take a seat.

"What's up with the door frame?"

"My husband got locked out the other day and kicked the door in. I haven't found the time to clean up the mess." I was so good at lying that I sometimes surprised myself.

"I don't know how to ask this, Ms. Carter, but . . . when did you last see Roscoe Jones?"

I looked at Gucci, who sat with her hands folded like she would fuck me up on sight if I had lied to her. "I was just telling my cousin"—I nodded over to Gucci—"that he got dressed yesterday and left here late afternoon. He hasn't been back since. I've called him over a hundred times. Now his phone is just going to voicemail. Is he in trouble?" I thought maybe someone else might've seen the car at the Eastern Market and called the police.

"What was he wearing?" the older detective asked while opening up a small note pad and pulling a pen from his shirt pocket.

"A yellow shirt, some jeans, and some Gucci loafers," Gucci said, and we all looked at her.

"How do you know?" I asked, forgetting all about the cops.

"He was at Club Vibe last night, and that's what he had on when I saw him," she said nonchalantly.

The two detectives looked at each other, then the older one jotted something down in his notebook.

"Well, we have reason to believe that Mr. Jones was one of the victims at that nightclub yesterday. There was a shooting last night shortly after 2:30 a.m., Miss— Um . . ." He looked down at Gucci. "I'm sorry, I don't know your name, but were you there around that time?"

"No, it was so packed that I couldn't get in. I only saw Roscoe as I was walking back to my car and he was getting out of his," she said, not blinking one eye.

I knew she was lying, because Gucci would never be turned away from any club in Detroit, packed or not, but what could I say?

"What do you mean, a victim? Was he shot?" I began to worry.

"Yes, he was, and unfortunately, he didn't make it. When the emergency medical technicians arrived, he was dead on arrival. I'm so sorry," he apologized.

I almost fainted. "How do you know it was him?" Tears began to fall.

"Well, that's why we need you. The body we found inside the club is sort of unrecognizable."

"What? Inside the club? I thought the shooting took place in the parking lot. That's what the news said." I looked confused.

"Yes, a shootout did take place outside the nightclub. However, at the same time, it appears that a small commotion went down in the men's restroom. Therefore, a few stragglers inside the club were shot as well. We found a gentleman in the bathroom, shot to death with multiple gunshots to the chest. The victim had Mr. Jones' identification on him, but his face appears to be . . . excuse the term . . . blown off. We need you to come down to the county morgue and make a positive identification."

Chapter 44

Gucci

I just had to go see for myself if the shit this cop was spitting was true. So, I went with Tonya to the morgue. There Roscoe was, laid on the table, still rocking his famous *I'm so hood* chain and his Gucci loafers, but his face was completely gone. Tonya almost had a heart attack. I was contemplating consoling her, but the thought of who shot Nikki wouldn't leave my mind, so I left. I was so perplexed as I got into my car that I went straight over to the Doll House instead of Tonya's, where I had meant to go back to so that I could retrieve my shotgun.

"If Roscoe was dead and still at the club, then Tonya could've been the only one to drive his car. But how would Tonya or Roscoe know where the truck was supposed to be in the first place?" I thought as I pulled into the club's parking lot.

"What up, Gucci?" someone said as they were getting out of their car.

I nodded and kept it moving. *No time for small talk.*

I entered the club through the back door because I didn't feel like talking to any of the customers that night. I saw three girls in the dressing room. They all looked scared as shit when I busted them doing lines of coke on the vanity tables.

"Oh, girl, you scared me! Shit, I thought you was William's ass," Dazzle said and then went down for a line. William was the old owner, and he would've given them a warning and put them on restriction. Restriction meant they were only allowed on stage but no lap dances or VIP dances, which meant they ass would go home broke, because the money was definitely in private dances.

I looked at the group and rolled my eyes because I personally didn't like none of them hoes. The fact they had to get high to dance really pissed me off. Hell, nobody wanted a wasted stripper that was too high to even look sexy. The Doll House was supposed to showcase the hottest women in Detroit, giving the customers the illusion of perfection. Things hadn't been like that for the last two years, but I was about to change that right now.

I walked toward the stoners and wiped the powder off the counter, spilling it onto the ground. "Take that shit and go work on Woodward some damn where," I said, referencing the street known for its high level of prostitution.

"Bitch, that was good blow! What the fuck you do that for?" Kenya asked, standing up like she wanted some of me, but we both knew better.

"'Cause I can, bitch! In case you ain't heard, I own this bitch now, and I don't want my dancers to look like zombies and shit. I don't care about how you fuck up your body, but when you fuck up my money, then there is a problem."

Dazzle, Kenya, and the other girl, Pretty, looked at me in shock. They knew I wasn't the one, so they collected their shit and got to steppin'.

"Yo, Prett," I called, and she looked back. "You can stay."

"Thanks, Gucci. Girl, I promise I won't bring that shit up here no more. I need this job. I got three kids. I knew that you had my back!" She reached for a hug, and I stepped back. I only called her back because she fit the Doll image to a tee. The customers loved her half black, half Asian look. Cutting her off would cut my pockets, and I couldn't have that.

"We ain't cool. You just make money, and like I said, I ain't fucking up my money." I dismissed her and walked out into the hallway that led me to William's old office, trying not to be noticed, but I failed.

"Gucci, aye! Some chick is here and wants to see you. She say her name is Mina or some shit like that." Randy, my bouncer, pointed over to Mina, who was sitting at the bar, looking as uncomfortable as the devil in church.

"Send her in here." I nodded at the office.

He hustled back toward her and pointed her my way. She walked with her mouth opened as she took in the sight of naked bodies everywhere. I laughed because I knew she wasn't cut out for this.

"Hey, Gucci, so you own this place now, huh?" She looked around the junky office that reeked of stale cigarette smoke.

"Yeah, I just got the papers to it yesterday, so you're in luck." We laughed. "So, show me your moves." I sat behind the desk in William's leather chair and rocked back and forth.

"Right here, right now?" She blushed.

"Yeah. Shit, if you can't dance for me, then you definitely can't dance for a crowd," I pointed out.

"But you're a woman," she shyly announced, and I rolled my eyes.

"Girl, I ain't no pussy eater. I'm strictly dickly! Plus, there will be plenty of women in that audience every night! Hell, dykes are the best customers."

"Okay." She stood and removed the jacket and slid out of her skirt, revealing a really pretty sheer pink baby doll top, matching thong, thigh-highs, and a garter belt with some pink platform heels. Her makeup was flawless. I decided that even if she couldn't dance, I would hire her anyway to be a waitress or something.

The sound of Ciara's song "Ride" flowed into the office through the speakers that were on the wall. She began to work it. She rolled her hips and eyed me seductively. Then she shocked me by even making her booty clap. Because those were the three necessities for this type of position, I had no choice but to give her the job.

"Pick a name for yourself, doll. Welcome to the Doll House."

"Oh my God, are you serious? I was nervous as hell!" she admitted.

"You did good, and once you learn some pole tricks, you'll be the shit."

"Um, am I supposed to pick the name of a doll that's out or what?" She looked at me for clarification.

"Well, we add Doll behind it, so when they announce me, they say let's welcome the Gucci Doll. We have a Pretty Doll, Satin Doll, Pynk Doll, Sexi Doll, Toy Doll, and Diamond Doll."

She thought for a minute, then smiled at me. "What about the most popular doll of them all, Barbie?"

"Barbie Doll does fit you, but I think you need a wig or something to go with your theme." I got up and took her into the dressing room, introducing her to the ladies that were beginning to arrive. I gave her my old locker. I even found a pink wig for her to rock for that night. Then I took her back into my office to give her the rules and regulations. I put her on game about the club, which customers to stay away from, as well as which dancers to steer clear of. I told her that I absolutely needed her to obtain a cabaret license in order to dance, but I would allow her a week to get her money together—which reminded me about why she was there in the first place.

"What does your husband think of this new profession?"

"Girl, he hasn't been at home lately. Just in and out. Also, he's been getting so high he can't think nothing, because his mind ain't all there." She tried to smile, but I saw the pain in her eyes.

"So, you need the job to feed his habit," I guessed.

"No . . . not at all! I would never support that shit. I need the job because he fucked over someone's product, and I'm trying to pay that bill. In fact, I think my life depends on it." She averted her eyes, and I knew she had to be talking about Mario.

"Well, once you pay it off, what you gon' do?"

"I'm leaving this place and his ass, never looking back again."

I smiled. I liked her even more because she could've run already. Because she stayed, it showed me she wasn't grimy.

"Well, I hope you do just that. Pay the debt off and never look back!"

Chapter 45

Nikki

Where am I? I thought as I heard voices that sounded distant. I blinked rapidly, but my vision was cloudy as I tried to focus. I felt like shit, but once I saw my husband, I was thankful I was still alive.

"Oh my God, baby. Thank God you opened your eyes." He stood at my side, looking as though he needed a nap, a shower, and a shave. "You been in here for seven days, baby. The doctors thought you wouldn't make it, but I knew you would, baby. I knew you would." Tears began to drop down his face and then mine.

He grabbed my hand and put it toward his face, then his lips, then on his chest right over his heart. "I swear on my life, we looking for the niggas that did this, baby. Sam said he saw a blue-and-black Marauder leaving the warehouse. Gucci thought it was Roscoe's old one, but when she got over there, the police showed up and said he was dead." He looked hurt about that. Then he continued, "Tonya was next on our list of suspects, but we waiting to make a move, since we don't even know how they would know about it in the first place. The truck was left untouched, and that really gets me. I know this was no random shooting. Whoever shot you thought it was me and must've known what was in it, so why did they do all of that just to leave it?" He looked up at the ceiling.

I couldn't speak because of the tube in my throat. I began to point at it, hoping he would call someone to remove it.

"Oh, you want to say something?"

I wanted to say, "Hell yeah, it was Tonya's ass," but I just nodded gently instead.

As Mario hit the call button for the nurse to come in and remove the breathing tube, a very large man with a security shirt burst through the room door like a gust of wind. "Mr. Wallace, your mother called and wanted me to let you know your son is not feeling well, so they won't be coming for a visit today."

"What she say was wrong with him?" Mario replied.

"I don't know, but it sounded urgent. She said she was taking him to the hospital. She wants you to call her as soon as possible," the man urged, pushing the cell phone toward Mario.

"Nikkita, don't trip baby, it's nothing," Mario said as he turned toward me and noticed my worried expression.

Hearing the mention of my son being in some sort of danger and having to be rushed to the hospital sent me into shock. I began pulling at the tube vigorously, while simultaneously trying to get up from the bed.

"Stay calm, Mrs. Wallace," the nurse said as she walked in.

The monitors were all going off, and my eyes began to roll inside my head. A loud, long beep sounded.

"We're losing her. Everybody out now!" another voice yelled.

"Baby, don't do this to me. Please don't do this to me. Nikki, stop it, please!" Mario screamed in panic as my body went into a seizure.

Before I knew it, it was lights out. I felt as if I were in another world as my inner spirit stood in that hospital room, crying and watching my outer body losing its lease on life. Although the medical team barked orders for Mario to leave the room, he never let go of my hand.

"Nikkita, stop this shit!" he screamed as the tears poured from his weary face.

"Baby, I'm scared. It's not me that's doing this," I wanted to say, but all that came out were gurgling noises.

"Oh my God. Nikkita, we got plans. Don't fucking do this to me. Baby, I can't breathe without you." He fell down on the side of the bed to his knees.

Someone climbed on top of me. I felt a volt of electricity, then another, and another.

"Sir, you have to step out and give us room to save this patient, your wife," the black, middle-aged female doctor said with a kind smile, placing a comforting hand on his shoulder.

"Nikki, baby, don't leave me. I swear, ma, I will fucking die without you!" he said as he backed his way to the door. "You hear me, baby? I'm dead out here without you! I fucked up, and I'm so sorry, Nikki. I love you!"

That was the last thing I heard, followed by the room door closing. I tried with all that I had to get back to my husband, but I was getting weak. There was some supernatural power forcing me to turn my back away from the hospital scene and make my way into the light. I wiped a tear and looked back at the lifeless body that those people were desperately trying to save.

"I'm sorry, Mario, and I love you too!"

Chapter 46

Tonya

"Brothers and sisters, today is not the day that we should mourn for the lost life of our dear brother, Roscoe Jameel Jones. Instead, we should be rejoicing, for he has earned his wings. He has gone on to glory to be with the Lord, our savior. He is now sitting on the right hand of God, and we know he is smiling down on us," preached Pastor King of Mt. Glory Baptist Church, which was my mother's home church.

I sat still and was numb as people passed by, wishing me and my kids well, telling us to call if we ever needed anything. I rolled my eyes at half of them because I knew they were just blowing smoke up my ass! Truth be told, I knew that if I ever decided to pick up the phone and dial their numbers, nobody would answer.

"You be strong, okay?" Someone patted me on the shoulder.

"Mommy, where is my daddy?" my daughter Ciara whispered and asked me in my ear.

I looked at her and smiled. She was so pretty in royal blue, which was also Roscoe's favorite color. I looked into her eyes and pointed up to the ceiling. "Daddy is in heaven."

"Well, where is heaven?" she quizzed.

"Heaven is where the angels live."

She looked at me in confusion, then replied, "How was daddy an angel when he did bad things? And plus, Mommy, he went to jail, remember?"

I didn't respond, but yes, I did remember. Part of me still wished he was there. At least I would know he'd have another opportunity to come home to me.

Ciara tapped me to remind me of her question. I didn't know how to respond to her. I was glad I didn't have to, because the pastor then asked us to bow our heads for a prayer. So, we did.

The memorial service was nice, but I felt incomplete because Roscoe's body wasn't there. He had been cremated. I watched as people flooded in, some still dressed from the night before and smelling like it too. They reeked of liquor, weed, and partying, and it made me nauseous, because that's how he'd died—partying!

At the thought of that selfish bastard, I smacked my lips. I twisted in my seat, getting up and retreating to the bathroom. The thought of him pissed me off because he wasn't a man! Real men don't leave their families behind in poverty while they go to a fuckin' party. If that nigga would've kept his mind on his money and been handlin' his business, then we would be chillin' somewhere on a got damn vacation! Instead, now I had bills to pay and no money to pay them with. I knew with Nikki being laid up in the hospital, right now wasn't the time to press my luck with getting some money from Mario, but I had to figure something out to get paid.

"Excuse me, Tonya." Someone tapped me on my shoulder. I swung around to see some young, dark-skinned girl with dark shades and a long weave smiling brightly at me.

"Yes," I said, pushing the door to the bathroom open with her in tow.

"I just wanted to say I'm so sorry about what happened to Roscoe. He will truly be missed."

I looked at her like, *How the fuck do you know my man?* She must've gotten my drift, because she quickly extended her hand.

"I'm sorry. My name is Amber, and I grew up with Roscoe. You could say he was like a brother to me. I moved away with my family years ago, and we lost contact," she explained.

"Oh, okay." I went into the stall, ignoring her extended hand. I mean, who does that? Were we supposed to become BFFs and share old memories or something? I don't think so! I had big girl problems and the bills to go with them. Therefore, if she wasn't talking about money, then we couldn't talk.

I opened the stall door and walked right past her silly-looking ass toward the sink. "You still here?"

"Yes, Tonya, I'm here, and I want to help you."

I gave her the screw face. "Help me with what? You don't even know me, so what could you possibly help me with, huh?" I shifted my weight over to my right leg and folded my arms.

"Well . . ." She stalled. "No, I don't know you, but I did know Roscoe. I know that you guys have children together. With him gone, can you pay your mortgage? Can you pay your bills or put food on the table? I want to help you, so please let me," she pleaded.

"What's the catch?" I rolled my eyes.

"No catch. I'm just doing what I know he would do for my family if the tables were turned. Here. Take this and call me if you need me, but I'll be in touch real soon, okay?" She handed me a manila envelope, turned on her Red Bottoms, and left the restroom.

I ripped the envelope open with my index finger. My mouth fell to the ground when I saw six thick stacks of rubber-banded money. *Who is this girl, and where did she come from?* I thought as I flipped through the bills.

Chapter 47

Chloe

"It's Robin, bitch!" I said under my breath as I walked away from the church and stepped into my new Mercedes Benz. I had just left that Tonya chick speechless and I knew it. Her ass didn't know what to think. I knew with her gold-diggin' ways that she would soon try to become my new best friend. I smirked to myself and let out a wicked laugh. If she only knew that she was a very big piece to my puzzle.

See, now that Nikki and Mario were out of the way, I really had room to do what the fuck I wanted. Sam was so busy trying to run the dope game that he wasn't paying little ol' me any attention. That was cool with me. I was doing my own thing and making shit happen.

This Chloe shit had been a front the whole time. I couldn't really care less about Sam and his new position. Shortly, he would be history anyway. Soon I'd have key evidence to turn the streets inside out. Shit, with an informant like Tonya, who would agree to testify to anything that I asked her to after I paid her off, I knew I was about to blow the lid off this drug case that I'd been working for the past six years. I didn't really want Sam or Mario. I wanted Zion, the head nigga in charge. He was supplying the streets with major weight and heavy arsenal. Kids were dying, and that shit didn't sit right with me.

I know that earlier I told you my name was Chloe, which I had been for six years, but before that life, my birth name was Robin Jones. I wasn't lying about the rest of my story. My father was a hustler, and my mother did die a hustler's wife. Year after year, it was the same story. I watched my dad go in and out of jail as my mother constantly looked over her shoulder. *No thanks*.

That lifestyle had never appealed to me. However, it did entice my big brother. You know him as Roscoe. That, in fact, is his real name. Growing up, he got mixed up in the street life early, due to our parents' influence. He left home when he was eighteen. I was only thirteen at the time, so we didn't keep in touch. I saw him a time or two after our mom's funeral, which was several years later. We were like two ships passing in the night. He stayed in his lane, and I stayed in mine. He resented me for becoming a cop and turning my back on the family hustle. I, of course, felt the same way about him and his profession. He was the scum that I put away on a daily basis.

So, why would I associate with the likes of him and his kind? A year after my brother went to jail, I constantly begged to be put on cases surrounding his associates. I wanted to put those muthafuckas away. Eventually, I got the break of a lifetime.

Things ended up coming full circle when my boss came in one afternoon and requested that I go undercover on one of the biggest drug cases in Michigan's history. After a notorious gangster named Lavelle Lucifer Brown was indicted a few years ago, Mario Wallace moved up as one of the top crime bosses in Detroit. He moved everything from China white to dog food.

My job was to infiltrate the organization and find out who the supplier was. I did research and learned that he was committed to his wife and loyal to the streets, which in turn were loyal to him. Infiltrating his circle was nearly impossible, until Sam unknowingly got me in. Events went off without a hitch and even better than I expected. No one knew I was cop or that I was Roscoe's sister. As time went on, Sam moved up the ranks, and I moved with him.

One day, my superiors called me in and told me we had to switch focus from Mario to Zion. They had later found out Zion was indeed the ringleader of the entire West Coast drug enterprise, while Mario's organization was just a small piece of the puzzle. That shit was going to be tough, but I knew I would eventually pull it off.

Well, much to my surprise, my brother ended up reaching out to me from behind the wall, stating he was ready to make a change. After some consideration, I pulled some strings and got him released early in exchange for his help in bringing down the crime boss. Hell, Roscoe was Mario's old partner in crime, so who better to get info from than him? He agreed. The shit was going smooth until Tonya started talking that shit in his ear and got him all confused. I had never met her personally, but from what I heard about her in the streets and from Nikki, I could tell she had my brother wrapped around her baby finger like an iced-out pinky ring.

Anyway, I almost blew my cover on the day she and Nikki had a run-in at the nail shop. She was so focused on Nikki, she wasn't studyin' me. I used additional precaution that day by wearing colored contact lenses and a wig. Therefore, I wasn't worried at all about her recognizing me. As many years as she and my brother were together, she didn't even know he had a sister. Roscoe told me he never mentioned it. As a matter of fact, he said he was done with her.

Once he was released, he was supposed to help me out, collect his kids, then bounce. But, like I said before, she fucked with his head, and he began to get shit twisted. I put him up on game about the details surrounding various matters of my case, which included Zion's truck full of dope. I thought he had changed and could be trusted. Boy, was I wrong. Dead wrong! Can you believe his dumb ass was really going to try to take the fucking eighteen-wheeler and kill Mario like I wasn't on to him? I had to cut his stupid ass off A.S.A.P. *Dumb muthafucka.*

Just like that, I had to pull his ass off the case and put him into protective custody overnight. The shoot-out at the club was beautiful. It couldn't have happened at a better time. My team and I had planted eyes and ears on him. They followed him throughout that night. During the commotion, we figured nobody would question his death if we made it appear like he had been shot at the club that night.

After the crime scene was cleared of all the local police, news reporters, and onlookers, my team got inside and went to work. We pulled a John Doe from the morgue that fit my brother's description—*minus a face, of course*—staged the body, and dressed him like Roscoe. Meanwhile, the real Roscoe was on the next thing smokin' out of the city.

I patted myself on the back for a job well done, then moved on to the next phase of my plan, not even missing a beat. I was sick of these scum-ass niggas giving crack to pregnant women and guns to children. It was time for me to take the law into my own hands and do something about it. Hell, everybody knew that street justice was way better than watching a nigga's lawyer get him off with probation or a punk-ass light sentence. I had no regrets.

I did, however, wish that I would've done something with Tonya's ass after she tried to shoot Mario that night at the warehouse. Yes, I said *tried to shoot*, because I knew she didn't pull the trigger. I did! The way I figured it was if I shot Mario, that would be one less dope dealer on the street. He was no longer the target of my investigation, so who would care? I planned to snipe him, then catch Zion and his men as they came to retrieve the truck. I would take them all out if I had to, leaving his ass holding the gun. Everyone would think it was just another drug deal gone bad, and that would be all she wrote. I didn't care that Mario was about to retire or that he had a family. Shit, we all have families. I didn't know that Nikki was in that truck instead.

Oh, well. She made the choice to get behind the wheel, so she must live or die with the consequences, I thought as I started up my engine. Some people would risk their lives and their freedom just for a taste of the lavish life, and that's pathetic.

"Hello," I answered my business cell, which had just snapped me out of my daze.

"Jones, it's Mitch. Did you make contact with Ms. Carter?" my boss asked.

"Yes. I'm leaving the memorial service now, and all is good. Those tears people were crying were real. No one will question a thing. The envelope I gave Ms. Carter will have her singing like a canary in no time." Again, I smirked at a job well done.

"Good job, Jones. I'll be in touch. Watch your back, okay? This case may be over real soon, and you can finally come on home."

Chapter 48

Gucci

"So, when are you coming home?" I asked Mario with tears in my eyes. Nikki had been in a coma for almost eight months now. Even though it was my bed that he ran to when his flesh was weak and hungry for lust and passion, he still couldn't let her go. He would come in at night and make mind-blowing love to me, but then he would be gone before the sun rose, to make sure he was at her bedside in case she woke up. The first few months of our arrangement were great. I was a love-'em-then-put-'em-out type of woman anyway. However, after him sleeping in my bed night after night, I let my guard down and got attached. To make matters worse, I was even more confused when my gynecologist told me I was pregnant.

I was scared as hell. I didn't tell him for three months, not until it became noticeable. I thought he would fly off the hinges and accuse me of trying to trap him, but to my surprise, he didn't. He rubbed my belly and told me he could never ask me to kill any life that he had created. Part of me was ashamed of what we had done, but then again, part of me was relieved. I found comfort in knowing this baby would make things right with the universe. I felt like I had been given a second chance to be the mother of Mario's child. I would die before I got another abortion.

A month or so later, he swore he would make peace with Nikki and finally send her to heaven. In spite of that, here we were four months later, and he hadn't let her soul rest yet. The doctor told him that her waking up would be a miracle. His reply was, "Jesus makes miracles every day." I knew he was desperate for his wife to wake up. Silently, I prayed she wouldn't, because where would that leave me and my baby?

"G, don't start, okay? I'll be there later like I always am!" he snapped, and I damn near jumped out of my skin.

"Don't start what? I need you." I began to cry after I'd promised myself that I wouldn't.

"My wife needs me more," he said through gritted teeth.

I hung up the phone on him and continued to cry. I wasn't crying because my feelings were hurt. I was crying because at that moment, I knew that whenever Nikki did pass away, he would die too.

He called back several times, but I ignored the calls. I decided that no one would have my back like me. I was tired of sitting around waiting on a man to decide if I was the woman he wanted. Pregnant or not, I wasn't no slob! *I'm Gucci Maria Robinson, bitch!* I shouted to the phone as his number flashed on the caller ID again. I got up, got dressed, and headed to the only place that never disappointed me, the Doll House.

"Oh, shit, y'all, we got royalty in the place tonight. And is that a baby bump I see?" The DJ shouted me out. I waved my hand in the air to acknowledge all the familiar faces. One in particular caught my eye. I had to do a double take.

"Gucci, girl, look at you!" Mina screamed as she ran over to me, looking like Detroit's Next Top Model. Her confidence level was through the roof. I was really impressed with her. She was all decked out in her gray spandex Dior dress, dripping with diamonds, and the matching gray Jimmy Choo shoes. They weren't meant for dancing on any poles, but they did look fierce. Damn, she put my simple black skinny jeans, black cashmere sweater, and Prada boots to shame.

"Look at you, girl. You're looking good, boo." I winked, and she spun around, doing a three-hundred-and-sixty-degree turn.

"Thank you, Gucci. I've been trying. The girls around here have been helping me out, especially your friend Satin. But any who, look at your belly! I knew you must've had a good reason for not being here."

"Yeah, I'm just trying to take it easy, ya know. What's going on with you and your husband? You leave him yet, or did he get his shit together? It has to be one of the two, because you look happy as a mutha," I acknowledged, and she blushed.

"No. I didn't leave yet, but there is a new guy in my life. Before you ask, I can't tell you his name, but I might be falling in love, girl." She smiled.

"That's good. I'm happy for you, girl," I said as Satin walked up.

"Damn, bitch, I ain't seen or heard from you in a month of Sundays. What's good? I thought we was better than that!" she half joked.

I told Mina I would kick it with her later, then pulled Satin toward my office. We went inside and closed the door.

"Satin, girl, I fucked up, and I don't know what to do."
I began to cry, which had become a frequent thing for me
to do since I had become pregnant.

She looked at me, genuinely concerned. "Girl, calm
down. What's the matter?" She took a seat in the chair
across from my desk as I continued to stand and pace
back and forth.

"I fucked around and slept with Mario, and this is
what happened." I pointed to my stomach. "I thought this
was just a once-in-a while thing. Nikki was in a coma
and all, but when he kept crawling into my bed more and
more, I became attached and got pregnant." I reached
for Kleenex and blew my nose while Satin stared at me.
"Every day it seems like I lose more and more of him. He
leaves early in the morning and doesn't come back 'til
late at night! He keeps saying he's going to pull the plug
on her. It's been so long, and the doctor says she's basically a vegetable, but he still hasn't done it yet." I paused
for a moment. "Satin, I can't compete with her!" I sobbed
even more and reached for more tissue in order to blow
my nose again.

"Gucci, don't take this the wrong way, but regardless if Nikki was in a coma or not, that's still his
wife. Even if she died tomorrow, you'll still be living in
her shadow." Her words hit me like a right hook. "You
know that you both crossed that line by letting him into
your bed. He was weak and vulnerable, but you—" She
pointed an accusing finger at me. "Shit, Gucci, you were
clothed in your right mind. You knew exactly what you
were doing."

I couldn't believe she wasn't on my side. *Damn,
nobody feels for me. Not Mario, not Satin, and especially
not Ms. Claudia.*

Ms. Claudia was beyond pissed, and I knew it even though she hadn't said anything to me about it personally. I heard her one night yelling and telling Mario how big of a fool he was and how he fell right into my trap.

"That damn girl couldn't wait to get her hands on you, and you fell right into her arms. Your wife is on her death bed. Your son has been taken out of his element and away from his mother while you over here playing house!"

"Mom, chill out, a'ight. Gucci has never come after me! I had a weak moment, and I went after her," Mario admitted.

"I bet she didn't put up a fuss either! Hell, she probably never said no. She just slid right over and let you in," she yelled. "Son, let me school you real quick. See, a woman will chase you until you catch her. Do you get my drift, son?" She left on that note, but her words lingered on long after she was gone. She also took Mario Jr. with her, and he hadn't been back.

"Ugh, Gucci, don't ignore me!" Satin snapped me back to reality.

"I wasn't ignoring you. My bad, girl. I just wish I could turn back the hands of time and—"

She cut me off. "Don't have regrets about anything that you did. It's exactly what you wanted to do at that moment . . . believe that!"

Chapter 49

Mina

"What's up, ma?" Sam walked into the hotel suite at the MGM Casino that he rented for me two weeks ago. I needed to get away from Tre', who was becoming more abusive whenever he was at home. A few times, he had even come up to the Doll House, threatening to kill me. I took his word for it. I didn't know what he was capable of anymore, and I wasn't one to take chances.

With a smirk, I watched Sam as he stood there eyeing me seductively. I was lying across the plush California king bed, reading *Still Deceiving*, another book by India. I had picked it up at a book signing the other day.

"Hey, you. What's up?" I flirted and put my book down on the nightstand. He was standing there with a dozen red roses and a bottle of champagne. I smiled. Sam was the man of my dreams, and until recently, I never knew I could be treated so good by anyone. About a month or two back, he began coming to the Doll House more frequently than his usual once in a while visit. In between my turns on stage and dancing with other customers, I would sit and talk with him.

One night I remembered our casual conversation growing a little more serious as he vented to me about the change in Chloe and how not having Mario around so much was really hard on business. "I want something more with my life, Mina. All of this shit was for Chloe." He pointed to the jewels that he was flossin' then nodded to his team of niggas who were standing around us.

"Like what? If you could go back in time and change your situation, what would you have done differently?" I quizzed.

"Man, I don't really know about changing shit. Erasing what I've been through only changes who I am." He took a gulp of the Jack and Coke that was in his glass. "I ain't the would've, should've, could've type of cat. I was thinking that moving forward I could do something to give back to the hood or go back to school or something. I always wanted to own a restaurant, but in the ghetto, dreams like that don't come true. For niggas like me, you either gotta be a ball player or a dope dealer to live a better life and put food on the table for your family, and that's real talk."

I looked at him and saw the conflict in his eyes regarding the lifestyle he desired to have versus the one he had chosen. "You still have time to change your life. Not to mention the money that you have saved won't hurt. You should leave the game and get away. Go somewhere far and start over." I fantasized more about me and my life than his.

"It ain't that easy, Mina. There's rules to this shit and consequences if you don't follow them." He smiled halfheartedly, and I knew he was about to change the subject as he so often did. "You got my money?" he joked to lighten the mood. We both laughed.

I pulled bills from my garter belt and off my arm bands. After counting out $400, I handed it over, but he refused to take it all. He took $200 and gave me the other $200, so as not to leave me broke. Sam was just good people like that.

I smiled at the thoughts of the past just as Sam slipped off his Mauri gator boots, sat down on the bed, and began kissing me on the cheek.

"What were you reading?" He looked down at the book on the nightstand.

"The sequel to *Dope, Death, and Deception*. You should read it. It's really good!"

"Is that so? Well, one day, I just might."

I saw that he was tense, so I moved over behind him in the bed and began to massage his neck. "What's wrong?"

He didn't speak at first, just exhaled. "I know you might not want to hear this, but it's Chloe. She's up to something, but I can't put my finger on it. She ain't never home. When she is there, she does nothing but question me about what I've been doing all day, then complains when I don't answer. She knows I can't tell her certain things, but she keeps pushing and pushing. My grandfather told me a long time ago, never trust a person that asks too many questions."

I rolled his neck from side to side. "Well, Sam, maybe she just wants to know where her man is. You can't blame a woman for that." I stood up and grabbed the bottle of champagne, filled two glasses from the bar, and came back over to Sam, who had moved over to the couch. He looked so sexy. It was getting harder and harder not to come on to him. He and I had not had sex. Although I wanted to, I didn't try, because he was incredibly committed to Chloe. Our relationship was nothing more than being each other's shoulder to lean on and an ear to listen.

"I've been thinking long and hard, and I've decided that I'm ready for change. Pretty soon I'll be finish paying you off, and I'm out of here," I said.

He looked up at me and took the glass that I was handing him. "Where you going?"

I sat on the sofa across from him. "I was thinking about ATL. Big things are happening there, and I need a new start. Thanks to you, I'm finally away from Tre'. Therefore, I feel like I can really start fresh." After taking a sip, I placed the glass on the coffee table.

"Where will you go when you get down there, and what will you do?" Sam leaned forward, fully engrossed in my plan.

"I don't know." I shrugged. "I would like to open a clothing store like the one we had here before my son died. I really like fashion. I have a little money saved from the club. I figure in a year or two, I'll be able to get out of here for good." I threw my hand in the air.

"Why wait a year or two and not tomorrow?" He looked me square in the face.

"Dang! Why you want me to leave so soon?" I joked, hoping he was too.

"It ain't like that, Mina." He smiled. "I'll be a li'l down about it, but if you think you have a good opportunity, I think you should go for it. Who knows? Maybe when I've had enough of the street life, I can come down there and look you up." With a serious expression, Sam downed his glass of champagne and stood to go get the bottle.

"Why wait? You should come too!" I blurted out before I realized it.

Without saying a word, Sam grabbed the bottle and came back over to where I sat before plopping down on the couch. He sat back with a cool demeaner, took a sip, and looked as if he was seriously considering my proposal.

Chapter 50

Chloe

Again, another late night! Sam hadn't come in until after five a.m., and I was pissed.

"Where the fuck have you been?" I snapped as he came out of the bathroom wearing pajama bottoms yet shirtless.

"Fuck you mean? I been hustlin'! You know the shit I do in order to keep this big-ass roof over your head and designer names across your ass!" He was being sarcastic, and it was agitating me.

"Fuck you, nigga," I spat.

"You know what, Chloe? I ain't want this shit. You wanted this, so fuck you too!" Sam grabbed a pillow and was about to walk out of the room, but I grabbed his arm.

"Listen, I'm sorry, Sam. Don't leave. I just get so frustrated because you're barely home, and when you won't tell me what you're doing or where you were all day, it just makes me crazy." I had to fix this situation, because my case wasn't getting anywhere. Sam wasn't talking. Even when my guys followed him, they always seemed to lose him. He used so many forms of transportation. He never took the same way to and from home. Therefore, I knew he never took the same route to make his runs or go to meetings with Zion.

"Chloe, you knew what you were getting into. Don't try to make me feel bad. I don't know why you trippin'. I've never discussed with you the things that I do when it comes to the streets. Sometimes, baby, not knowing things are for your own good. The less you know, the better." Placing his pillow back down on the bed, he pulled the covers back.

"Yeah, it just never seemed like you was gone that much when you had Mario with you, but now things have changed." I sat back down on my side of the bed.

"Yeah, they have changed. I accepted the position, so for better or worse, I gotta ride this one out. I got a lot of shit on my mind. The last thing I want to do is come home and argue with my lady." He turned to face me, and I knew I had found a way in.

"What kind of stuff, baby? What's wrong? You ain't in trouble, are you?" I gave him the concerned face.

"No, baby, nothing like that. I guess it's just what they say—more money, more problems. I got niggas on my team fucking up. I got other niggas expecting me to be Mario. It's hard as hell to walk in his shoes. Besides, I think I got a tail on my ass."

At the mention of the police, I tensed up. "Why would you think the hook is on you?" I tried to calm my shaking hands.

"Because some clown-ass detectives follow me around all day and night. But don't worry, they won't catch your boy slippin'."

I felt nauseous. "How do you know it's the police and not just some random coincidence?"

"When you grow up in the projects like I did, you can spot a cop with your eyes closed." He laughed. "I ain't really worried. Like I said, they won't catch me slippin'. I just hope we don't have a leak in our foundation, though."

"A snitch?" I confirmed.

"Yeah, because it seems like them niggas only show up when I leave for meetings with Zion. Not to mention the fact they know where I live. Nobody know where I lay my head except a small handful of people. This shit is buggin' me out, trying to figure out who snitchin' and bringing heat on us."

I wanted to bust his bubble and tell him that I was a narc just to see the wack-ass look on his face. Instead, I turned over and told him good night.

Chapter 51

Tonya

Life without Roscoe was hard, but it was what it was. Instead of sitting around crying and being miserable, I was gettin' it in. I decided to let my mother have custody of the kids shortly after the funeral to fully move on with my life. To be honest, up until Roscoe died, I thought I wanted to have a lot of kids. Since he'd been gone, though, I'd come to the conclusion that the single life was better for me. Hell, me and my new friend Amber were partying like rock stars, and tonight was no different.

"Girl, where we going tonight?" She walked into my front door wearing a black Spandex cat suit with gold accents and gold platform boots.

"We're headed to Club Amnesia. I heard it's bumping. Tonight, I want to get fucked up and find someone to bring home." I noticed that she frowned, but I paid her no mind. It seemed like whenever I mentioned getting with someone else, she would act or look at me a certain way. I knew it was because Roscoe was her friend. Hey, life goes on. She also flipped the script when I told her I was leaving the kids at my mom's for good, but they were my kids, so she left it alone.

About three hours later, we were getting it in at the club. All the men were buying us drinks.

"Damn, slow down. You gotta drive us home," I yelled over the music. Her ass was getting wasted, and I was concerned.

"I'm . . . good," she slurred as she took one more shot to the head.

"Girl, this is like your ninth shot. Not to mention those three tequila sunrises you had when we first got here, nor the Long Island that you downed twenty minutes ago."

"Damn, is you the po po? Yo' ass clocking my shit tough." She rolled her eyes.

"Naw, I ain't the police, but I'm your friend. As a friend, I want you to know you're getting sloppy."

"I'm a G, so don't worry about me. I got this." Her eyes were so glossy.

I watched her sway from side to side. "Let's go sit down." I pulled her away from the bar and over to the lounge area.

"Damn, Tonya, normally you the party girl. Now you all uptight 'cause I'm having all the fun." She laughed a little too long at her unfunny humor. It was annoying the hell out of me. How could I pull a nigga and babysit her drunk ass at the same time?

"Oh, I'm having a good time. I just don't want you to get all sloppy and embarrass me." I laughed, and she flipped me the bird. Just then, Toni Braxton's song "Seven Nights" came on. Amber began to sing along. I laughed at her facial expressions because home girl was really into her performance.

"Seven whole nights and I'm just about through. I can't take it, won't take it. I had about enough of you." She swayed from side to side off rhythm. I was rolling.

"So I guess that's your song, huh?"

"Shit, you just don't know. My mama used to jam to that song on full blast for days at a time when my daddy was out hustlin'. Now it's become my song." She smirked.

I listened closely because very seldom did she ever talk about her life. Therefore, whenever she did talk, I made sure I didn't miss a beat.

"Girl, my man be out in them streets day in and day out. I never see him anymore." She stared off.

"Does he handle the east or the west side?" I was trying to see if I knew him.

"He handles Mario's old crew." She looked at me in horror, like she knew she had fucked up the minute she said it. To be honest, *she did*.

"Mario? How do you know Mario?" I asked, knowing now that her story was flawed.

Chapter 52

Chloe

"Ain't this a bitch!" I wanted to shout after Tonya asked me about Mario.

"Well, the dude that I'm kicking it with was already working for him when we met. I guess he got bumped up or something when Mario retired, I guess." I was stumbling over my words, but I continued to ramble on like it was nothing. "I really don't know too much, but we been kickin' it since I came back in town. It ain't gon' work out, 'cause I think he got somebody else. . . . Do you know him?" I played that shit off, giving her the best excuse I could come up with in my inebriated state of mind.

She looked at me doubtfully then answered with a sinister look on her face. "Yeah, his name is Sam. He do got somebody else. Her name is Chloe. I met her once at the nail shop with Nikki. I don't know her personally, but I do know that is definitely his main chick. Girl, you're being played."

"Are you serious? I need to leave now! Me and Sam got something to talk about." I pretended to be disappointed. She stood with me, and we headed to the door.

In the car, I pulled myself together and prepared to get behind the wheel. Tonya knew I was fucked up, so she grabbed the keys and took control of the situation. On the ride back to her house, I continued to rant and rave while she just drove and listened intently. I didn't know what she was thinking, but something was definitely on her mind as she sped to her house.

I needed a way to fix this and clear my head. I was blowing my case. I planned to tell Tonya everything so she could help me close this case, but I had to gain her trust. Her ass was sneaky, and I feared if I let her in on my plan too soon, she would use it against me. I didn't want her to find out now and put my work in jeopardy. I had to regroup. I was close to being an epic failure.

Maybe I should just explain now and put her onboard with this just get it over with . . . but what if she ain't down? I fought with myself all the way until we reached her house.

"Can I come in?" I asked, and she nodded. We walked into the living room, and both took seats on the couch. Before I could speak, I was interrupted.

"So, bitch, who the fuck are you?"

"Well . . ." I began, but she kept going.

"See, I may not be book smart, but my street knowledge is through the roof!" She removed her shoes, never taking her eyes off me. "I knew that something wasn't right with you, how you just showed up out of the blue and all, throwing money my way and shit. But believe this—Tonya can't be bought." She reached for the ponytail holder on her table and pulled her hair back.

I didn't know how to read her, but I was ready for whatever.

"On the ride home, I started putting two and two together. You set this whole thing up, didn't you?" she accused me.

"Set what up?" I played dumb.

"Before Roscoe died, he told me he had an insider telling him where the truck was going to be and what time it was supposed to be there. I wondered how he got that info. Now I know it was yo' ass." She lit a Newport cigarette and took a long drag. "You and Sam sucked up to Mario, making him think when he retired, he was giving the game to a loyal, trustworthy friend, but this whole time, you just wanted what was his." She blew smoke in my direction.

"No, Tonya, I swear it's not like that." As I tried to explain, she cut me off again. This girl thought she had it figured out, but she was way off. Yes, I pushed Sam into this business, but not for the reasons that she thought. Hell, I wanted to get more insight on the new case that I was assigned to, and Sam was my way in.

"You and Sam plotted to kill Mario, didn't you?"

Now that accusation had me sober and up out of my seat. "What the fuck are you talking about?"

"You wanted that truck, didn't you? With all the dope in it, who wouldn't?" She sat back on the couch and gave me a knowing smirk.

"Bitch, I ain't none of you! You wanted that dope so bad you came down to the Eastern Market yourself." I pointed back at her. "Yeah, that was your greedy ass with the gun pointed at the truck." Now it was my turn to smirk as her mouth dropped.

"So yo' ass was there then, huh? Well, I wonder what I could get if I called Mario and told him that you and Sam shot his wife." She reached for her cell phone.

I had to think quick. "Here. Use mine," I said, tossing my shit straight at her face.

Her natural reaction was to reach up and catch it in order to stop it from making contact with her face. "What the fuck! I don't want to use your shit."

"Look at what you're holding, dummy." I could barely contain my laughter. I hadn't tossed her a cell phone at all. I had tossed her my Beretta, a throw-away gun that I'd purchased off the street.

"Oh, shit!" was all she could say as she looked down at the gun that now had her fingerprints all over it.

"See, I was just trying to help your stupid ass. All I wanted you to do was testify about certain suspects in my case. I was going to pay you big with all the money that I've been stashing from Sam, but no, you just had to jump the gun."

"What case?" She looked puzzled.

"The one that I'm building on crime boss Zion." I pulled my badge from the inside lining of my jacket and placed it on the table.

The look on her face was priceless. I always kept a concealed compartment in all of my jackets and purses just in case I needed it. Right now, I was so glad that I had it.

"You're a fuckin' cop? I didn't know that, Amber. I'm sorry. I swear I won't say nothing to nobody. I can get you info on Zion. I have a few girlfriends that have niggas in his circle. Just give me a few days." She was about to cry as she pleaded her case. No matter what she said or how good it sounded, I'm sure she knew what was about to go down.

"See, Tonya, it's too late. Now the deal is off the table, and the game is over." I stepped back and pulled my government-issued gun out of my purse and pointed it at her. "Tonya Carter, put down your weapon now. I am an officer of the law. I repeat, please lower your weapon," I said in a calm tone.

She looked confused and stood, dropping the gun to the floor. "Please, I have kids. Don't do this."

"Oh, now your kids are important, huh?"

Two shots to the chest ended Tonya's life as she fell to the floor. Once she was down, I staged the house to look like she had fired at me first. Then I grabbed my cellphone to put the cherry on top.

"Nine one one. What's the emergency?"

"Undercover officer involved in a shootout. In need of assistance."

Chapter 53

Gucci

I awoke to the smell of breakfast. I smiled because I knew Mario was still there.

"Good morning. How did you sleep?" He walked in, carrying a tray of bacon, sausage, eggs, grits, and French toast.

"Wow! All of this for me? What did I do to deserve this?" I sat up in bed, sliding the tray up to my protruding belly.

"Well, it's sort of a peace offering. I know that I've put you through a lot. I just wanted to say that I'm sorry. This morning, I woke up and decided that today is the first day of my new life. I'm ready to get Junior back from my mother and bring him home where he belongs. I've come to peace with the fact that Nikki ain't never coming home. In life, we lose people all the time. Knowing that never makes it easy, but it's God's will. It's just that much harder when the life of the one you love is in your hands."

As he spoke, a tear slipped down my cheek. I had never even thought about it like that. I really felt bad for making him choose. "Mario, I'm sorry for trippin' on you. I guess I never saw your side in this. I struggle with the fact that this was never supposed to happen, but trust me, I'm okay if you want to leave. I know that you'll be a good father, but we don't have to be together. I don't want you to feel obligated to be with me. No matter what, you'll always be my best friend, and I love you."

The night before, I had come to the conclusion that I didn't want to lose Mario as my friend. If that meant letting him go as my man, then I was prepared. He meant too much to me to lose him over something like this.

He didn't respond. He just got down on the floor with tears in his eyes. I thought he was finally about to break down and vent about his emotions, so I moved the tray aside, slid to the side of the bed, and placed my hand on top of his hand.

"G, I want you to be my wife." His words stunned me into silence as he pulled the biggest chocolate diamond that I had ever seen out of a black box. "I want my new life to include you as my new first lady, my son as my prince, and our daughter as my princess. My family is complete again. I don't want to let this blessing from God get by me. He is giving me a second chance, and I'm going to take it. I'm going down to the hospital tonight. I'm going to send Nikki to heaven because I want her to finally have peace."

Chapter 54

Chloe

"Got dammit, Robin! You're off this case!" my boss yelled seconds after getting into my car. I'd called him an hour after reporting the incident. Once I gave a statement to the first responders, I left the scene, got in my car, and drove down the street. I parked and decided to stick around to survey the area.

"Sir, it was self-defense," I tried to explain.

"You've got a dead witness and barely enough evidence to arrest anybody. I don't see how we're building a case against somebody. All of the people that can get you one step closer to him are all doing other things now. For some odd reason, you pulled your brother off the case, and I can't understand why. He was supposed to be your nail in the coffin. Not to mention that your make-believe boyfriend is at the top of the food chain and rubbing elbows with our target daily, and we still haven't bagged his ass."

Though I wasn't looking at him, I could see him through my peripheral vision, shaking his head in disgust. "I told you that I pulled Roscoe because he wasn't getting any rhythm with them. They had removed him from their circle by the time that he got out of prison. Tonya messed up their relationship. Therefore, he was not offered another position within Mario's organization. Even if he was, they would've never let him anywhere near the head honcho again. He would've been made to start at the bottom." I didn't want to tell him that my brother got greedy after I let it slip about the drop.

"Okay, what's going on with Sam? From the reports Carver and Swift are giving me, he's sending them on one hell of a goose chase. The only thing your pretty-boy boyfriend is doing on the regular is visiting with someone at the MGM Casino Hotel."

"Well, maybe that's where he's visiting our target." I thought I had hit the jackpot. I hadn't known about this information before, but now I was sure that was where he had to be doing business with Zion. "The only thing that I have to do now is set up surveillance at the casino and find out when the next big transaction is, so I can catch this bastard red-handed."

"Unfortunately, Robin, the room is registered to Sam himself. We checked it out one night when the room was vacant. It appears to be a woman staying there. So again, we're back to square one." He puffed on a Newport while the medical examiner exited the house with Tonya's body.

"He has a hotel room with a woman staying there?" I snapped, not really meaning to show that emotion to my boss. It wasn't a good look, but fuck it. I was pissed.

"Robin, you do understand that this Sam and Chloe thing is pretend, right? You do understand that as an officer of the law, you swore not to take your assignments personally." After rolling down the window, he flicked the cigarette.

"You're right. You're absolutely right. It just gets too confusing sometimes." Though I was putting on a straight face for my boss, I couldn't wait to light into Sam's ass the minute that I got home.

"Yes, I understand. Jones, you're a good cop, but lately, I've noticed that your head isn't in the game. It happens to the best of us. As of now, you are officially off this case. Almost a year ago, I got the vibe that your angle was heading toward a dead end. I've been putting together a plan B."

"A plan B?"

"Yeah, I have another cop working it from a different angle. This will be his case from now on." Without another word, he opened the car door.

"Nobody can get as close as me, sir. Zion has a very tight grip on the police. They know these faces and are familiar with our whole undercover department. The only reason I was cleared was because I had been a cop for less than a year, and my files were deleted." I tried to get him to see it my way.

"I know all of that, Jones. That's why I pulled some strings and had an undercover cop from another state put on the case."

"Another state? No disrespect, but he probably don't know shit about Detroit being that he's fresh off a plane from God knows where."

"Actually. he has been here for quite some time. He was an undercover in his hometown, and a damn good one from what I hear. His own family doesn't even know what he does for a living. His cover was blown, and he had to get out of dodge. He's been underground for quite some time, but he's back and ready to put in work."

"I don't think it's a good idea to change up now."

"You're off the case, and that's final! Are we clear?"

"But, sir—"

"Are we clear?"

"Yes!"

"I know you gave a statement to the first responders, but now I need you to return to headquarters immediately and give your sworn statement to IA. Then you'll need to report to our office in the morning for debriefing. All of your knowledge and insight will be passed on to the other undercover officer by me. Of course, you understand that his identity must remain anonymous, even to fellow cops."

"Of course I do," I said with an attitude. I couldn't believe all of my hard work was down the drain. This was my first and only big case, and I was a failure.

"Do you need a ride home? If so, I'll arrange for an officer to drive you."

"Um, why would I need a ride? We're sitting in my Benz." I waved my hands around like Vanna White.

"Jones, you do understand that the car, the house, the jewelry, and money were all belongings of Chloe, not you, right? I arranged for this car to be dumped at a junkyard. First thing in the morning, we're going to put the word on the street that you and Tonya were both killed here tonight." Leaving no time for a rebuttal, he turned and walked away.

Chapter 55

Mina

"What the fuck happened to you?" Sam rushed into the hotel suite and assessed the damages on my face.

"I went home like you told me to. I had to get all of my important stuff, so I sat across the street until he left the house, then I ran in to get my things. I couldn't have been in there six minutes before I heard the front door open and him running up the stairs."

"Bitch, I know you're in here. I can smell your raggedy ass!" He burst through the door.

"Please, Tre', just let me grab what I came for and let me go." I tried to block him out, but he grabbed me by my neck and threw me down on the bed.

"Let you go?" He sent a punch to the lip, causing it to split. "Why would I do a silly thing like that?" Then he landed a punch to the nose, causing it to bleed. "Look, I got another gig, okay, baby? Since you've been gone, I got my act together, baby. Please believe me."

"What type of job, Tre'? Another one that's going to end up getting me killed?"

"No, Amina. It's a real job. I'm chauffeuring now for this cat named Z. Ain't no drugs involved, baby. I'm strictly a driver." He was still pinning me down.

"Sounds good, but I'm leaving. I can't let you continue to treat me like this, take our money, and risk my life."

"Listen, I promise, Mina, I can make it up to you. Don't you still love me?"

"Yes, but I love me more. I have given up too much to be with you, and I'm done with that."

He tightened the grip on my neck.

"Just let me go, Tre'." I tried to fight.

"I ain't never letting you go."

"Well, you might as well kill me, because no matter what you do to me, as long as I have breath in my body, I'm leaving." Lord knows that was the truth.

He shook me violently. I was beginning to feel sick.

"Please, Tre', stop it!" I cried out in pain.

He spit right in my face. Some had even gotten into my eye. "Bitch, you too good for me now, huh? I hear about you at that club, and it really pisses me off." He punched me in the jaw, I heard it crack.

"I took the job to pay your bill, don't you remember?" I said, barely able to move my mouth.

"Whatever, bitch. You took the job so you can show your pussy—my pussy—to them young-ass li'l ballers." Pulling my dress up, he reached for my panties, ripping them off.

I couldn't speak because his hands were now over my mouth. All I did was cry while he forcibly jammed his penis inside of me.

"And you know what?" My eye twitched as I looked at Sam, who was standing before me, full of anger.

"What?"

"The son of a bitch didn't even have the decency to penetrate me vaginally. He raped me in my ass," I cried as I recalled the pain.

"I swear to God, I'ma kill that son of a bitch." He punched a hole in the wall.

"No, Sam. I can't have you do that for me. Just take me to the airport. Please, I need to get out of here."

"Yeah, I'm going to get you out of here, but first I got to handle something."

"Please don't go. I'm begging you."

"Mina, I despise any man who puts his hands on a woman. My mother was a victim of domestic violence. She died at the hands of her abuser. I was too young to get my mama's killer, but I'm a grown-ass man now, and your husband is about to feel it!"

"I didn't die, though, Sam. I'm right here. Once these bruises heal, I'll be okay." I tried to smile, but it hurt too bad.

"Mina, that muthafucka don't deserve to live." Sam grabbed his keys.

"What if someone sees you?" I asked, coming to the conclusion that he was going to do what he wanted regardless.

"It don't matter. When I come back to get you, we leaving."

"We're leaving?" I questioned

"Yeah, Mina, I'm going with you. Fuck this game! I want to start over and finally open my restaurant, giving my mama something to smile at up in heaven."

"What about Chloe?" I asked before I knew it.

"Chloe is strong. She knows what she wants, and I ain't it! She'll find a way to get back on top." With that, he stormed out the door, and I said a prayer for him.

Chapter 56

Chloe

"Lying muthafucka!" I spat as I followed Sam through the casino, still dressed in my Amber disguise. I knew my boss would have my ass if he knew I was disobeying his orders. I also knew I was putting my job in jeopardy, but I couldn't turn my Chloe switch off. Deep down, I loved Sam. It really pissed me off that he was fucking around on me, even though by tomorrow my alias, Chloe, would turn up dead. I followed him to his truck in the parking lot and was thankful that my personal gold Camry was parked on the same level.

After my interrogation about the shooting with Tonya, I had one of the officers take me to my apartment. When I was sure they had pulled off, I exited the back door and got into my old car, which was still parked under the awning with the cover on it. I started it up and flew to the casino. It didn't go as fast as my Benz, but it did get me from point A to point B, and I was thankful. I tried to call him on my cell phone, but he didn't answer, which pissed me off even more. As I merged onto the Lodge Freeway, I called one more time.

"Yeah!"

"Where are you?" I asked, and he paused.

"Look, Chloe, it's over between us, a'ight."

"Why?" I was losing him as he merged in and out of traffic. He was doing 90 miles per hour, and I could only get up to 65 miles per hour.

"Drop the act. No bullshit, you know why!" he yelled as I cut on the GPS tracking system that I had on my department phone. I had placed the device up under his car when I first pulled up to the casino. It was sending a signal to my phone just in case I lost him. As the signal beeped and began to pick up his location, I was glad to be a cop, because I loved gadgets like this.

"What act? What are you talking about? Don't try to switch this shit up on me while your ass is cheating and shit. Yeah, nigga, I know!"

He began to laugh. "Bitch, please! Is that some shit your cop friends told you?"

He'd caught me off guard with that one, and I had to swerve to avoid almost hitting this Astro van in front of me. "What cop friends?"

"Don't play stupid. Them dumb fucks that was following me. I know that you sent them. You fucked up!"

I was speechless, yet he continued.

"So, what did they offer you? Matter of fact, don't tell me. Whatever it is, I hope it was worth it." There was pause. "I loved you. I wanted you to be my wife, but I guess you made your choice!" Sam hung up.

I tried to call him back several times, but he no longer answered my calls.

After pulling up to the location where his truck had stopped ten minutes earlier on the GPS, I parked down the street and started a stakeout. It was about twenty minutes before Sam emerged from a condo on the block and went back to his truck. He fumbled around for something, then went back into the condo again.

I stepped from my car, mad as hell. *This nigga must be crazy if he thinks I'm going to let him go like that.* I'd recognized the address from some of my files. It was Mina's house. Therefore, my mind told me that he had probably just grabbed some condoms from the glove compartment to go in there and give her my dick.

It's not your dick. It was just a job, I told myself. For some reason, though, I kept walking. *That's my man!* I replied to myself. I knew I was beginning to lose my mind. Instead of going into the house, I decided to get inside the truck and wait on him to come out. If I went inside, I would shoot both of them and wouldn't think twice about it.

After a few minutes of waiting, my mind told me to get into the driver's seat and pull off.

When he comes out to find his truck missing, he will most definitely call you to pick him up. I gassed myself up for the mission, and my getaway was smooth, with the keys still being in the ignition. Without a second thought, I backed out of the driveway and sped off down the block like a bat out of hell. I opened the glove compartment to see if the condom box was empty, but there were no condoms. Just a nickel-plated nine. I closed the compartment and sat up, refocusing on the road.

I heard the sirens before I saw the police cars in pursuit. I pulled over to allow them to pass, but to my shock, they blocked me in.

What the hell? I know he hasn't reported the truck stolen that fast. Probably ain't even bust a nut yet.

"Driver, turn the vehicle off and put your hands up!"

As I did what I was instructed to do, I had no clue that I was about to be accused of murdering an undercover cop. Unbeknownst to me, a neighbor reported hearing gunshots from the condo next to hers. She told them the assailant was driving a black F350. What I didn't know was that Mina's husband, Tre', was my undercover replacement. During his career, he'd worked with the Feds and had taken various roles in the drug industry. He was my boss's secret weapon.

Karma is a bitch, and payback is a mutha!

Chapter 57

Nikki

"Baby, I just wanted to come by and hold one last conversation with you before you go."

I heard my husband's voice just as I'd heard for months now.

"Nikki, I guess you retired without me, huh?" He sniffed, and I could tell that he was crying. "I beat myself up every day. I should be the one laid up in this bed, baby. You don't deserve this. I need you. Our son needs you, but I guess God needs you more. Nik, I love you, and I always will. Those doctors tell me every day that you're gone. At first, I couldn't believe that. I refused to let you go. But now I see I'm doing you more harm than good. People said your soul needs peace, but I needed you. I guess I kept you alive this long just to know you were here with me in the flesh. I can still touch you, see you, and kiss you."

Rio, I'm here. I hear you, baby, and I love you too. My mind was saying what my mouth couldn't.

"Nik, you know that I've always been truthful. I need to come clean with you, baby."

What's the matter, Rio?

"Baby, I was weak. I slept with Gucci. I'm so sorry. I . . . I . . ." he stuttered

My heart began to beat really fast.

"I tried to stop after a few times, but I'm a man, baby, and men make mistakes. I ended up getting her pregnant, and I couldn't bring myself to ask her to get an abortion. Baby, please forgive me. I can't have any of my creations being flushed."

My chest moved up and down as my heart rate increased.

"I asked her to marry me, baby, and she said yes, so Junior will have a mother figure around. Don't worry."

My eyes fluttered.

"Anyway, I just wanted you to hear this from me. I messed up, baby, I know, but a man handles his business, so I got to do this. I love you from now into eternity. Please don't ever forget that. You're my world, but it's time for me to say goodbye and let you go get your wings. God knows you deserve them. Please watch over us and hold us a spot in heaven right next to you."

He kissed my lips. I heard him walk away then come right back.

"Junior, we have to let Mommy fly with the angels, okay? Say bye-bye to Mommy and give her a big kiss."

I felt my son's breath as he leaned toward my face. I wondered how big he was now and what he looked like. I knew that at his age, he wouldn't even remember me. He would think Gucci was his mother, and I couldn't have that!

"Bye . . . Bye, Mommy."

I snapped up, causing him, his dad, and the doctor, who was inches away from unplugging my breathing machine, to look at me like they'd seen a ghost. That's right, I was back, and I was madder than a muthafucka!

Chapter 58

Nikki

One year later

Whoever said life's a bitch and then you die has obviously never met a woman like me. I survived multiple gunshot wounds and almost a year of being on life support. I went through rehabilitation for my injuries and took it all in stride. I was not the woman I was a few months ago; I was better. I pressed through these trying times like a warrior. However, the only curve ball I couldn't handle was the divorce from my husband of ten years. Mario and I were like greens and cornbread; we just went well together. I thought our love would last a lifetime, but little did I know our fairytale would become a nightmare.

While I lay in the hospital on life support, Mario sought comfort with his "best friend," Gucci. That trifling bitch sat back all those years, silently praying and wishing for a chance with my man. She couldn't wait to offer him her body, and once her legs opened, my husband dove in deep like a dumbass. Truthfully speaking, I possibly could've forgiven Mario's infidelity, but the game changer was the baby. Yup, you heard me right. My husband and his mistress made a baby while my ass was in a coma. *Ain't that some shit!*

The betrayal I felt was indescribable, and I wished that kind of pain on no one. Because of the harsh reality called my life, I slipped into depression, but through God's grace, it only lasted a hot second. I learned that one monkey don't stop no show, and it was time to keep it pushing. I could've sucked it up and took him back because I loved him. However, no matter how much I loved my man, I loved me more, and the shit he did was unacceptable.

All I asked for in my divorce was child support because my son, Mario Jr., deserved it. As for me, I didn't want one iota from his scandalous ass. He and Gucci ran the drug operation that funded my glamorous lifestyle. Therefore, I refused to ask for any of the money they made going forward. I'd die before I let them live guilt free because they paid my bills. If I had to get a nine-to-five, then so be it!

The day of the divorce ruling had finally come, and I was a train wreck. My nerves were shot, and my stomach was in knots. Within a matter of minutes, my ten-year marriage would be terminated. After being shot, I was left with a slight limp. As a result, I maneuvered into the courthouse like a pimp with a mean gangster lean. My cousin Anjela walked beside me like a woman on a mission with a coal-black Coach briefcase and a manila folder in hand. She was there for moral support, but most importantly, she was my lawyer.

"Everything will be okay, cuz," she reassured me with a pat on the back and a huge smile.

"I know it will. I'm just ready to get this over with." I frowned.

On the way to the ruling, Anjela had informed me that Mario would be in attendance that day. I hadn't seen him or his whore in a few months, and I wasn't thrilled about the reunion. Just as we approached the oversized brown doors, I paused and tried to catch my breath. I was on the verge of a panic attack and knew it.

"Girl, go to the restroom and get your shit together," Anjela whispered out the side of her mouth.

"I'm good."

"You're not good. You're on the verge of passing out. I would rather postpone this ruling than to let you have a breakdown in the courtroom, cuz. That only gives Gucci the satisfaction of seeing you sweat."

"You're right." I sighed. "Give me five minutes." I turned on my heels and headed toward the bathroom.

Chapter 59

Gucci

"So, why are you acting like you don't want me here?" I had to compose myself from screaming at Mario as we walked up the stairs toward the courtroom. All day his attitude had been stank, and I wasn't feeling it. I could've stayed my ass at home with our daughter, Maria, instead of dealing with this shit.

"G, please just be quiet," Mario barked. "I have too much shit on my mind to be listening to you yap."

He blew me off, and I smacked my lips. Ever since Nikki served him with divorce papers, he had been on edge. I asked him if he wanted to postpone our wedding, which was in a few months, but he said no. Part of me didn't think Mario was ready for another wife, but I also knew he wouldn't have asked me in the first place if he wasn't ready.

"Okay, baby, I'm sorry. I'll be quiet." I leaned in for a kiss. Compromising wasn't one of my strong points, but I learned it was necessary to maintain a happy home.

"It's all good." He kissed me back as Joseph Kiefer, our attorney, walked over to greet us.

"Okay, lovebirds, break it up," he teased then embraced me for a hug and bumped fists with Mario. "How are you feeling today?"

"I'm good, Joe. Just ready to put this shit to bed." Mario removed his Detroit Tigers snap-back baseball cap and handed it to me.

"I hear you, man. This will all be over shortly." Joseph held open the courtroom door for some tall woman with an all-blonde weave. I was usually against black women wearing that color hair, but I had to admit homegirl was rocking it well.

"Joseph." She smirked.

"Anjela," Joseph replied. The two must've faced off before, because they appeared very familiar with each other.

"You don't see me, Anj?" Mario asked, and I did a double take.

"I do see you, Mario, but I'd rather pretend that I didn't," she remarked and approached her side of the bench.

"Who is that?" I asked with attitude. I typically wasn't the jealous type because I was a bad bitch my damn self, but old girl was super cute, with a big ass and large breasts; therefore, I needed to know where my man knew her from.

"Chill out, girl. That's Nikki's cousin." Mario approached his side of the bench with Joseph, and I hung back with the spectators. Earlier, I'd been asked by Joe not to come to the ruling at all, but since I did come, he instructed me to sit as far from Mario as possible. It wouldn't look good for him to be at his divorce ruling with another chick, so I played my position as always. A quick glance at my Movado timepiece told me that we had ten minutes until showtime, so I decided to use the bathroom.

Chapter 60

Chloe, a.k.a. Robyn

"Will the defendant please rise." Judge Harvey Mason sat like a giant towering over the small courtroom. To say a bitch was nervous was an understatement, yet I took a deep breath and rose to my feet like a boss. It had been six months since the murder of Tre' Townsend occurred, yet it seemed like yesterday. I chose to forego my right to a trial because I already knew what the deal was. I'd been caught red-handed leaving the crime scene in the getaway vehicle with the murder weapon. Although I was innocent, no jury would see it that way, because I couldn't even convince my boss of this.

The night after being arrested, I used my phone call on him. When he came to the holding cell, I gave him a play-by-play of what happened. Naturally, he was upset that I sneaked out to follow Sam, and then he accused me of being so involved in the organization that I decided to kill my replacement. I reminded him that he never told me who Tre' was, but it didn't matter. I'd already lied and screwed shit up so many times that he didn't believe that I was as clueless as I was portraying.

With no one on my side, I decided to save myself the trouble of a trial.

"In the case of murder in the first degree, how do you plead?" Judge Mason's voice boomed like thunder.

Right at that very moment, shit got real, and I could've passed out. Instead, I used the last of my energy to glance around the courtroom one more time. Out of all the thirty or so faces in attendance, only one mattered, and his was nowhere to be found. Sam was the love of my life, yet he chose to leave me high and dry. I stood there bewildered by his absence, because my case had been all over the media. There was no way he didn't know about it. I honestly thought he would at least come and support me. After all, I was taking the rap for a murder that he had actually committed. However, the surprise guest today was Mina, and my jowls tensed. I couldn't believe the pussy nigga sent his side bitch to my hearing instead of showing up himself.

"Robyn, answer the question." My public defender nudged me. When I didn't respond, he called my government name again. "Robyn."

"Oh," I stuttered. "I plead guilty, Your Honor," I stated for the record without removing my eyes from Mina. By the look on her face, I could tell that my staring had made her uncomfortable, but who cares? She was lucky I didn't want another murder charge that day, because I would've wiped the floor with her dusty ass. I had hated that simple bitch ever since day one, and that day was no different.

"Sentencing for your malicious act grants you life in prison without the possibility of parole." Mason banged his gavel. "Bailiff, please place this woman into custody."

Just like that, it was over. I'd spent the majority of my adult life as a police officer, only to end up in handcuffs on the wrong side of the law. As the sheriff started shackling my ankles and wrists, I pondered what would happen if I grabbed his gun and shot my way out of this bitch. I changed my mind and laughed it off, because court officers were trained to snipe a nigga without breaking a sweat. I didn't want to die for many reasons, the number one being that I was pregnant.

Two months after being in lockup at 36th District, I had begun to feel ill. At first, I thought it was due to my new environment and the nasty food. Then I noticed my period hadn't come, so I asked for a pregnancy test, and the rest is history. It must've happened the last time Sam and I were together before I got arrested.

"Chloe, I'll be praying for you." Mina walked up behind me with a saddened expression.

"Bitch, you better save those prayers for yourself, because if I ever get out of here, I'm coming for you." I smirked.

"No threats, inmate. That could earn you a violation," the sheriff warned, and I rolled my eyes. I was already going to prison for life, so why in the fuck would I care about some punk-ass ticket adding more time to my sentence?

"I don't make threats, Sheriff." I stood with the officer as he attempted to escort me out.

Chapter 61

Mina

"I only make promises, Mina. Do you hear me? I promise to watch you die a slow death for fucking with my man!" Chloe screamed like the crazy psycho she was.

"Good thing you are never getting out," I retorted.

"Never say never." She laughed like a mad woman as they carried her out of the courtroom.

I stood there, stunned, to say the least. I had actually gone down there because I felt sorry for the dumb broad. I was probably the only person besides Sam who knew she was innocent, and that was the thanks I got for showing support. No matter what she thought about me and her man, she could've given me credit for showing up when no one else did. Nikki and Mario had disowned her for being an undercover cop. Gucci didn't fuck with her period, and Sam was nowhere to be found. I knew she didn't have any family, so I put my own feelings aside and went there to support her in her time of need.

Just as I turned to exit the courtroom, they started calling another case, which meant I had to sit back down until it was over.

"Lovely Brown, you've been charged with two counts of murder. How do you plead?"

I watched as the young pregnant woman stood with tears in her eyes. She looked sick and scared as hell. I couldn't help but wonder how she could be capable of murder. A crowd of folks gathered behind her. I assumed they were family members.

"Your Honor, I plead not guilty," she cried.

"This case will go to trial, and you will be judged by a jury of your peers," the judge announced.

Some redhead attorney spoke up. "Your Honor, the state requests that bond for Ms. Brown is denied."

"My client is not a flight risk, Your Honor. She's already done several months in county lockup awaiting this hearing. Please let her go home with her family until trial." The woman's attorney defended her.

"Ms. Brown is the head of a very lucrative drug operation, with huge amounts of money at her disposal.," the state prosecutor declared.

"Correction!" the defense attorney snapped. "My client was associated with the organization, but the fact that she was the head of said operation has yet to be proven."

"Her father is Lavelle 'Lucifer' Brown."

At the mention of such a name, many eyes widened, including mine. Lucifer was public enemy number one in his heyday.

"That's unfair. My client can't help who birthed her."

"Enough!" Judge Mason yelled. "Bail has been denied. The defendant will remain in state custody until a trial date has been set."

Chapter 62

Lovely

"Oh my God!" I screamed. "I can't do jail."

"Baby, you've got to be strong," my boyfriend Jermaine called out to me. "I swear we will get you out of this shit!"

"Ain't nobody but God himself gon' get you out of this." Detective Vilan smiled. He was a major thorn in my ass, and I desperately wanted to get rid of him. Vilan had had it out for me ever since his brother was killed.

Long story short, my niece was kidnapped for ransom, and I didn't have the money. I hit the streets with my crew, prepared to get the money by any means necessary. We hit a spot to stick up some local drug dealers. Vilan's brother, who was also a cop, just happened to be in the wrong place at the wrong time. Shit went sideways, and he was killed. I wasn't the actual shooter, but guilty nonetheless for even being there. My right-hand man, Meechie, sold me up the river for his own twisted reasons. Without a second thought, he handed evidence from that shooting and another over to Vilan, and the rest is history.

Speaking of Meechie, if I had a gun right now, I would blow his muthafuckin' head off! He was the real killer in both situations, but he turned state's evidence on my ass, setting me up to go down for it all. Meechie had it out for me because I killed his son Spooky a few years back. At the time, I didn't know Spooky was Meechie's son, and I had reason to believe that Spooky had killed my fourteen-year-old sister. Needless to say, I did what I thought was necessary.

Meechie ended up joining forces with Detective Vilan, and now my ass was about to be put up under the jail! I'm talking real-life state property. To make matters worse, I was pregnant and devastated. I planned to tell Jermaine on our honeymoon, but Vilan killed that dream. The bitch-ass nigga had the balls to arrest me at the altar, just before I said I do.

With instructions from my attorneys, I decided to take my chance at trial. I needed to buy some time for my team to build me a rock-solid case. I couldn't fathom raising my child from behind a jail cell, and I prayed I didn't have to.

Chapter 63

Gucci

"Ain't this a bitch!" I smacked my MAC-covered lips. Upon entrance into the restroom, I spotted Nikki at the sink. She looked up from the mirror and into my face but remained silent.

"You ain't gon' speak, Nikkita?" I knew I shouldn't have provoked her, but what the hell.

"I don't speak to dogs." Nikki tossed her paper towel into the trash and limped toward the door.

"At some point, we have to communicate. You do know that, right?" I blocked the doorway.

"The only thing I know"—she paused and peered into my eyes—"is that you've got five seconds to step to the side."

"Or what?" I had to stop myself from laughing. I doubted she could whip my ass, especially with her new handicap.

"Gucci, don't let my limp fool you." She bluffed then walked around me and out the door.

"I just want to make one thing clear." I followed behind her. "Mario is my man now. Don't fuck with me, Nikki, because you don't want beef like that."

"Bitch, is that a threat?" Nikki stopped with her back to me.

"Call it what you want." I shrugged as she turned around to face me.

"I want you to know that I don't take kindly to threats, and you need not write checks that your ass can't cash. You might be a gutter bitch, but make no mistakes about it. I come from the hood too! I can throw those thangs just like the next bitch, and I will if I have to."

"Like I said, Mario is mine. After this divorce, I don't want to catch you sniffing around my man."

"First of all, I'm a grown-ass woman. If I want to call my son's father, please believe I will. Second of all, the only reason you have Rio is because I gave him up. And let's be clear, I'm no back door bitch. That's your title, remember?"

Chapter 64

Nikki

I stepped into the courtroom with my game face on. Anjela was right! I couldn't let Mario see me sweat, and my sidebar conversation with Gucci was just what I needed to put the homewrecker in her place.

"Where you been?" Anj asked as I approached the table.

"It's a long story." I nodded back at Gucci, who had taken her seat near the back of the room. Anjela rolled her eyes just as the judge began to call the case.

I tried to ignore Mario's stares, but it was hard. Up until this moment, we'd had no direct contact. All of our dealings happened through a third party, which was Ms. Claudia, his mother.

"Mr. and Mrs. Wallace, I've reviewed all of the information provided by both parties, and I have one question." The small Caucasian man with gray temples frowned. "Have you thought about counseling?"

"Your Honor, my client feels that this marriage is irreconcilable," Anjela spoke up.

"I'm curious to know why your client feels this way after ten plus years of marriage." He removed his glasses.

Anjela looked over at me and sighed. "Well, for starters, the other party is already in another relationship."

I glanced over at Mario, who shifted nervously.

"Mr. Wallace, is this true?" The judge was astounded.

"Yes, sir," Mario mumbled.

"But do you love Mrs. Wallace?"

"Of course I do, judge."

Mario looked at me, and I caught Gucci out the side of my eye. She was pissed.

"Are you willing to fight for your marriage?" Before Mario had time to respond, Anjela jumped in.

"No, your honor, Mr. Wallace doesn't have time to fight for this marriage, because he is busy planning another marriage with his mistress." She pointed at Gucci.

"Well, in that case, let's proceed." The judge put on his glasses and grabbed a few documents off his desk. "I'm granting joint custody of Mario Antonio Wallace, Jr.; therefore, no child support will be rendered. Both parents will come together and decide on a schedule that's best for both parties. Should you not reach an agreement, you will be ordered to meet with a mediator. I'm awarding sole possession of the property in Bloomfield Hills, one limited edition custom Maybach, and the sum of five hundred thousand dollars to Mrs. Wallace."

At that point, I'd zoned out, because the only thing I asked for was child support. How in the hell was he awarding me with all these things I didn't ask for? Anjela squeezed my hand tight, and before I knew it, my divorce was granted, and court was adjourned.

"We did it, cuz!" She beamed.

"I didn't ask for that stuff, Anjela. Why did he give it to me?" I was still in shock.

"Girl, you know me better than that." My cousin rolled her eyes. "You've been with that nigga way too long to walk away empty-handed. I wasn't about to let you live in the poor house while that nigga took everything, so I did what I thought was necessary," she whispered while tossing a manila folder my way. I scanned through the paperwork and noticed several forged documents with my signature allegedly asking for the money and possession of the expensive home and car.

"Nikki, can I holler at you?" Mario approached the table, and I closed the folder.

"Go ahead."

"Whether you believe me or not, I never meant to hurt you." He appeared saddened.

"That's the funniest thing I've heard all day." I let out a laugh.

"I swear on my kids." Mario raised his right hand as if that meant something.

"Speaking of kids, how is Maria?" I smirked at the mention of his daughter with Gucci.

"She's fine!" Gucci snapped. "She's waiting on her mommy and daddy to come home right now. Let's go, Mario."

"G, please let me handle this, damn." Mario was bothered. "Anyway, Nik, I just wanted to apologize again. I know I fucked things up, but I don't want any bad blood between us. If there is anything you need, please don't hesitate to call me."

"If there is anything you need, please call me and not my husband," Gucci chimed in.

I was about tired of her mouth, so I stood, but Anj was already on it.

"Bitch, don't get your ass beat."

"Who gon' whoop me? Not you, and damn sure not the cripple," Gucci teased, and I lost it.

"I don't know what I've done to make you not like me, but you've got some nerve. You fucked my husband and made a baby, so I should be the one with the grudge. I tried my best to blow you off, but like a pesky gnat, you just keep coming back. You wanted beef, and now you got it."

"Ain't shit between us but air and opportunity, Nikki." Gucci squared up, but Mario pulled her away from me.

"Next time I see you, I'm spanking that ass," I warned her, and I meant it.

"Bitch, you ain't gon' do shit." She laughed.

"Best believe I can show you better than I can tell you." That was the truth, so help me, God. Right then and there, I vowed to give that girl the ass whooping she'd been asking for. Detroit wasn't that big. We were bound to run into each other sooner than later.

Chapter 65

Mina

"Surprise!" we yelled as Gucci and Mario walked through the doors of the Doll House. Earlier, she'd called and informed me that the divorce was final and she wanted to celebrate. Instead of going out, me and Gucci's best friend, Satin, decided to throw an impromptu party at Gucci's strip club. In a pinch, I called around for decorations, food, and for some of their closest friends to show up. The place looked like a celebration, and everyone was ready to party—except Mario.

"What the hell is all this?"

"Baby, I thought it would be a good idea." Gucci looked shocked by Mario's disapproval.

"Why in the fuck would this be a good idea? Do you think I want all these people up in my business?"

"I just thought we could celebrate." She stuttered on her words.

"You celebrate, and I'll come pick you up later." He turned around to face the door as Satin and I looked on in silence. Good thing the DJ had started the music after we yelled "Surprise!" because Gucci would've been mortified if everyone overheard his tone with her.

"Baby, please don't leave." She pulled at his arm. "Let's have a drink and enjoy the party."

"G, I'm not in the party mood, but don't let me stop you."

"I don't want you to be mad at me." She looked over at us, and we averted our eyes.

I knew the party probably wasn't going to go over well, but Gucci was my girl, so I did what she asked me to. I believed once the divorce was final, she expected Mario to be as excited as she was, but things like this take time.

"I'm not mad. I just have a lot of shit on my mind. I'm going home, but you enjoy the party."

As Mario walked out the door, I approached my friend and handed her a much-needed drink.

"Thanks, girl." She sipped on the pineapple moijto.

"It's all good." I smiled as Satin walked over to join us.

"Just give him some time, Gucci. You don't want to scare the nigga off before the wedding, do you?"

"Speaking of wedding, do you have a location in mind?" I knew time was winding down until the event, but Gucci wanted to postpone planning anything for fear that Mario may back out.

"I'm thinking we should fly to Las Vegas or something."

"I thought you wanted a big wedding?" Satin quizzed.

"I do, but Mario has already been there and done that," Gucci explained.

"That shouldn't stop you from having it the way you want," I chimed in.

"Yeah, but I'm good either way as long as he says *I do*."

"So how did everything go today?" Satin asked.

"Nikki was awarded the crib, the Maybach, and five hundred racks!" Gucci proclaimed, and my eyes widened.

"Not to be nosy, but how in the hell did she get all of that?" I asked. "The money is dirty, and the possessions were purchased with drug money."

"Mario and Nikki owned several front businesses. On paper, the money and property are legit," she explained. "Enough about me. Tell me what happened at Chloe's hearing."

"Girl, that crazy bitch told me she would kill me if she ever gets out." I laughed.

"Don't worry about her ass! I got people on the inside ready and willing to handle her, and if she does get out of prison, I got a bullet with her name on it, believe that."

We all laughed, but I knew without a shadow of a doubt that Gucci wasn't joking.

Chapter 66

Chloe

The moment I stepped onto the transport bus, I felt trouble brewing. Every inmate on board was giving me the side eye. They were probably aware that I used to be a police officer, and that shit was frowned upon. Don't ask me how, but for some reason, people behind bars found out information faster than those on the outside.

"Ain't no room for you on this bus!" Some big, burly woman spoke with a deep voice.

"Is that so?" I asked while taking a seat despite what she had said.

"You must've not heard me." She stood from her seat across from me.

I glanced through the bar-covered window to locate a corrections officer but quickly gave up. I'd forgotten that I just pleaded guilty to killing a fellow cop. No officer would help me after that confession.

"I heard you, but I just don't give a fuck!" I turned my attention back to the bully just in time to see her knee smash into my face. I tried my best to block her, but the cuffs prevented me from fully protecting myself.

As she tried to mangle me, I took notice that she didn't have any handcuffs on. Someone had set me up for the ass whooping.

"Where is that tough tone shit now?" she asked after one more blow to the face.

"All right, Gwen, have a seat." A gold-toothed officer stepped onto the bus with another prisoner.

"Damn, Johnson, it was just getting fun." Gwen smiled and retreated to her seat.

"They said hurt the bitch, but not kill her." The officer laughed and placed the cuffs back onto my assailant.

My face was in serious need of medical attention, but I shrugged it off.

"You've got balls, bitch." The cop stood over me and pulled out her camera phone to take a picture.

"What the fuck are you taking pictures of me for?" I wiped my face on my shoulder in an attempt to clean up the mess.

"Smile so Gucci can see what she paid for," the officer said.

I spit blood to the ground and made a mental note to get at that bitch the minute I broke out of here.

Chapter 67

Lovely

The ride to Women's Valley Correctional Facility was long and silent. I used the time to reflect and pray about my situation. I was not a cut-throat criminal, and I didn't belong behind bars. Some of these women were monsters, and I was scared to death. I'd heard so many horrible things about inmate rapes and other violent offenses. Not only did I have to protect myself, but I needed to protect my son.

After the bus pulled up to the rear of the prison, we were unloaded and placed into single file. Up until that moment, I'd only been in county lockup, so this was different.

"Put that pretty bitch in the cell with me, C.O." Some old raggedy, dingy-looking chick called out from a room labeled LAUNDRY as we entered the facility.

"Which one?" the gold-toothed C.O. asked to entertain the old broad.

"I want that one right there." She pointed in my direction, but I didn't take it personally, because I wasn't easily intimidated. I knew that the women in there could smell fear like a blood hound, so I wore my game face like an old war wound.

"This one right here? Yeah, she is a pretty one, huh?" the C.O. continued, and I kept staring straight ahead, not giving her the time of day. Within a few seconds, she was on to her next victim.

"Girl, you look like you are about to pee on yourself." She teased the pregnant chick that was in front of me in line. The young woman appeared to be my age, with brown skin and short hair. She was still bleeding from her run-in on the bus, but no one seemed to care. I could see she was sweating bullets while swaying from side to side.

"I have to pee because I'm pregnant, Columbo," she spoke, soft yet firm.

"Did I say that you could talk?" the C.O. yelled, causing li'l mama to jump so hard that she almost pulled me forward with her. We were all connected by the chains around our waists, so when one of us moved, it was inevitable that another one of us would move also. This time, li'l mama didn't reply to the C.O., which caused her to yell again. "You better answer me when I'm talking to you!"

Before li'l mama could answer the officer, she was unchained by another guard and directed into a small room off to the side.

While waiting for my turn to be unchained, I surveyed the area. There were stale gray walls, security cameras, and several TV monitors behind a large circular desk being watched by a young Caucasian officer.

"You're up," a young Hispanic officer said to catch my attention while she wrestled with my chains. I followed her into the room that everyone before me had entered, and she closed the door. "Take off all your clothes," she demanded.

"What?" I asked for clarification.

"Strip!" she once again demanded.

I was at a loss for words. Up until this very moment, I'd been kept in a cell at the county precinct. There were no strip searches, just bad food and a large room with women coming and going as they got booked or released. The only displeasure was having to share a toilet and pissing in front of everyone. So, this whole strip-down was for the birds.

"Inmate, do it now!" She raised her voice an octave.

"Diaz, you good in there?" another guard called from the other side of the door.

"Am I good, inmate? Or should I call for backup?"

"You good. I got you," I said, reaching to remove my pants and panties.

"It's all good, Shack," Diaz called out as I removed my top. I didn't have to deal with a bra since it had already been taken from me because of the underwire in it. "Spread it." The officer flexed her rubber gloved hand.

Oh, hell no!

Biting my tongue and holding my breath, I bent over, spread eagle. Not only did she look though my shit with a flashlight, but she had the nerve to damn near finger fuck me while searching for whatever it was she thought I could possibly be hiding.

After she searched between my fingers, toes, ears, hair, and mouth, the longest five minutes of my life was finally over. I was given a dark green outfit with WVC on the front in bold black letters, then taken into another room, where I was photographed and returned through the door I entered.

As I exited the strip search, the gold-tooth officer started in on me. "How did you like that?"

"It's all good," I replied.

"Oh, so you like for girls to play in that kitty kat, huh?" she purred.

"Not even!" Was what I said, although I wanted to tell her bisexual ass to get the fuck out of my breathing space pronto!

"Okay, Barbie, I hear ya. Now step over to that white line for me."

On the walk over to the line, I noticed li'l mama was crying. I didn't know her situation, but she looked like she could use a friend and some words of wisdom. While no one was watching, I whispered, "Girl, you need to save them water works for the shower. These officers and inmates see that and you're dead! Do you hear me?"

"I–I can't help it. I feel so violated." She sniffed then wiped at her face.

"So does everybody else in this damn line, myself included. Get your shit together. Don't you know where you at?" I said as an officer looked in our direction.

"You're right." She wiped her eyes on the sleeve of her shirt. "I'm Robin, but you can call me Chloe." She smiled, happy to have met a friend.

"I'm Lovely." I'm not fond of many females, but there was something about this girl I liked. I wasn't looking for a bestie, but having an acquaintance in there did put my mind at ease.

Chapter 68

Nikki

"Hello," I answered after searching for my phone in between the stack of boxes I had sprawled across the lawn. Less than two weeks ago, the judge had awarded me possession of the home I shared with Mario, and already I'd cleared it out and set up an estate sale. The place was a mess, and I was trying to straighten up before customers started arriving.

"Nikki, are you sitting down?" Ms. Claudia asked.

"No." I paused and pressed the speaker phone button so I could continue cleaning.

"Well, you will be after I drop this news." Ms. C smacked her lips. I loved her to pieces, but at times she didn't know how to make a long story short.

"Claudia, I don't have time for guessing games. Are you okay?" I paused and awaited the reply.

"Yeah, I'm fine, although I almost died of a heart attack about twenty minutes ago when I received a text message from my son, inviting me to his wedding."

"What?" I was heartbroken but tried to sound normal.

"I just received a text message from my son, requesting my presence at his wedding this afternoon," she repeated with disgust.

I was at a loss for words because the bastard has only been divorced from me for less than two weeks.

"I'm so upset with Mario that I have half a nerve not to show up," Claudia vented.

"No, Ms. C, you have to go, because that's your son." As much as I was pissed with the situation, I wasn't about to give her any bad advice.

"I'm grown as hell, and I do as I please, Nikki." She was fuming. "I get an invite through a damn text message, and I'm supposed to drop everything for him and the little wench I can't stand?"

"I hear you, but you will regret it if you don't show up." I sighed. "Look, Ms. C, I've got to go, and you need to get ready. Love you. Call me later." I ended the call before she had a chance to catch her second wind.

I was just about to call Anjela when her champagne-colored Mercedes-Benz E350 pulled into my driveway. She blew the horn as if I didn't already see her.

"What's up, cuz! I told all my friends about your sale, and I even had my assistant run an ad in the paper. Today should be all about the Benjamins." With a laugh, she rubbed her fingertips together.

That afternoon, I was selling every item I owned, including Mario's Maybach. I'd already found a buyer for the house, and the deal was set for thirty days from then.

"Girl, do I have some news for you." I wiped sweat from my brow. It was the middle of July, and the sun was baking me.

"Spill it." She took a seat on the folding chair behind the table with the makeshift cash register.

"Claudia just called to tell me that she received a text message invitation to Mario's wedding in a few hours." I took a seat beside her.

"Are you fucking kidding?"

"Real talk." I laughed but silently wanted to cry.

"Where is the wedding going to be?" Anj looked like she was already plotting.

"I didn't ask, because it ain't like I'm going." I uncapped a bottle of water and took a swig.

"Bitch, please! I would've gone." She rolled her eyes. My cousin was a bona fide hood chick. Sometimes it was hard to believe she actually graduated from Harvard at the top of her class.

"Why would I go there? I'm over here trying to sell everything that reminds me of Mario, so showing up to bear witness to his wedding is not on my list of things to do."

"I hear you, cuz, but I'm just saying, if you want to do a drive-by and egg that bitch, I'm game." She shrugged her shoulders. "Anyway, I know you ain't selling those red bottoms over there." Anj pointed to a long row of shoes on display across the manicured lawn.

"Yes, I am." I laughed. "Everything must go."

"What about these Alexander McQueens?" She stood with her mouth open.

"Everything must go," I repeated for clarification.

As Anj walked around the lawn to glance at my inventory, her mouth dropped several times. Amongst the items for sale were custom pieces of artwork, furniture, expensive jewelry, and designer shoes, purses, and belts. I'd chosen not to put a price tag on any of the merchandise, hoping the items would move faster with my "best offer" marketing strategy. Anjela thought I was out of my mind, but I was on a mission to clear my life of all those unwanted items.

Within an hour, almost everything except the Maybach was gone. I was about to close down shop when a black Yukon Denali pulled up.

"How much for the whip?" a familiar voice asked after rolling down the window.

"Mario, what are you doing here?" Instantly, my hand went to my hair as I smoothed back a few loose strands. It wasn't that I was trying to look good for him. I just didn't want to look bad. He needed to know what he was missing.

"I heard my shit was for sale, so I'm coming to retrieve it." After stepping from the car, he put his hands in his pocket and pulled out his wallet.

"Please believe it's selling for more than what you've got in that wallet," Anj chimed in.

My voice was caught in my throat because I was caught off guard. Mario looked good in his black dress slacks and button-down shirt. He face was cleaned up really well, and his long black hair free-flowed in the air just the way I liked it.

"Nikki, I got somewhere to be, but I do want the car. Just tell me how much it is, and I'll take it off your hands."

"She should give it to you as a wedding gift." Anjela smirked.

I smiled too, but he didn't find the joke amusing.

"Here you go." He handed me a blank check with his signature on it. "Just put what you think is a fair amount and cash it. I'll be in touch to collect my whip, all right?"

"Okay," was all I could muster as Mario threw Anj the deuces and returned to his vehicle.

Chapter 69

Mina

"Where in the hell is Mario?" Gucci yelled from the bathroom of her hotel suite. She had called him several times, but he wasn't answering.

"Girl, he's probably getting ready." I tried to calm her down.

"Do you think he changed his mind?" She opened the bathroom door, and I could tell she was nervous.

"No!" me and her friend Satin said in unison. "After all, it was his idea to have this wedding today, remember?" I added.

Mario had called us that morning on a three-way call, explaining that he didn't want to wait until the end of the month. He was ready to get this show on the road and wanted us to help him surprise Gucci. I was shocked, to say the least, because Mario had made it clear that he didn't like me on several occasions. Gucci tried to sugar coat things between us, but I knew the beef was because of what happened with Sam. Mario felt Sam left him high and dry, and because Sam was nowhere to be found, he took his attitude out on me. Nonetheless, Gucci was my girl, and I wanted her day to be perfect, so we immediately went to work and booked the Roostertail, a premier wedding venue located downtown off the water.

"You need to calm down before you ruin your hair and makeup," Satin advised the nervous bride while she dressed Maria in a pretty lilac ensemble.

"You're right." Gucci relaxed and took a deep breath. "Mina, please help me slide this dress on."

As I went to assist her, my cell phone rang, and I saw PRIVATE on the ID. "I hate private calls." This had been a recurring thing lately, and I was on the verge of getting my phone number changed. It would've been changed already, but for some reason, I still believed Sam would call.

"Me too," Gucci replied and stepped into her beautiful beige Demetrios dress. It was mermaid style, halter up top and fitted around the thighs down to the ankles. Her hair was pulled back into a tight bun, which was perfect for the small tiara and veil.

After zipping up the dress, I carefully placed the beautiful crystal necklace Mario had given her around her neck. "Gucci, you look gorgeous." I smiled.

"Yes, you do." Satin handed her the bouquet.

"Thank you."

"Now, come on so we can get you married."

Chapter 70

Gucci

I couldn't believe Mario had gone out of his way to surprise me with a wedding. Honestly, up until that morning, I thought he would find a reason not to marry me, but I was wrong. As we walked into one of the ballrooms at the Roostertail, my stomach felt queasy. I'd waited for this moment for most of my life, and I couldn't believe within minutes my dream would come true.

The music started, and on cue, Mina and Satin took turns walking down the aisle. As I stood there waiting for my turn, I was once again shocked out of my mind. My father, whom I hadn't conversed with in over fourteen years, walked up beside me.

"Daddy?"

"Baby, can I please have the honor of walking you down the aisle?" He was an alcoholic who had seen better days, but I wasn't going to ruin my day by holding a grudge. Without a word, I wrapped my right arm around his and used my left arm to cradle Maria. There was no greater feeling than approaching the altar and seeing my man standing there with a Kool-Aid grin. At that moment, nothing else and no one else mattered.

Once I was positioned across from my husband-to-be, I handed my daughter to Mina and my bouquet to Satin, who was right behind me. Occasionally, I glanced over to see a couple of familiar faces but noted Ms. Claudia was missing in action. Part of me wanted to believe that Mario neglected to tell her, but I knew better. She wasn't there because she didn't agree with our union.

"Mario Wallace Senior, do you take this woman to be your lawfully wedded wife, to have and to hold, from this day forward, for better, for worse, for richer, for poorer, in sickness and in health, until death do you part?" the minister asked.

"I do."

"Gucci Robinson, do you take this man to be your lawfully wedded husband, to have and to hold, from this day forward, for better, for worse, for richer, for poorer, in sickness and in health, until death do you part?"

"I do."

"By the power vested in me by the state of Michigan, I now pronounce you man and wife. Mario, you may kiss your bride."

Just like that, Mario and I were man and wife, and life couldn't have been better. After years of playing sidekick, I was now the main bitch, with a rock-sized diamond to prove it. Mario had outdone himself with this, and I was pleased.

Nothing could ruin my moment, but something was upsetting Mario.

"What's wrong baby?"

"Nothing," he lied.

"Well, whatever it is, don't let it kill this joyous occasion." I kissed him seductively. "What do you think about leaving these people here and coming back to the room with me?" I winked.

"You don't have to ask twice." He winked back and pulled me toward the door. Satin had already offered to care for Maria, so I had no worries.

Chapter 71

Mina

"Don't leave the party just because we're leaving. Stay and enjoy the fruits of your labor," Gucci said while being whisked away by her hubby.

"I'm tired, plus I need to prepare for my interview." I followed them out toward their waiting limousine. I had recently made the choice to leave the Doll House as a stripper and go into real estate. Honestly, I was tired of taking my clothes off for money, no matter how good the pay. I needed an honest living if I was going to find me a decent man.

A few months earlier, I thought I would be with the man of my dreams, living somewhere in the ATL, but boy was I wrong! Just after Sam and I purchased our tickets to get out of dodge, we caught the news broadcast announcing that my husband Tre' and his girlfriend Chloe were both undercover police officers hired to take down the Hand Over Fist drug operation. I swore to Sam that I didn't know about Tre', and he swore the same about Chloe. In my heart, I knew he was telling the truth, but I think he doubted me.

Hell, after being married to someone for six years, I couldn't believe I didn't know my husband was a cop either. With my own eyes, I had watched him hustle.

Back home in Cincinnati, Tre' was the man. His motto was *kill or be killed*, and he had pulled his fair share of triggers. I stood by while he did a few months of jail time, and I've even bailed him out a time or two. At most, I knew he had a drug problem, and I justified it by the amount of time he spent around the narcotics. However, to find out his ass was a cop had me speechless. Millions of things went through my head. *Was our love real? Was our marriage legal?* Needless to say, I felt bamboozled.

After Sam and I split up at the airport, I decided to return to Detroit, because I needed answers. However, it was a wasted trip, because the police department marked everything confidential. I didn't even get the chance to plan a funeral for my fake-ass husband. I was told his body was flown home to his family. For as long as I'd known Tre', I'd never known him to have any family.

Anyway, after the shock wore off, I began to focus all my attention on waiting for Sam to reach out. That night at the airport, he promised to call in a few days. Well, days turned into weeks, and weeks had turned into several months. I could have kicked myself for falling for another man's lies. Sam was full of shit just like Tre,' and I was over it. It was time to start over and start fresh. I was finally on my own, and it felt good.

Chapter 72

Lovely

The WVC housed roughly 4,000 inmates. Their program was strict, and they ran the facility like a well-oiled machine. Before we could get our cell assignments, we had to actually go through what they called a transition period. During transition, you're not allowed any phone calls. You're placed in one large room with approximately one hundred inmates. You attend daily workshops and informational meetings about the site, and you're given the rules. Counselors monitor your behavior for about two weeks before finally allowing you into what they call general population.

Today our transition period was over, and we finally moved to the "big house," so to speak. We were taken on a tour to see where the cafeteria, showers, and recreational rooms were located, then finally escorted to our destination, which was where I was greeted by my cellmate.

"I'm Benita, but the girls on the block call me Benny. I roll solo. I don't need no friends and don't want none. If you stay out of my way, then I'll stay out of yours, but if you get in my way, then I'll get in yours. I'm in here for life, so I don't mind getting another murder rap. You get my drift?" Benny asked, and I nodded my understanding.

"Well, I'm facing double life in this muthafucka, so finding a beef ain't on my bucket list either!" I had to let Benny know that I wasn't a punk, although I spoke with more confidence than I actually had, because Benny looked like a monster, and I was a tad bit scared. She was about 5 feet 8 inches, caramel-toned, with sandy brown hair that was beginning to turn gray at the temples. She was a petite woman, but due to her athletic build, I could tell she worked out. Her arms were toned and covered with a boatload of tattoos. She had to have gotten them before she became state property, because they weren't jailhouse style.

Benny had a youthful face with about a dozen scars, but I knew she had to be in her late forties or early fifties. Neither her gray temples nor her few wrinkles gave her away. It was the look on her face that spoke volumes. The look told me that Benny had lived one hell of a life, and I knew she had a story to tell. It was something about her eyes that said she wasn't nothing to play with.

"Hot damn, did you say double life, green eyes?" She stood from her bed, which was the bottom bunk.

"Not a day less!" I replied, trying to read her thoughts.

"What could a pretty little girl like you have done to earn that type of sentence?" she asked while pulling her pants down and squatting over the metal toilet that was positioned in the corner about five steps from where I was standing.

"I pissed somebody off," I said, turning my back to give her the privacy she needed to wipe her ass. I climbed up to the top bunk and began to make it up using the paper-thin sheet set and pillowcase that I was given earlier.

"Green eyes, you ever did a bid before?" She asked as she flushed the toilet.

"It doesn't matter. I'm doing this one!" I said with an attitude. This chick had just told me to stay out of her way, and now she was all up in my business.

"Listen, youngster, the only reason I asked is because you turned your back to me. In a place like this, that could be a deadly mistake. If you want to survive your double life bid, don't do that shit again! The wrong bitch will use that as an opportunity to take you out." She washed her hands then sat back down on her bunk and prepared for lights out.

Chapter 73

Nikki

"What's up, cuz?" Anjela spoke as I answered the phone.

"Nothing much. Just sitting at the computer, trying to think of what to write." I stared at the blank screen in front me.

"Are you still thinking about becoming a writer?" she asked, partially interested.

"Yeah, I am, actually. I have a story to tell," I explained.

Lately, I'd had a lot of free time on my hands, with Junior splitting his time between me and Mario. Recently, I decided to break out my computer and give writing a try. It was something that I'd always wanted to do.

"Will it be a how-to book for hustlers' wives?" She laughed, and I did too.

"Whatever, tramp. What can I do for you?" I leaned back in the leather chair.

"I have tickets to the Battle of the Beauticians, and I would love to have my favorite cousin accompany me."

"No way!" I shook my head as if she could see me.

"Nikki, your ass has been on lockdown far too long. Can't you just come out this one time?" Anjela begged. "Everybody will be there, and you need to have some fun."

"Girl, I'm not in a party mood. I have too much to do. I have to be out of this place in a few days, and I haven't even found a new home yet," I tried to explain, but she wasn't having it.

"Girl, I'm not taking no for an answer, so you better have your ass dressed and ready by eight," she said and hung up.

I sat there for a minute and pondered going to the hair show. There would be a bunch of familiar faces in the crowd, and I didn't feel like all the questions or sympathy about my divorce. No matter what my cousin said, I was not going to that hair show.

Just as I prepared to leave the house to do some much-needed grocery shopping, there was a knock at the door. "Who is it?" I called out, thinking my cousin had made her way over to beg in person.

"It's Rio," Mario replied.

I contemplated not answering, but quickly changed my mind. He was persistent as hell and wouldn't leave until I came to the door.

"What's up?" I swung the front door open.

"Can we talk?" He stepped inside the foyer before I had the opportunity to extend an invitation.

"Talk about what?" I shrugged my shoulders.

"Me and you," was his reply.

I blew out an audible breath and rolled my eyes. "Mario, there is no me and you. Remember, you're married." I sighed and grabbed my purse off the coat rack. I was done with this conversation already. I hadn't seen him since the day of his wedding, and the sight of him still sent chills through my body. He was finer than I remembered, standing there in a pair of 87 jeans and a True Religion T-shirt. He must've been hitting the gym, because his muscles were flexing hard. I really missed his companionship, and although I was pissed off about his infidelity, part of me wanted to forgive him so we could at least be friends, but that wouldn't happen today.

"As long as I got breath in my lungs, there will always be me and you, Nikkita." He towered over me like a giant. Moments like this, when he professed his love for me, used to make my heart melt, but now it was downright irritating.

"Look, I've got somewhere to be." I turned away from him and put my hand on the door handle.

"Nikki, I've been trying to get at you for months, but you keep blowing me off," he protested.

"Yeah, I have been blowing you off, and I'm going to continue to blow you off now that you're married," I reiterated.

"Nik, we really need to talk." He placed his hand on top of mine.

"You really need to leave." I snatched my hand away.

"Why are you doing this to me?" His eyes were misty, which caught me off guard. He was a newly wedded man who should've been somewhere with his wife, yet here he stood, begging me to talk.

"I didn't do this to you, Mario." My voice raised an octave as my blood began to boil. "You did this to me! You did this to us!" Spit flew from my lips, but I wasn't bothered one bit. "You fucked that bitch raw and got her pregnant, Mario."

"I've apologized over and over again. What else can I do to fix this?" His tone matched mine. True, he had apologized time and time again by way of voicemail, text message, cards, flowers, and other expensive gifts, but I was unfazed.

"Saying I'm sorry won't mend this fence. Saying I'm sorry won't stop the pain I feel every night when I lay in bed alone. Saying sorry won't stop the mental pictures of you and that bitch!" I paused to catch my breath. "Saying sorry does nothing for me Mario, and neither do you. Now get the fuck out!" I yelled at the top of my lungs, and the empty house made my voice echo.

I don't know why I lied, but it was much easier than admitting I was wrong for letting him go. I know he fucked up in one of the worst ways imaginable, but ten years ago, I vowed to love him through the good, bad, and ugly.

"Straight up, it's like that?" He was shocked because I'd never come at him like that.

I didn't say one word as I watched him walk out of my house and down the porch steps.

Chapter 74

Mina

"What's up, Gucci?" I tilted my head and placed the cell phone between my ear and shoulder. I was trying to get dressed and fix my hair all at once. A quick glance at the clock told me that I was about to be late for my meeting with Hilda Rodgers, real estate guru. I'd been preparing for this interview like my life depended on it, because I needed the money. After bringing home between a few hundred to a few thousand a night, I couldn't survive a nine-to-five type of job that paid close to nothing. So, real estate was the next best thing. I didn't have a formal education, so I doubted I would land a well-paying career. I'd also depleted my savings account trying to make ends meet, so going back into the entrepreneur field of fashion would be on pause for the time being.

"I know you're on your way to the big meeting, but I just called to tell you how proud I am of you." She spoke with wind blowing in the background. "You don't know how many women say they're going to walk away from the strip club but stay forever. I was one of those women." She laughed.

"Aw, thank you." I smiled. Over the past few months, Gucci had definitely become a very close friend of mine. We'd spent a lot of time together, and she was actually pretty cool. The only thorn in our friendship was Mario. He didn't really like me and made no effort to conceal his feelings. I was sure it was because of the whole Sam thing, but whatever.

"Um, hello?" Gucci chimed in.

"My bad, girl." I apologized for zoning out. "I'm trying to get out the door. Can I call you back later?"

"Yeah, good luck with your meeting." She hung up, and I scanned the cluttered living room for my keys. I'd only been at this new place for about three months. I still had boxes to unpack and pictures to hang on the walls.

Just as I spotted my keys on top of my MK purse, my cell rang again. I looked at the caller ID, and it read private, so I didn't answer.

I arrived at the real estate office and flew inside like a bat out of hell. Hilda Rodgers was a well-known celebrity agent with offices in Michigan, LA, Chicago, ATL, and Las Vegas. Her approval could make or break me, and right now, I couldn't afford to be more broke than I already was.

"You're late," Hilda snapped as she met me at the front door.

I glanced down at the Coach watch on my wrist and noted that I was actually on time.

"Mrs. Rodgers, it's six on the dot." I cleared my throat.

"To be early is to be on time. To be on time is to be late." She stared at me and shook her head. "In the world of real estate, timing can make or break you." She spun on the heels of her red bottoms and proceeded to re-enter the freshly decorated office. I'd heard through one of my clients at the Doll House that Hilda's new office would be in Michigan, and she was looking for worthy agents to represent her.

On cue, I followed behind the well-built fifty-some-thing woman and tried to keep my eyes from bugging out of my head. The place was immaculate and really resembled a well-to-do law firm instead of a real estate office. Warm earth tones were throughout the entire place, and there was even a fireplace. As we headed down the hall into her office, I admired the pictures of Hilda and her clients standing in front of their new properties. I smiled to myself because I could definitely picture my future with this company.

Chapter 75

Gucci

"Hey, baby." I kissed my husband on the lips and set my shopping bags down. He was lying across my suede coral sofa with his feet up and shoes on, playing the Xbox.

"What up, G." He nodded, and I slid his feet to the ground. "Damn, Gucci, you made me miss the ball!" he yelled.

"You shouldn't have your feet up on my shit then."

"Don't nobody give a fuck about this hoe-ass couch!" He put his feet back up, and I moved them again.

The newlywed phase had only lasted about a week, because we were back at each other's throats. I could tell something was on his mind, but I wasn't about to baby him by asking him what was the matter. Lately, he had been getting on my reserved nerve, and I just wished he would get his attitude in check.

"Mario, why are you being like this?"

"Like what?" He paused the game and looked at me like he was ready for an argument.

"You know how I feel about shoes on the couch." I put my hands on my hips.

"And you know that I hate being treated like a kid." He turned the game off.

"Anyway, did you remember to pick up the carry-out for tonight?" I glanced at my watch. His mother would be arriving for dinner any minute. I'd invited her over with hopes of mending the fence between us. Ms. Claudia wasn't a fan of our marriage, and rightfully so. She loved her son, but she loved Nikki more. In her eyes, I was a homewrecker, and I was tired of the animosity between us. I just wanted to clear the air and start over if she was willing.

"Mario, did you pick up the food?" I asked again. The blank expression on his face told it all.

"Damn, G, my bad. I got sidetracked," he said just as the doorbell rang.

"Sidetracked doing what?" I snapped because he knew how important this was for me. "How in the hell are we supposed to have a family dinner with no damn food?" I was fuming mad.

"Just go upstairs and get Maria ready. We'll go out for dinner." He winked and went to answer the door. I sighed because he was sabotaging my effort to make things right with his mom.

On my way up the stairs, I stopped to eavesdrop. I often wondered what Ms. Claudia said about me when I was out of earshot. Today was the perfect time to find out.

"Hey, Mama," I heard Mario say.

"Hey, son. How've you been holding up?"

"I'm good, and you?" Mario asked, and I frowned. *Enough with the small talk,* I thought silently.

"Oh, I'm hanging in there. Where's my granddaughter?" Ms. Claudia took a seat on the couch.

"She's upstairs. Gucci is getting her dressed now."

Mario sat down beside her. I rolled my eyes because obviously, this conversation was going nowhere fast. Just as I took another step, I heard something that caught my attention.

"Son, to say that I'm disappointed in you would be an understatement," she started. "I never in a million years would've imagined you falling for the trap that girl set for you."

"Mama, please don't start with me." Mario stood from the couch.

I bit down on my jowl to keep from chiming into the conversation.

"You're a man, and I understand that men make mistakes, son. What I don't understand is why you let this foolishness continue. That girl ain't what you want, and you know it."

"Mama, that's my wife now. You've got to let my relationship with Nikkita go, all right? It's unfair to Gucci." Mario had my back, and times like this reminded me of why I loved him the way I did.

"Unfair to Gucci?" Ms. Claudia raised her voice. "What's unfair is the fact that Nikki had her whole life stolen while she was on her death bed."

"Mama, don't come at me with that. I waited several months for Nikki while she was in that coma, and you know it! Yeah, what I did with G was wrong, but I thought my wife was a damn vegetable. I would've never done what I did if I thought Nikki was going to wake up." Mario defended himself.

"I get that, son, but why did you still marry that girl after your wife woke up from her coma?" Ms. Claudia asked the million-dollar question.

Honestly, I held my breath waiting for the answer, because I'd wondered about this myself.

"I married Gucci because Nikki didn't want me anymore," Mario whispered.

His words hit me like a ton of bricks, and I had to take a seat on the stairs to calm down. I was mad as hell but hurting even more. I felt like a fool, and the joke was on me. So many times, I'd convinced myself that Mario and I belonged together. He was always my first choice, and I hoped to be his now that he was my husband. However, I saw that I was, and would forever be, number two in his book.

I went into our bedroom to grab my purse, cell phone, and car keys. My destination hadn't been determined, but I knew I had to get the hell out of there. On my way back downstairs, the conversation between Mario and Claudia stopped abruptly.

"Where's Maria?" Mario asked.

"She's upstairs still napping. I'm going to head out for a while." I walked past them both.

"I thought we were going to dinner," Mario grabbed my hand. He knew I'd overheard them, and so did his mother.

"I guess the plan has changed. I'll see you later." I walked out of the door, leaving both of them speechless.

As I sat in my pink Dodge Charger, prepared to zoom off, I had a change of heart. There had been so many times that I let this thing with him and his mother happen and not say a word, but not today. I slammed the car door and flew back into the house.

"Look." I pointed at Ms. Claudia. "I don't know what your beef with me is, or what muthafuckin' trap you think I set out for him, but I do know that I didn't ask him to marry me." I pointed at my chest. In hindsight, I probably shouldn't have cussed at my husband's mother, but it was too late to take it back, so I continued. "I didn't invite him into my bed. That nigga invited me into his!" I snapped. "Yeah, maybe I could've denied him, but that would've been denying me and the love I've had for your son since I was sixteen. I sat by for years when we were growing up and waited for Mario to love me the way I loved him. But instead of him loving me, I stood there and watched him love another bitch!" I wiped the tears and snot coming out of my face.

"Little girl, you better mind your damn manners and show some respect." Claudia stood from the couch like she wanted to throw some blows.

"Respect is a two-way street," I snapped. If she wanted some, I was ready to serve it up proper, mother-in-law or not. "I invited you here with good intentions, yet you came into my home and talked about me like I'm nothing. If that's not disrespectful, I don't know what is."

Without another word to me or Mario, Claudia grabbed her purse and walked out of the front door, and I was right behind her.

"G!" Mario started, but I cut him off.

"Don't say shit to me!"

"Why are you trippin'?" He blocked the door so I couldn't leave.

"You tell your mother that you're only with me because Nikki didn't want you anymore, but I'm the one trippin'." I rolled my eyes.

"I didn't mean it like that." He tried to embrace me, but I wasn't having it.

"It's hilarious how everybody puts that bitch on a pedestal like she's something special." I laughed because it was too comical. While she was pretending to be a hustler's wife, I was actually living that life. "I've never seen her cook crack! I've never seen her pop a pistol! As a matter of fact, I've never seen her ass anywhere near the trap! So, tell me why the fuck that bitch is so got-damn special?" I squared up to Mario. As I watched him fumble with the answer, I shook my head. "That's what I thought."

Chapter 76

Chloe

Lucky for me, my cellmate was in the infirmary; therefore, I had time to myself. A few hours of alone time did a body good. I hadn't slept a wink since my arrival because I was afraid of being shanked in my sleep.

Just as I stirred from my catnap, a corrections officer approached my cell door and opened it. "Shower time, inmate."

"Huh?" I yawned.

"Let's go before your ass be stankin' 'til tomorrow."

I looked up to see the gold-toothed corrections officer standing in the door. I jumped down, grabbed my toiletries, and headed down the hall behind the other women. Honestly, I thought I wouldn't get the chance to shower until the next day, so this was a pleasant surprise.

As we entered the medium-sized area, it reminded me of a bootleg high school locker room. I removed my clothing with a lot of discomfort because there were about twenty other chicks in there, naked as well. I had never seen so many vaginas in my life. Some were white, black, small, big, bald, hairy, wrinkled, and everything in between. This was something that I would never be able to get used to, and I prayed I didn't have to.

After hearing the corrections officer yell out that we only had eight minutes remaining, I quickly shrugged it off. Having no other choice if I wanted to get clean, I briskly walked into the shower. My mission was to get in and get out. I washed everything but my face because I was too scared to close my eyes. Instead, I dabbed my face with the towel. By the time we were down to four minutes, I had dried off, put on a fresh uniform, and was standing back in line when li'l mama from the other day walked up and stood behind me.

"What's up, girl?" I asked with familiarity.

"Just getting settled, and you?" she asked.

"Same here, I guess."

"Nobody speaks in this bitch unless they ask me first." A black woman with dreads walked up to the line. She looked like a man and had the mannerisms of one too.

"Are you some sort of bathroom bully?" I laughed, and li'l mama did too.

"Oh, it's funny?" she spat at my new acquaintance.

"Yeah, bitch. I laughed, didn't I?" Lovely squared up.

"Yo, Cupcake, I say that you should teach that green-eyed bitch a lesson!" Another black woman hyped up the Li'l Wayne lookalike.

"I should, shouldn't I?" Cupcake stepped really close to us as the gold-toothed corrections officer took the opportunity to look away in the opposite direction.

"Hell yeah, show that bitch that prison ain't no place for Barbies," the hype woman said as a small crowd formed around us and cheered.

"Fight, fight!"

"Bitch, you got so much mouth, then you come and get some!" Lovely pointed at the high yellow girl with the big mouth. "In my youth, I learned to take the one with the biggest mouth and make them an example."

"Oh, shit, Red! Barbie done called you out," Cupcake stated.

"Fuck that bitch! I'm only doing a year. I ain't got time for no more charges." Red then closed her mouth and walked away.

"Well, I'm doing a twenty-year stretch, so I got time to spare." Cupcake turned to face me, and I squared up, looking her right in the face.

"I'm in this bitch until I die," I confirmed.

"And I got from now until eternity, so what's up?" Lovely stated as a matter of fact. Because we were pregnant, other inmates probably thought we were handicapped.

"Barbie, don't have me fuck you up," she said before turning back toward the crowd for encouragement.

I was tired of the word games, so I took that as my opportunity to take the first shot. I reached back and knocked the hell out of Cupcake. She blinked a few times, spit the blood from her bleeding lip down onto the floor, and charged toward me full force. She attempted an upper cut, but her fist failed to connect with my face. Not backing down, I came with a vicious right hook, a quick left, and then finally a jab to the ribs that sent her falling backward into the crowd.

I was about to finish her off when the sound of a whistle blowing caught my attention. All of the inmates dropped down to their knees and placed their hands behind theirs heads, so I followed suit.

"Ladies, what the hell is going on in here?" the Caucasian correction officer asked, but no one uttered a word.

"Who started this shit?" She elevated her tone, but still no one said a word.

"All right, I see there are no talkers today, so how about I charge all of you with this locker room brawl." She walked around the group of women. There were a few moans and groans, but still no one spoke.

"What about you, Cupcake? Are you going to tell me who did this to you?" She kneeled beside Cupcake, who was bleeding from the face and doubled over in obvious pain. To my surprise, Cupcake shook her head no, but she continued to stare directly at me.

"Okay, that's not a problem. Since you probably started this one like you do all of the others, I'm going to send you to the hole. You can cool off there for three weeks, but first, you need to go the infirmary. I won't charge you with a violation this time, because it looks like somebody has punished you enough." The guard laughed, which probably pissed Cupcake off even more.

Chapter 77

Mina

My meeting with Hilda went well, and she decided to give me a try. As a test, she gave me a new client. I was so anxious to get started, because I had already begun to count the future commission.

As I navigated through the city, I noticed a black BMW on my trail. It had been behind me for twenty minutes and had even blown a few red lights to keep up with me. This had been happening more and more lately, along with the private calls, and I was beginning to get annoyed. I didn't take the stalking too seriously, because it was probably one of my clients from the strip club, but enough was enough.

I pulled over at the Mobil gas station on West Seven Mile to see if my stalker would stop too, and sure enough, he did. Without a second thought, I stepped from my black Chrysler 300 and proceeded to the window-tinted vehicle idling about three pumps over. Just as I approached the BMW, it sped off and back into traffic. I laughed to myself and headed back to my car.

Not wanting to lead the maniac to my crib, I circled a few blocks and took several unnecessary side streets. Not long after I returned home, there was a knock at the door. Instantly, I became paranoid but checked the peephole and answered the door for Gucci.

"What's up, boo?"

"I need a drink, A.S.A.P.!" Bum-rushing herself past the front door, she went straight to my bar rack.

"Well, hello to you too." I laughed and closed the door behind her.

"I'm sick of Mario's ass!" she spat while sipping Don Julio straight from the bottle.

"What happened this time?" I watched her drink the potent alcohol like it was tap water.

"Too much shit to talk about." She wiped her wet mouth, and I watched the liquid spill onto her pink fishnet top. It was sort of breezy that day, but Gucci didn't care, because skimpy clothes were all she had.

"Okay." I laughed. I'd seen this side of my friend more and more since her and Mario had become an item. Normally, she held her shit together, but every now and then she let her situation get the best of her.

"Am I crazy?" She put the bottle down and came over to my sofa.

"No, you're not crazy," I reassured her.

"The love of my life is in love with somebody else. I knew the shit when I said I do, but I thought he would change. I told him we didn't have to get married, but he insisted." She wiped her eyes.

"Gucci, it will be okay." I patted her back.

"When will it get better? Nikki got some type of death grip on him." She went back to retrieve the unfinished bottle and took another swig.

"They were together for a long time," I tried to explain.

"Fuck that! I have been with him, running the block way longer than he was with that bitch." Slamming the bottle down, she almost chipped my stone coffee table.

I could tell she was getting too tipsy, so I casually removed the liquor while making light of the situation. "Mario is Biggie, Nikki is Faith, and you're Kim." We both laughed at my referral.

"Look at me, girl." She smiled. "I'm over here cryin' and shit! This ain't me, Mina. I ain't ever cried over a nigga."

"But Mario is your husband and your daughter's father. It's okay to cry a little over him, because you love him." I rubbed her back.

"Husband or no husband, baby daddy or not, I'm done with playing the sideline bitch." She sprang up from the couch. "The only way to get over one nigga is to move on to the next. We're going out tonight," she declared.

"Hell no! Are you a psycho with a death wish? I'm not helping you find another man." I shook my head adamantly. Mario barely liked me enough as it was. I was not about to give him another reason.

"Girl, I'm not going out to look for someone to bring home." She rolled her eyes. "I just want to dance and have a good time. I promise to keep it PG." She winked.

I knew we were playing with fire and sure hoped Gucci wouldn't get burned. "Well, as long as you keep it clean, I'm game."

"Oh, shit! How was the meeting?" She flopped back down onto the couch.

"It went well. She's putting me on thirty-day probation. If I do well, then I'm hired." I smiled hard.

"That's good. I might know a few people looking for property. I'll refer them to you." Gucci slurred a bit.

"So, where are we going?" I asked.

"I'm not sure, but bring your A-game." Gucci snapped her fingers. "Speaking of which, I need to call Satin for something to wear, since I ran out the house in my jeans and this shirt." What she already had on was club gear for most people.

"I have plenty of stuff for you to try on. We're about the same size." I glanced over her body. Giving birth had definitely added a few extra pounds on Gucci, and to be honest, her 125-pound frame needed it.

"No, that's okay." Gucci smirked. "Your stuff is too goodie-goodie." She made air quotes. "Tonight, I need a freakum' dress!"

Chapter 78

Gucci

After chillin' with Mina for another hour and letting my buzz die a little, I left her apartment and went up a floor to my girl Satin's crib. Good thing they lived in the same building, because I wasn't for drinking and driving. Just as I raised my hand to knock, the door opened. I almost pissed myself when I saw my old flame, Cartier, standing there.

"Gucci?" he asked in shock.

"Cartier!" I raised an arched eyebrow. The last time I seen this fool, I was dropping him off at the police precinct fifteen years ago. He was wanted for murder and went to turn himself in. Back then, I was young and loved him more than I loved myself. It wasn't until after he left that I started hanging with Mario, and the rest is history.

"What are you doing answering my best friend's door?" I folded my arms. Jealousy is a mutha, and I had no right to floss my attitude, but fuck it.

"Damn, girl, I missed your sexy ass." He licked those lips I loved to death.

"Answer the muthafuckin' question." I bossed up. I don't know if it was the liquor from Mina's house or my old feelings, but I was pissed.

"Chill out. Damn! I came over here to find you." He leaned against the door frame. "I went by the Doll House looking for you, and they told me you don't dance no more. I asked where Satin was, and they said at home. My partner be fucking with her, so I asked him to bring me over here." He smirked.

"Whatever, nigga!" I pushed him aside. "Let me find out y'all fucked and it's gon' be trouble." I barged into the house, sniffing the air like a blood hound. I would hate to beat Satin's ass in her own house, but if she crossed me, then so be it.

Once I made it into the apartment, I heard moans coming from the bedroom, which confirmed that Satin was busy with someone besides Cartier. I relaxed and turned around to see him standing there with a Kool-Aid smile.

"I'm glad to see you still care for a nigga." He laughed.

"Don't get it twisted." I raised my ring finger so he could take in my rock.

"Yeah, I heard about that bullshit." He frowned. "I guess that's what happens when a nigga is sent upstate." He reached into his pocket and pulled out a blunt then lit it.

"Yeah, I guess so." I shrugged. "I thought you were sentenced to thirty-five years?" I made small talk to avoid the sex sounds invading my space.

"Let's just say some shit came up missing and my case was dropped." He came over to the living area and sat down beside me.

I pretended not to catch the whiff of Armani that crept into my nostrils as he passed by. I also pretended not to notice how tall and buff he'd gotten over the years. Not to mention the Italian loafers on his feet and the custom-made suit he was rocking. In all honesty, Cartier was a boss in every sense of the word and had been since he was about ten years old. When other niggas went left, he went right. When other cats talked about it, he was about it, and that shit was hella sexy.

"So, how is married life?" he asked, passing me the kush.

"It's all good." I inhaled. "We just recently tied the knot, and we have a daughter named Maria." I smiled.

"Although you're smiling, you don't look happy." Cartier sat back and stared at me.

"I'm happy, Cartier. Today was just a bad day." I sighed.

"If you were my woman, all your days would be awesome." He slid close to me and rubbed my inner thigh.

I was so nervous that I had to force my hand to stop shaking. "Well, baby boy, you're a dollar short and a decade too late." Although I kept my composure on the outside, my stomach was doing back flips. It was something about him that made me very intrigued. I liked being in his company, although I knew it was wrong.

"Gucci, you know my money long, so it's impossible to be a dollar short on anything." He puffed on the blunt. "As for being a decade late, you're right, but I never stopped thinking about you when I was locked up." He passed the blunt to me again. "I wrote letters to you for almost six months straight, and one day, they all were returned."

"After you left, I started hustling harder than I did when I was with you, and I eventually left my father's house. If the letters were returned, he was the one who sent them back, because I never saw them." I flicked the ashes into the ashtray on the coffee table.

"So why didn't you write me?"

"When you left, I was fourteen. I didn't know the first thing about the prison system." The weed had calmed my nerves, so I relaxed a bit. "How many years did you do?"

"Five."

"Well, why didn't you come and look for me?" I asked. Hell, had Cartier come back, my life would have been totally different.

"When I got released, I had to lay low and go underground. This is my first time back to Detroit in years. You were the first person I came looking for. Doesn't that mean something?" He peered into my eyes, and I looked away.

"I'm married," I reiterated.

"That don't mean shit! People leave their husbands every day." He grimaced.

"It ain't that type of party, and even if it was, that would be unfair to my daughter."

Leaning in close to me, he whispered in my ear. "I'll raise her. She should've been mine anyway." He smiled and grabbed my hand. "I'm a gangsta, and you are my gangsta girl!"

I ain't gon' lie, I was turned on and prepared to press my lips up against his. Just then, Satin and some dude walked into the living room, so I snatched my hand out of Cartier's like it was on fire.

Chapter 79

Nikki

I heard the car horn and knew my cousin was outside. I went to the door and opened it.

"Damn, you ain't dressed yet?" she snapped.

"I told you I was not going." I went back to the kitchen table and wiped up my son's mess.

"And I told you that I was not taking no for an answer." She placed her hand on her hip. "Go upstairs and get dressed."

"No." I was starting to catch an attitude.

"Look at you." She pulled me over to a mirror on my wall. I stared at the oversized jogging suit, fuzzy socks, and bonnet on my head.

"What's wrong with this?" I asked.

"Nothing if you want to remain old, single, and lonely."

"Bitch, I'm not even thirty yet," I snapped. "I keep telling you I ain't looking for love, and I'll never be lonely as long as I've got Junior." I smacked my lips.

"Nik, you're in a frump, and I'm going to pull you out if it's the last thing I do." She hugged me.

"Girl, bye! There is nothing wrong with me." I shook my head. "It's you that needs to be checked out."

"I'm serious, Nikki. Ever since you had your ordeal, you haven't been the same." She sat down on my couch and removed her red bottoms.

"Well, after you've been shot multiple times, damn near died, and came back to life only to find out your husband cheated and made a baby with his mistress, can you tell me how to go back to acting normal?" I rolled my eyes.

"I didn't mean to upset you, cuz." She sounded apologetic, "I just don't want you to waste your second chance at life. You've been through hell and back, but you're still here. Your life could've ended the night you got shot, but it didn't. The doctors thought you may never walk again, but you went to rehab, and now look at you." She smiled. "Yeah, Mario did some foul shit, and Gucci got your leftovers, but to live like a hermit only gives them the victory. Tyler Perry once said, 'Everybody loses their lease on life. It's up to you to renew it or let it expire.'"

As I listened to my cousin preach, I had a revelation. She was absolutely right! Tonight, I was going to renew my lease on life and praise God for second chances.

"Okay, girl, you got me. Now, call Claudia to see if she can babysit while I go and get dressed."

Chapter 80

Mina

"Damn, this hair show is all the way turned up," I said to Gucci as we pressed our way through the thick crowd inside of Cobo Hall. We had decided to scrap the club scene and head out to one of the most anticipated events this year, Battle of the Beauticians. Detroit was known for fabulous fashion and hairstyles. The hair battle was to our city what fashion week was to New York. Hairdressers came from all over the city to display their work and compete for the most coveted prize: bragging rights and the golden blow dryer.

We stopped by the makeshift bar and grabbed something to sip on as the music bumped. After speaking to a few familiar faces, we finally made our way to our seats. Thanks to Gucci's hairdresser, we were sitting up close and personal.

"When does this thing start?" Gucci's friend Satin asked.

"The ticket said nine p.m., but you know we're on colored people's time. I'll give it to ten," Gucci replied and sipped on her mojito. I glanced down at my cell phone for the time and noted it was already 9:34, and the technical crew were still assembling the lighting.

"It feels good to be out tonight," I spoke over the noise.

"Yeah, it does." Gucci nodded. "I've been on lock-down with Maria, but tonight she is all Daddy's problem." Gucci laughed.

"I miss hanging with you, girl." Satin put her arm around Gucci. "Let's toast to a good time and old friends." She raised her plastic cup, and we followed suit.

"Let's also toast to being drama-free." Gucci laughed.

On the ride downtown, she'd finally gone into detail about the drama with Mario and his mother. I felt bad for her, but, like I said before, she was playing with fire from the beginning. I didn't speak much on the situation at the time, because I had my own issues with Sam.

Speaking of Sam, I knew it was time for me to move on. It had been more than long enough, and I was tired of loving a ghost. Like some damn movie, I thought he would come back for me and we could live happily ever after. My ass was probably the furthest thing from his mind right now. I was sure he was laid up with the next bitch at that very moment. I needed to get my life back on track and focus on rebuilding a new me anyway.

My new real-estate license was the best thing going for me, and I was determined to put it to use. While dancing at the strip club, I was able to make a few promising acquaintances. Every last one of those men was a sucker for a big butt and a smile. Luckily, I happened to have both; therefore, I was bound to sell real estate and show Hilda Rodgers what I was working with.

"Hello, did you hear me?" Some chick waved her hand in my face just as the lights dimmed.

"I'm sorry. What did you say?" I snapped back into reality.

"I said you and your friends are in our seats." She smiled, but I could tell it was phony.

"These are our seats." Satin stood up into the woman's face.

Gucci searched her purse to produce the ticket stubs, and that's when all hell broke loose. Standing right beside the woman claiming our seats was Nikki.

Chapter 81

Nikki

"Don't tell me you're stealing seats now too, Gucci?" I laughed. Hell, what else was there to do? The one time I let my cousin drag me out of the house, I ran right into the broad that I couldn't stand.

"I ain't no thief!" She stood and produced the tickets. "Row A, seats four, five, and six. See for yourself." She pushed the tickets into my face.

"You're right about what these tickets say." I smirked. "However, Row A is on that side of the room." I pointed to the other side of the stage. The look on her face was priceless. "Now, take your thieving ass over there." I couldn't help but trash talk. Deep down, I'd waited patiently for this showdown ever since the courthouse incident. I'd dreamt over and over about the ass whipping she had coming.

"Let me tell you something." She got in my face.

"You can't tell me shit!" I spat as the announcer informed the audience the show would start in five minutes and asked everyone to take their seat. "Now, run along." I smiled.

"Who in the fuck do you think you are?" Gucci stepped up closer to my face.

I prayed for restraint, but the Lord must've been busy. Before I knew it, I had grabbed the bitch by the collar of her Christian Dior blouse as one would do a child. I held her with my left hand, and I removed my stiletto with the other. Her friends tried to save her, but nothing except death would keep me from striking this bitch, and that's exactly what I did over and over again. *Wham*! I hit her ass twice in the face with the heel on my shoe. She fought like a man, trying to break free, but I wasn't done. *Wham!* I hit her again, and before I knew it, we were tussling on the floor.

I was not sure what Mina's intentions were, but Anjela shut her down when she got too close to us. "One on one is a fair fight. Ain't nobody jumpin' in!" I heard her say just as Gucci went for my hair like a sucker, but I moved my head in the nick of time.

"Ahh!" she screamed as I pressed my finger into her eye socket. "You bitch! Let me go."

"You have been asking for this beat down for a long time. Don't act scared now." Spit flew out of my mouth as I sent two shots to her face.

The crowd began to disperse as police raced toward us. I was determined to get a few more licks in before I was taken to jail. I slammed her head up against the cement floor, and I was sure it hurt. Just as I was being pulled by two male officers, Gucci got one in. She caught me in the face and started kicking me. I wiggled free and slipped from their grasp long enough to take my other shoe off and hit that bitch again.

"Break it up!" the cop yelled and grabbed me with much more force this time.

I laughed like a mad woman as Gucci picked her things up from the floor. Her face was a bloody mess, and I was satisfied.

"I got you next time, Nikkita!" she screamed.

"Bring it on, bitch!"

"Oh, I will, and when I do, I'm going to kill yo' ass!" she threatened.

"I'll be waiting! Just let me know the time and place!" I yelled back. "Gucci, Detroit ain't big enough for both of us! Every time I see you, I'm spankin' that ass! I swear on my son, bitch!"

Chapter 82

Lovely

After showers, we were able to have recreation time. Some inmates watched the news on the 56-inch television which was mounted to the wall and caged in. Others hit the gym to work out, while a few inmates played Uno or checkers. I opted for outside, because I desperately needed some fresh air.

"You got some nerve, Barbie," someone called from behind me.

I turned quickly to see who was talking trash and put my dukes up, prepared to whip ass. I thought it was the yellow girl from earlier, but to my surprise, it was my home girl, Tiny.

"Tiny!" I screamed because I was elated to see a familiar face in this godforsaken place.

Me and her went way back to my days as a dancer. When the club we danced at burned up, it was her that got me into the female escort service. My girl Tiny was also the get-money bitch that I kept on my payroll when I was in the streets selling dope. She would set a nigga up in a heartbeat for me, and she always did dirt heavy, so it really didn't surprise me that we were having this reunion on this side of the gates.

"Lovely, girl, I don't know what to do with you." She smiled and hugged me tight.

I stood back and smiled because this was the first time I had seen her without makeup, eyelashes, hair extensions, and a really expensive outfit. I laughed to myself because I was sure that she was thinking the same about me.

"Tiny, what the hell are you doing in here?" The last time I saw her was the day I was supposed to get married.

"Bitch, I got caught slippin'." She laughed. "I fucked around and got caught fuckin' this white boy at Belle Isle."

"What? So, you got sent to WVC for getting busy in public?" I said in amazement.

"Girl, they slapped my ass with a prostitution charge!" she spat. "I went before the judge that following Monday, and his old ass hit me with six months in this raggedy muthafucka." She rolled her eyes. "My attorney tried to get the case dismissed, but they had a recording of the white boy paying me." She laughed.

"So, he set you up?" My mouth dropped.

"Yeah, he set me up! He approached me and asked how can he be down with a fine-ass woman like me. I looked at him and decided that he wasn't half bad. I told his ass that he had to pay to play in this kitty kat. He offered a rack, and I was like, hell yeah!" She cracked up laughing. "I thought he was some wealthy businessman doing business in the city. I didn't know his white ass was a cop.

"You can't be serious." I laughed hard.

"Girl, I been in this hell hole for a week already." She motioned for us to take a seat on the grass near the basketball court.

"Well, at least you only have six months to do, maybe less for good behavior. My ass is looking at double life, T." I looked away and quickly brushed a tear from my eye.

"Lovely, I don't know what to say, boo." She shrugged her shoulders. "I can't say that it's going to get better, because I doubt it. I won't say that it will all work out, because I'm not that bitch. You know me. I don't sugar coat things." She leaned over and placed her arm around my neck, pulling me in for an embrace. "What I will say is, no matter what, as long as I'm in here, I got yo' back, just like when we were on the streets!"

Chapter 83

Gucci

"Aw, shit!" Mario exclaimed as he entered the hospital room. I'd been in the emergency room for three hours and was ready to go home. I didn't want to come here anyway, but Satin and Mina insisted.

"I can't wait to see that bitch again!" I yelled, completely forgetting I was in a hospital. My blood was boiling, and I was irritated. Not only had she caught me off guard, but she actually beat my ass. I had to give it to her. She wasn't by far the lame I once thought she was.

"Damn, Nikki did this?" Mario was shocked.

I didn't even acknowledge him with an answer. Lying back on the flat pillow, I closed my eyes in an attempt to calm down and stop the pounding in my head.

Just as I was getting comfortable, a doctor popped her head in. "Hi. May I come in?"

"I guess," was my reply as Mina held a freezer bag filled with ice on my face.

"So, I went over your x-rays and didn't find anything to be concerned about. There's nothing broken or fractured," she explained.

Mario looked relieved, but I already knew everything was all good. I'd been in enough fights to know the difference between minor injuries and major ones. My face appeared worse than it actually was.

"Can I go now?"

"Sure, Mrs. Wallace. Here is your prescription for pain medication should you need it. Here are your discharge papers, and remember not to overdo it with the ice. Too much ice numbs the cells and prolongs the healing process."

The ride home was silent. I was sure Mario didn't know what to say, and I wasn't up for talking. After stopping to fill my prescription, we picked Maria up from her grandmother. Ms. Claudia must've heard what happened, because she came out to the car.

"Are you okay?"

"Yeah, this is nothing." I smiled as best I could. Even though I was sure my husband's mother was silently cheering for Nikki, it meant a lot that she came out to check on me.

"Can I get you anything? Tea, water, or something stronger?" she joked.

"No, I'm okay, but thanks for asking." I laughed.

Ms. C patted my hand and walked back into the house. Mario strapped Maria into her car seat and pulled back out into the night air. Within twenty minutes, we were pulling into our driveway. I laid my precious daughter down and went into my bedroom to undress.

"You wanna talk?" Mario unbuttoned his Polo shirt.

"Maybe tomorrow." I sighed and headed into the bathroom. I smiled when I saw that Mario had already run my bath water and added my favorite scented bubbles. Walking over to the sink to remove my wedding ring and earrings, I assessed my face in the mirror. There were more lumps than I cared to count, so I turned away from the mirror and stepped down into the water.

"Is there room for one more?" Mario asked from the doorway.

I smiled at the sight of my husband. I took him in from head to toe, starting at the long, black braided hair he sported, down to the six pack at his mid-section. Next, I glanced over his tattoos and smiled again. The picture of our daughter on his chest warmed my heart. However, there was one tattoo across his ribs that nagged me. It said *Forever and Always* and was meant for Nikki.

"So, you just gon' leave me hanging?" he asked.

"I'm sorry, baby. There is always room for you." I sat up so he could get behind me, then I fell back into his arms.

"You know I love you, right?" he asked while stroking my hair.

In that moment, all of my pain was gone. I realized right then and there that I may have lost the battle, but I'd already won the war. Here I was in the arms of my husband as he nursed my wounds, while Nikki was in a damn jail cell. Tonight, when she got home, there would be no one to love and hold her like Mario was doing for me. The irony of the situation made me laugh.

Chapter 84

Nikki

"You've got street credibility now," my cousin teased. The mayhem had taken place almost three days ago, and she was still talking about it. That night, I'd spent forty minutes at the police station and was released with a ticket. They said I was being a public nuisance and fined me $150. I paid the bill and threw them the deuces. Honestly, I would've paid triple the amount if they would've let me hit the broad a few more times.

"Did you see her face?" I laughed as I pulled into the driveway. I'd replayed the moment over and over in my head. "I wish someone would've recorded it so I could've watched it on YouTube." I stepped from the car just as my mailman walked up and handed me the mail.

"That girl probably needed to see a doctor." Anjela laughed.

"She's too stubborn to see a doctor. She probably went home and licked her wounds." I flipped through the bills that I'd just picked up from my post office box. I knew I was moving and wanted to get a jump on the mail, so I had it forwarded a month ago.

As Anj continued to talk, I came across an envelope from the Women's Valley Correctional Facility. The original envelope had been ripped opened and placed inside of a newer one with a stamp indicating it had been inspected. In prison, there was no privacy. Everything was scanned on the way in and out.

"What do you think Mario said about what happened?" my cousin asked as I unlocked the door.

"He probably didn't say anything! How can he?" I laughed. "She had it coming. They both knew that."

"You just better make sure you watch your back out there, cuz. I heard her say she was going to kill you." Anjela got serious.

"Trust and believe I ain't even worried about her. But let me call you back, cuz." I ended the call so I could focus on the letter.

I stared at the sender's name and rolled my eyes because it was from that snake, Chloe. I didn't know what she could possibly have to say to me, and I contemplated throwing the envelope in the trash. I had loved her like a sister and treated her like one of my blood relatives. To know that she was an undercover cop assigned to set my family up was one of the most heart-breaking things I'd dealt with outside of my divorce.

For years, I took her under my wing to show her the ropes of a street boss's wife. I felt proud and accomplished watching her grow from a baller's chick into a true hustler's queen. I'd laughed with that broad, cried with her, and even shared some very personal details about my life. Many times we broke bread together, and to know that Judas sat at my table with every intention of bringing harm to my family killed me.

I looked at the letter and opened it against my better judgment. Curiosity was killing me. I needed to see what she had to say.

Nikki,

First and foremost, let me start by saying I hope all is well in your life. I've been praying to God that you've had a full and speedy recovery and that He brings justice to the person that shot you!

I know you're very angry and upset by the things you've learned about me. I know you probably hate me, and I can't say that I blame you. I want you to know that I'm very sorry for causing you pain and wanted to explain myself. I know an undercover officer was the last thing you'd believe I was. I came from a family of crime, so everyone was shocked. I only took the assignment because I've wanted to take down drug dealers ever since my parents let drugs destroy our family. Nikki, it was nothing I had against you or your husband, because I didn't even know you all at first. Honestly, Mario was just a name and a picture on the board in my headquarters. My boss assigned me to the case, and I went to do my job, nothing personal!

Along the way, I met you, and we became very close friends. I love you like a sister, and that will never change. After six years, you and Mario became my family, and it was impossible for me to bring him in on charges, so I didn't. Much to my boss's dismay, I switched the game up and turned everyone's attention on Zion, Mario's supplier. You've got to believe me when I say I did everything in my power to keep the heat off your husband. I wanted to protect you and him so much that I went out and killed Tre'. He was also assigned to the case, and once I found out that information, I had to do what was best for "our" family!

Unfortunately, I was caught and placed here in this women's institution for life. I want you to know that I'm not telling you I killed Tre' to save Mario for your sympathy. I don't regret what I did, and I wouldn't change a thing, because that's what you do for "family."

However, I am writing you because I do need help. A few months after I got here, I found out I was pregnant! I need to find Sam and tell him the good news so he can take custody of our baby when it comes. I've tried to contact him several times, but it's only so much I can do from behind these walls. You know I don't have any other family, and if I can't get anyone to take my baby, she will become a ward of the state. Nikki, I can't let that happen. As a mother, I know you understand my situation. Please find it in your heart to forgive me long enough to help me out of this jam. I did what I had to do in order to save your family. Please try to help me save mine.

Love,
Robin a.k.a. "Chloe"

I folded the letter and placed it back into the envelope. I sighed heavily and rubbed my temples. I was at a loss for words after reading her letter. I didn't know she went out on such a huge limb to save Mario from jail time. This girl had murdered someone in exchange for Mario's freedom. If that wasn't loyalty, I didn't know what was.

Chapter 85

Gucci

"This damn baby is heavy. What have y'all been feeding this girl?" Mina joked as she pulled Maria from her car seat.

We had just returned from Somerset Mall, and my daughter was beat. Milk dripped from her lips, and an empty bottle lay at her side. After some much-needed retail therapy, I was tired myself and ready to join Maria with a nap of my own.

"I'll get her if you get all these bags." I popped the trunk and began to unload the merchandise. This was my first time out in a few days because I had to let my bruised face heal. There was no way I'd be caught dead in the streets with proof that I'd gotten my ass beat. People would think I was weak, and that was far from the truth. If the bitch hadn't blindsided me, things would've turned out differently.

"I'll pass." Mina took Maria up onto the porch and waited for me.

As I set the bags down, I noticed someone rapidly approaching from the side of my house through my peripheral vision, and I yelled for Mina to call for help. Without a second thought, I made a mad dash back to the car to retrieve my purse, which housed the .22 I carried at all times. The stranger beat me to the punch by pulling his weapon first—a semi-automatic shotgun.

"Slow your roll, little mama."

"What the fuck you want from me?" I asked with my hands in the air, not wanting to make any sudden moves. I'd been robbed before and knew the best way to handle the situation was to play it cool, give him what he wanted, and then hunt his ass down like a rabid dog later.

"Look, I ain't here to hurt nobody," he explained. "I need to talk to Mario."

"About what?" I asked the unmasked, handsome stranger who stood before me dressed to the nines in an all-black Armani Exchange hookup. I could tell this man wasn't there to rob me, but he was there for some serious business.

"Mario has an uncle named Demetrius, who is a key witness in my girl's murder trial. I need Mario to make Meechie disappear in order to set my girl free," he explained with a stone-cold straight face.

"Let me get this straight. You want my husband to hand over Uncle Meechie to save some bitch we don't even know?" This fool was buggin'.

"That's exactly what I want." He nodded in agreement.

"News flash, playa, there's no sellouts over here! We ain't giving up nobody! Fuck your girl. If you want Uncle Meechie, then you need to go get him your damn self, and if you do, just know we'll be coming for you." I may be small, but I was no pushover. I handled my business better than most men when it came to the streets. If this fool thought I was some damsel in distress, scared and ready to agree to what he said, he would learn today.

"Look, bitch!" He backhanded me, and I went flying up against my car. Blood rushed from my nose. "I don't have time for games. I'm asking you nicely, but don't make me angry." He gritted his teeth.

"Well, you can ask however you wanna ask, but the answer is still no." I wiped blood from my busted lip. "Now, get your whack ass off my property." I turned quickly and tried to walk away but was caught by my neck and hemmed up against the car.

"Stop it! You're hurting her!" Mina yelled. She was rocking Maria back to sleep to keep her calm during the commotion. "Her husband is on the way, and he will fuck you up."

I knew she was bluffing, because Mario was out of town, but hopefully it would be enough to scare the stranger.

"Look, bitch, I ain't the one to be fucked with! You better ask somebody." The man leaned down into my ear. "Meechie ain't shit but a punk-ass coward who sent my girl upstate behind his bullshit. Tell Mario if my girl don't come back home, then his won't either."

"Is that a threat?" I asked.

"I don't make threats, only promises." He pushed me away forcefully and tossed me a cell phone. "Tell that nigga I'll be in touch."

Chapter 86

Chloe

My cellmate had passed away in the infirmary a few nights ago, so I was still alone and grateful. The time by myself gave me time to think and devise my plan. I'd written and stamped my letter to Nikki over a week ago. I knew snail mail could be even slower in prison, but I didn't have computer access. I was certain that once she read it, she would be here with bells on.

As I hopped down off my bed and went to use the bathroom, there was a rap at the cell door. I heard some keys jingle, and I tried to wipe and wash my hands before someone came in and saw what I was working with. However, the door never opened. A small rectangular flap opened, and someone slipped in a pre-made cereal packet of Cheerios and a carton of 2 percent milk. I grabbed them and frowned. I didn't like Cheerios, especially without sugar, and I damn sure didn't drink milk—2 percent, skim, whole, or anything in between. I slid the tray to the side just as the cell door opened. I thought it was a C.O., but in walked Cupcake.

"What you frowned up for? That right there is the breakfast of champions."

"I'm frowning because I didn't have another ass whooping for you on my schedule, but I guess I can pencil you in." I knew this was the doing of that gold-toothed C.O.

"Chill. I don't want to fight you." Cupcake threw her hands up in surrender.

"Well, what do you want then?" I stood in position just in case she tried me.

Holding up her bedroll, she shrugged. "I'm your new cellie."

"Give me a break." I shook my head. "This can't be for real."

"Bitch, I don't want to bunk with you either!" Cupcake threw her items down.

"So why in the fuck are you in here?" I knew she was close to the gold-toothed officer and wondered if Cupcake was placed here to harm me.

"Chill out. I'm in here because I don't have any other choice. Me and you are in the same boat. I'm told when to eat and where to sleep just like you. Obviously, someone put us together so that some shit will break out. Maybe they placed bets on who would last the longest. All I know is I don't need another trip to the hole, so I'm willing to squash this." She extended her hand.

"So, you're telling me that you're willing to end our beef without retaliation?"

"That shit in the locker room was for shits and giggles. I have to keep my reputation up on the yard, so I pick on the new inmates, so to speak. You proved you weren't a punk, and I respect that," she said while fixing up her cot.

Chapter 87

Mina

I waited patiently outside of the brand new two-story, four-bedroom home for my new client. The area was immaculate, and I made a mental note to stack enough money so that one day, I too could live in the new subdivision. Just as I checked my watch for the second time, a black SUV pulled up.

"I'm so sorry for being late. My son spilled orange juice all over his clothes, and I had to change him," the woman explained as she hopped out of the driver's seat and went to retrieve her son from the back.

"Nikki?" My mouth dropped. I couldn't believe my luck.

"Mina?" She removed her sunglasses and smacked her lips. "Hilda didn't tell me you would be the agent." She paused, no longer attempting to get her son out of the SUV. I knew she was half a second away from getting back in herself and pulling away.

"I just started." I attempted to smile and put her at ease. The last thing I needed was for her to leave, because Hilda would fire me and toss my commission out the door. I slowly walked up to her. "Look, Nikki, I don't know you, and you don't know me. Please don't let your beef with Gucci stop you from handling your business with me and run the risk of missing out on this beautiful home." I continued to woo Nikki for an additional ten minutes by mentioning every last detail about the new model home from the cathedral ceiling to the Grade-A school district. Mario Junior was still in diapers, but it was never too early to plan for his education.

My plan worked! Nikki agreed to put the drama aside and tour the home. Within an hour, we were back at the agency signing a contract.

"Thank you so much for allowing me the opportunity to work with you. Enjoy your new home." I grinned from ear to ear, because this house placed a guaranteed four racks in my pocket.

"You better not tell your friend where I live," she scolded.

"I wouldn't do that, Nikki, and besides, I told you that's not my beef. Please believe me, I've got my own issues."

"Can I ask you a question?" She stopped at the doorway.

"What's up?" I asked from the fax machine. I needed to fax over Nikki's cash offer to the sellers before someone else sent a bid.

"Where is Sam?" She raised an eyebrow and awaited my response.

"Honestly, I don't know." I shrugged.

"Well, if you see him, send him my way. I have something to tell him."

Chapter 88

Lovely

As I walked through the corridor, I stopped to ask one of the officers what time I would be able to make a call. She didn't answer me. Instead, she pointed over her shoulder to the line behind her. I turned in that direction and went to stand in line behind some huge white woman with missing teeth, dirty hair, and a mustache. I held my nose during the entire fifteen-minute wait. Her ass was rotten, and it was beginning to make me nauseous.

Finally, it was my turn to use the phone, which was three booths away from her, and I was thankful for the separation. Quickly, I dialed my house and anticipated someone picking up.

"You have a collect call from a Michigan State inmate," the operator started once the phone was answered.

"Lovely," I spoke to the recording.

"To accept this call, press one. To reject this call, simply hang up," the operator instructed.

"Lovely, baby, I've been waiting on your call," I heard in the receiver after my call was accepted.

"Maine, I miss you. I'm ready to come home," Were the first words to come through my mouth.

"I miss you more, baby. How are you holding up? How is my baby?"

"I'm okay, and the baby is too." I sighed with a lump in my throat.

"I'm going to get you out of there, baby. I swear on my mother I'm going to get you out," he confessed, and I believed if he really could get me out of there, he indeed would.

"Where is everybody?" I missed my niece, Shawnie, and my brother, Do It. I also missed my best friend, Coco. I was sure that they were missing me too.

"Shawnie is right here doing homework with her dad."

"How is Do It?" Do It was my play brother and my right-hand man. He was shot and left for dead by that nigga Meechie, but real niggas don't die easy. After being shot, he suffered minor brain damage, had a colostomy bag, and was placed in a wheelchair. Recently, I was informed that he had recovered some, and neither the wheelchair nor the colostomy bag were part of his life anymore.

"That nigga is one hundred. He wants to holla at you." He passed the phone.

"What up, Lo? Are you all right?"

"Hey, bro. Yeah, I'm good. I ain't got no other choice." I leaned up against the booth and closed my eyes for a brief second. Like Dorothy in the *Wizard of Oz*, I tried to click my heels, because there was no place like home. I desperately wished I could turn back the hands of time. I missed the 500-count Egyptian cotton sheets, hot bath water, clothing options, and having a refrigerator full of food. I missed coming and going as I pleased, and I missed making love to my man.

"If I could do that bid for you, you know I would, Lo." Do It snapped me out of my thoughts. "I can't believe that nigga Meechie played us like this. As soon as I'm able, I'm going to see that nigga."

"You don't mean that," I said, although I knew he did mean it. "Don't forget we're on tape, my nigga. Don't be playing like that." I reminded him that our call was being monitored and recorded.

"Yeah, I know. My bad. I can't see that nigga anyway. His ass is in lockup too, remember?"

I did remember. How could I forget? Meechie was taken into custody the night before I was. He was arrested for the murder of my ex-friend, White Girl, and the attempted murder of me. He would've killed my ass had an FBI agent by the name of Detective Nichols not jumped in front of me and taken the bullet. Currently, they had Meechie under high security in an undisclosed facility, and I heard through the grapevine that he was about to get a cake walk for turning State's evidence on my ass.

"Five minutes remaining," the automatic phone operator chimed in.

"Keep your head up, Lo. We are going to figure this shit out," Do It said, and then Maine was back on the line.

"Baby, I will be there tomorrow. Me and Nichols. On my word, it's going to work out okay. I love you!" he said, and I hung up.

I wanted to say that I loved him too, but love would get you killed up in this place. I didn't want anybody to think I was weak or vulnerable, so I placed the phone back on the hook and put my game face on.

Chapter 89

Nikki

It had been almost two weeks, and Chloe's letter was still fresh on my mind. I wanted to talk to Mario about it, but all my calls went unanswered. I was sure the fight between me and Gucci had played a part in that.

Without Mario's input, I decided to go see Chloe, because she was a friend, and I wanted to help her. So, I called Ms. Claudia and was on my way to drop off Junior.

"Hey, Rocky," Ms. C teased as I came through the front door, and I laughed.

"Hey, Mom. Thanks for watching Junior. I should be back in about three hours." I placed his toys, sippy cup, and a few Pull-ups down on the table.

"Take all the time you need. I miss my little man. I don't see him that much since you moved," she said while chasing my son around the living room.

"Have you and Rio talked since you missed the wedding?"

"Chile, I went over to their house for dinner, and all hell broke loose." She stopped chasing Junior and turned her attention to me.

"What happened?" I begged for details.

"You know I'm a straight shooter, so I came right out and told him that I was disappointed."

"No, you didn't." I covered my mouth.

"Yes, I did. I asked him why in the world he would marry that thang." She rolled her eyes. "He responded by saying he only married her because you no longer wanted him."

"What! Are you serious?" I was outdone.

"Honey, Gucci overheard us talking and gave me a piece of her mind." She laughed.

"What did she say?"

"She said I was being disrespectful, and I left."

"Well, you probably should've talked to Mario when he was alone." I would've been mad too if someone tried to disrespect me in my home.

"Well," was all Claudia said. She was stubborn like that.

"Okay, I have to get going. I'll see you guys later." I waved bye and headed out the door.

Just as I put the SUV in reverse, Mario pulled into the driveway. He was alone; therefore, I knew he was going to say something to me.

"Open the door." He tapped on the window, and I let him inside. "So, you're a fighter now?"

"Man, don't come at me with all that. Why haven't you been returning my calls?"

"My bad. I've been out of town handling some shit," he apologized.

"Look, when I call, you better answer. Anything could've been wrong with Junior," I warned.

"You're right, and I'm sorry. What's up?" He reclined back in the seat.

"I'm going to see Chloe today."

"What the fuck are you going to see her rat ass for?" Mario groaned.

"She mailed me a letter and explained that she killed Tre' for you. She said she didn't have the heart to bring you down, so her boss replaced her. When she found out Tre' was her replacement, she took him out to save our family," I explained.

"Once a cop, always a cop in my book." Rio rubbed his goatee.

"Anyway, she's pregnant and wants me to help her find Sam. He needs to take custody of their child when it's born."

"Do you know where Sam is?" He looked at me.

"No, but—"

He cut me off. "Well, ain't no need in going to see that girl if you can't do anything for her."

"I can't leave her hangin'," I protested.

"Well, you're grown. You do what you gotta do and let me know what happens." He reached for the door handle, but I stopped him.

"Are you okay? You look stressed."

"I'm good, just dealing with a lot, that's all." He sighed.

"Is it something you may want to talk about?" I knew Mario kept a lot of things to himself. At times it was a good thing, but sometimes it really took a toll on him.

"It's all good. Just the typical stress that comes with the streets."

"You need to leave those streets alone," I warned.

"You're right, but I can't, because too many people depend on me to eat." He stared into the distance.

"Rio, not to sound rude, but you are not the only drug supplier in Detroit. If you stepped away from H.O.F., I guarantee all your workers will be selling dope for the next nigga tomorrow." I shook my head.

"It's more than selling dope, and you know that. I've built a family unit, and we help the community, believe it or not. I know our means are ill gotten, but our intentions are good. We feed the homeless, take books to the schools that don't have them, and we even give out Christmas gifts in the ghetto, which you already know."

"Yes, I know all the good you do, but I also know the bad that comes with it. The drug industry is dog eat dog, Rio. The streets aren't what they used to be. This new generation ain't trying to work under a boss. They want to be the boss. If that means taking you out, then it is what it is."

"All right, Nik, go head and handle your business. I'm going in here to holla at my li'l man, and then I'm going home. Be safe out there."

He wasn't trying to hear what I was saying, so I respected his wishes and pulled off.

Chapter 90

Gucci

"That nigga said what?" Mario was beyond pissed.

I had waited to fill him in on the details of what happened the other day because I didn't want to upset him while he was on a business run. In the dope game, you had to have a clear head in order to watch your surroundings and make smart moves. He'd just walked through the door ten minutes ago, and I hit him with the news I'd been keeping.

"He said if we don't stop Uncle Meechie from testifying about his girlfriend, he is coming for me." I paced the living room floor.

"I wish I was here!" Mario punched the wall, which cracked the drywall. "Fuck!"

"Baby calm down. We'll figure this out." I tried to reassure him, although I wasn't completely confident myself.

"Where is your uncle now?" Mina asked from her seat on the sofa.

Mario looked at her and said nothing; therefore, I took the chance to speak up.

"Meechie is in lockup at an unknown facility under federal protection."

"Can you guys get in contact with him?" As Mina spoke again, I could see the vein in Mario's neck pop out.

"Why in the hell are you asking so many questions?" he snapped, and Mina jumped to her feet.

"Look, I was just trying to help, but I see that I'm not wanted in this conversation." She grabbed her purse, obviously shaken and disturbed.

"Thank you, Mina. I'll call you later, okay?" I gave her an apologetic look.

"That's fine. I hope everything works out. I have a meeting to show another house anyway." She hugged me.

"Good luck with your showing," I said and closed the door behind her. "Why did you have to yell at her like that?"

"Fuck her," was Mario's reply.

"Like it or not, that's my friend." I rolled my eyes. This was not the first rude exchange between him and her.

"Friends will fuck you over faster than enemies. Didn't you learn that by watching me and Sam or Nikki and Chloe?" He laid back in the recliner and pulled a blunt from the pocket of his navy blue Dickies pants and lit it up.

I was not about to have this conversation again for the millionth time, so I changed the subject. "What are we going to do?" I sat down on his lap.

"First, I'm going to assemble a team that will sit on the house. Then I'm going to hit the streets and find out who this cat is. Next, I'm going to try to contact Uncle Meechie and get the back story. Last, I will wait for the asshole to call."

"Let me go with you. Two heads are better than one."

"No. You stay here with Maria and wait for my call." He stood and lifted me off of his lap.

"But I always go with you," I whined.

"Not today, G." He blew a smoke ring and walked past me into the kitchen.

"What's different today from the last decade?" I asked, because I had never been excluded from his dealings. We were a team!

"Years ago, we were young and dumb. Today, you're a wife and a mother." Mario grabbed a bottle of water from the refrigerator.

"But—" I started to fuss.

"You got a damn mark on your head! What part of that don't you understand?" He slammed the fridge closed, which knocked a few magnets to the tiled floor. "You're my wife, not a god damn gangsta!" he yelled.

It's funny, years ago when I was his sidekick, I longed to be his wife. Now that I was his wife, he treated me like some fragile porcelain doll, although he knew I was capable of handling my own in the streets.

"Okay, baby. I understand," I lied as an attempt to be the loving, patient, understanding woman he wanted. "But since you just got home, can you at least take me to a late lunch before you hit the streets?" I smiled seductively. "After lunch, maybe we could do that thing you like." I rubbed his manhood.

"Let's do that thing I like right now, and depending on how good it is, maybe I'll take you out to eat." He unzipped his pants and followed me up the stairs.

Chapter 91

Mina

Mario was beginning to piss me off with his rudeness. I thought after he asked for my help planning the wedding that our beef was squashed. Eventually, he would have to get over himself and put the grudge behind us. I would've called him out about it, but I had plans.

An hour after I showed up at Gucci's, I'd received a call from the agency asking me to show an expensive property to a potential client. Hilda congratulated me on a job well done with Nikki and offered me this deal as a bonus. The sale of this home could make or break me. The commission would be more than enough to stay afloat for at least three months.

I drove up to the beautiful waterfront property and pressed the code to enter the ten-foot wrought iron gates. With less than twenty minutes before meeting my new client, I needed to get prepared. The lights needed to be turned on, the scented candle needed to be lit. The blinds needed to be drawn, and the Jacuzzi needed to be turned on. The owner of the house lived out of town, so there was no telling what else I had to face once I unlocked the doors and started my staging process.

Pulling into the circular driveway, I stared at the black Yukon Denali and frowned.

"Damn. They beat me here," I said aloud, upset with the fact that Hilda had given them the code to the gate. I hoped they hadn't gotten out and inspected the property without me. Grabbing the manila folder from my passenger seat, I stepped from my car and put on my business face. Selling this three-hundred-thousand-dollar house would be a task, but I rolled up my sleeves, prepared to get the job done.

"Hello." I tapped on the triple-black tinted window to get his attention. The driver's window rolled down, and there was a Caucasian male behind the wheel.

"Hello. My boss is waiting for you in the backyard. He got a little antsy." The driver smiled, and I nodded.

Heading to unlock the door, I cursed myself under my breath. I knew how much this potential sale meant to me. My dumb ass should've been there an hour ago instead of stopping to kick it with Gucci. Reaching for the lock box, I punched in the code and retrieved the key. Turning the knob, I prayed everything inside was ready for viewing.

"Wow!" I exclaimed, stepping into the grand entryway. There was a spiral staircase, marble floors, and gold columns. I flew through the house like a breeze, cutting on the lights and scanning the area for misplaced items. All was well inside the house, so I stepped into the amazing chef's kitchen and out onto the connecting deck.

Closing the French doors behind me, I stopped dead in my tracks when I noticed what was all over the lawn. My heart rate quickened, and I lost my breath. I didn't know what was going on, but I was anxious to find out. Stepping closer to the edge of the two-tiered deck, I squinted to make sure I was reading this correctly. In white rose petals across the grass was the most beautiful message I've ever seen in my life: *I'll take it . . . if you'll take me.*

"Mina, it's been too long since I've seen you. I miss your laugh, your smile, and your beautiful brown eyes." Sam stood there like a thugged-out Prince Charming with a dozen red roses and a Kool-Aid smile. It was hot outside that day. Therefore, all he had on was a pair of black raw denim jeans and some red Adidas gym shoes. I pinched myself for fear that I was dreaming.

"I thought you forgot about me." I blinked rapidly.

"Forgetting you is impossible . . . especially when you're on my mind all day every day." He smiled, and I blushed. It had been so long since I'd seen him, but he still looked the same. Deep waves, beautiful teeth, and so many tattoos I didn't bother counting.

"I can't believe you're actually standing here right now!" I exclaimed, jumping into his muscular arms. I'd waited for this moment for a very long time.

"I came back for you, Mina, and this time we're going to do this right! No more Chloe, no more Tre', no more hustlin', and no more games."

He kissed me on my lips, and I felt my juices flow. It would be a bold-face lie if I said I hadn't wanted him between my legs since the first time I saw him. I knew he wanted me just as bad, but we had never crossed that line. Now that he was back, I was definitely going to find out what I'd been missing.

"No more hustlin'?" I repeated.

"That's not me, and I'm tired of pretending. I thought the life of a trap star was what I wanted, but that was Chloe's dream." He frowned. I was elated to hear the good news.

Previously, Sam had mentioned that he loved to cook and wanted to own a restaurant. I wondered if he still planned to follow through on his dream.

"So, what do you have in mind?"

"Right now, all I want to do is lay low and chill with you." He leaned back on the deck rail and looked me over seductively. Good thing I'd dressed in a sexy Bebe dress that accented my curves.

"I think that's a great idea." I flashed every tooth in my mouth. "What about Mario, though?" I knew the minute word got out that Sam was back, things between him and Mario would blow up.

"Honestly, baby, I can't worry about it. I'll see that nigga when I see him. Hopefully, he understands why I left the H.O.F. organization." Sam sighed. "And if he doesn't understand it, I hope he at least respects my decision."

I nodded my understanding, although silently, I worried about the outcome.

Seeing the perplexed look on Sam's face, I decided to switch gears and change the subject. "How did you know I would still be here? By now, I could've been anywhere in the world."

"That day at the airport, an hour after we decided to split up, I had a change of heart. I approached the ticket counter and asked if I could get a ticket to wherever you went. The lady told me that you had cashed your ticket in and headed back out the front door." He laughed lightly. "Girl, I was ready to follow yo' ass to hell if that's what it took to be with you . . . but coming back to Detroit was a different story."

"Well, I'm glad you're here with me now." I smiled.

"I'm here, and I ain't ever going anywhere unless you're with me, Mina."

Chapter 92

Lovely

I fixed my hair as best I could with the small comb provided me. Next, I smoothed some of the wrinkles out of my uniform and put on my best smile. Maine was waiting for me in the visitor's lounge, and I was elated.

As I walked through the hallway, a feeling of sadness came over me. I'd spent my whole pregnancy without him, and I was very afraid that once I had my son, he would have nothing to do with me.

"Baby, why are you crying?" He stood to greet me, and I sobbed harder. He looked and smelled better than ever. He was the man of every woman's dream, and I looked a mess. "What's wrong?"

"Maine, I love you." was all I could muster.

"I love you too." He squeezed me tighter, and then we were told to break it up by an officer. I wiped my eyes and took a seat across from him.

"I'm sorry I messed this up for us." I sniffed.

"Lovely, you didn't mess up anything."

"Yes, I did. I should've married you when I had the chance. I should've given you a baby when you asked. I just should've done a lot of things differently."

"That's in the past, and we can't do anything about it. We can only look forward to the future and move on." He smiled. "You are about to have my son in a few months, and we will get married, believe that."

"How, Maine? Let's be realistic. I'm in jail for life!"

"You haven't gone to trial yet. Don't give up now." He grabbed my hand. "I will get you out of here, I swear."

"It ain't that easy." I shook my head.

"Baby, you've got to trust me. I have something lined up."

"My meetings with the lawyers haven't been reassuring at all. They have all of that evidence on me, not to mention the testimony of Meechie." I sighed and thought about the gun with my fingerprints and the clothes I wore during the murder. I kicked myself every day for trusting my so-called friend with crucial pieces of evidence. I knew some of the things I'd done in life were wrong, but they were done with good intentions. Everything I did was to protect or avenge a member of my family, and this was the price I had to pay.

"Baby, I'm working on that. This will be all over before you know it." He patted my hand. "I've got plans for me and you, girl."

"Look, if this plan doesn't work out . . ." I started, but the words got lost in my throat.

"Shh. Lovely, you've come too far to give up now. All you have to do is stay focused in here, and I'll handle the rest."

Chapter 93

Chloe a.k.a. Robin

"Jones, you have a visitor, and so do you, Cupcake," the C.O. announced as she opened our cell.

"I hope it's my man, because I can't take another visit from my mama," Cupcake said.

Since we'd reached an understanding the other day, I hadn't had an issue with her or any other inmate for that matter. I was sure our locker room brawl had let them know that I wasn't to be messed with, pregnant or not.

"Well, I'm not sure who would be here for me, but anybody is appreciated." I stretched as we walked in the open room. Cupcake ran toward her visitor as I scanned the room for mine.

"Damn, it hasn't been that long. I can't believe you don't recognize me." Nikki smiled, although I could tell that my appearance shocked her. There wasn't much you could do to fix yourself in a place like this. Even if there was, you don't want to walk around in an all-female institution looking like a beauty queen.

"It's been long enough." I smiled back. "How have you been?" I took a seat across from her at the plastic table.

"I should be asking you the same thing, mama," she said as she pointed to my belly.

"I'm good, but I'll be better once I know my child will be with her father in my absence." I sighed.

"Chloe—I mean Robin." Nikki corrected herself.

"Please, call me Chloe. I've kind of adapted to that name, and besides, the other inmates even call me Chloe."

"Okay." She looked at me like I was crazy. "I have to be honest with you. I have no idea where Sam is, but I promise I will do everything to locate him for you."

"I'm sure that bitch Mina knows. After all, aren't they together?" I picked Nikki for any information she had.

"No, they're not together," she informed. "As a matter of fact, Mina is still in Detroit. Sam is the one that took off and hasn't been seen or heard from since."

"That's shocking," I admitted.

"Look, besides this thing with Sam, is there anything else I can do for you? Do you need any money?"

"No, I'm fine."

"Chloe, I'm so sorry you're going through this." Nikki stared at my face, and I stared back at her. She needed to absorb my tired face so the guilt would set in.

"That's enough about me. I'm just glad you came out of your coma. You look healthy and healed," I said, referring to her gunshot wounds.

"Yeah, thank God! It's been a long road to recovery, but I'm here." She smiled.

"I wonder why Tonya shot you."

"I don't know, girl. It could've been any number of reasons, although jealousy is my guess." She shifted nervously.

"It's a shame she was killed before you could ask her." I smiled on the inside because this dumb bitch had no idea that she was sitting across the table from the person who had actually shot her.

Chapter 94

Nikki

The meeting with Chloe actually felt like old times. Things started off awkward but ended up like a trip down memory lane. We reminisced about this and that and shared a few laughs. By the end of the forty-minute visit, I missed my old friend terribly and wished I could bring her home.

There was only one thing that struck me as odd. When Chloe mentioned Tonya's death, I was a bit taken aback. The news didn't surface until about a week after Chloe was locked up, so how did she know Tonya had been killed? There was also a twinge of something in the way that she spoke that told me she knew more than she was letting on.

"Damn!" I cursed as I approached my whip and noticed that my tire was flat. I stood there for a second and assessed what had caused the flat. Upon further inspection, I noticed a nail was the culprit.

"Do you need any help?" A fine-ass gentleman approached me. He was tall, dark, and handsome, well-built, and dressed to the nines.

"No, I'm going to call roadside assistance, but thank you." I smiled and pulled out my phone.

"That's nonsense." He removed his Armani blazer and rolled up the sleeves on his collared shirt. "I can get this changed and have you out of here in no time." He smiled.

"That's okay. I don't want you to get your nice suit dirty." I smiled, trying not to stare too hard.

"This suit means nothing to me. Besides, if I don't help you, it will be on my conscience all day. Now, pop your trunk." He handed me his jacket.

As I watched the stranger handle his business with my tire, I admired the sight before me. This man was clean-cut and polished. Secretly, I wondered why he was at the prison but quickly came to the conclusion that he was probably a lawyer. Within minutes, my spare tire was on, and I was handing the gentleman back his jacket.

"Thank you so much, Mr. . . .?"

"My name is Jermaine, and the pleasure was all mine."

"Jermaine, I'm Nikkita, but my friends call me Nikki." For some reason, I wasn't ready to let this man out of my presence, so I made small talk.

"Nikki, my friends call me Maine."

The CK fragrance drifting off of his body had me turned on.

"Well, it was nice to meet you, Maine. Do you come here often?" I instantly wanted to kick my own ass for such a corny line.

"Actually, I do." He smiled. "My sister is in there." He nodded back at the facility. "What about you? Do you come here often?" Maine mimicked me.

"No, this was actually my first visit. I came to see an old friend," I explained. "I thought you were a lawyer or something."

"No. I own a few businesses here and there, nothing major." He was being modest, because I could tell this brother had bank.

"A business owner. I'm impressed," I admitted. I was relieved to know that Maine was on the straight and narrow. No matter how fine he was, if he was into the streets, I couldn't mess with him.

"What do you do?" He leaned on the Aston Martin parked next to my parking spot.

I hesitated for a minute, because I didn't know how to respond. "Um, right now I'm working on becoming an author." I thought fast.

"That's impressive." He laughed. "What is your book about?"

"I haven't actually started it yet, but I think it will be a story about my life." As each moment went by, I felt closer and closer to this fine-ass stranger.

"Some life you must've lived to write a book about it." He flashed his pearly whites.

"You have no idea."

"Well, I would like to find out more about you if that's okay." He smiled.

"Yeah, that's cool," I said and rattled off my phone number. He gave me his number, and we said our good-byes.

On the way home, I called Anjela to see if she wanted to meet for a late lunch, and she agreed. I wanted to tell her about my new friend and discuss Chloe's situation with her. I didn't know what I expected her to do, but I knew lawyers had ways of making people surface. Sam needed to be found before this baby was born. As a mother, I could only imagine what she had been going through.

I pulled into the parking lot at O'Reilly's and stepped out into the rain. I spotted my cousin's car; therefore, I knew she was already inside.

"Hey, cuz." I hugged her, and we were shown to our seats.

"You look cute." She smiled. "I love those shoes."

"Can you believe these aren't name brand?" I flexed my foot so she had a good 360-degree view. Lately, I'd been trying to live without labels and prove to Anjela that things didn't have to be expensive to be deemed fabulous.

"Cuz, I don't mean to cut you off, but is that Mario and Gucci?" She pointed to the corner booth.

I strained my neck to get a good look and frowned at the sight. "Damn! There are a million and four lunch locations in the city. Why in the hell did they choose this one?"

"I'm about to send that bitch a bottle." Anjela laughed and waved over the waitress.

Chapter 95

Gucci

"Compliments of the ladies over there." Some Asian chick placed a bottle of red wine down on our table with a note on a napkin.

I picked it up and unfolded it.

Please accept my sincere apology for beating that ass. Drinks are on me. ☺

I threw the napkin to Mario, and he chuckled.

"What the fuck are you laughing at?" I snapped, ready to go sucka-punch that bitch right in her mouth.

"Y'all are acting like kids." He reached for the bottle, prepared to pour a glass, but I popped his hand like a child.

"I told that bitch!" Grabbing the bottle, I stood from the table.

"Where are you going, G?" Mario's question fell on deaf ears as I marched over to Tweedledee and Tweedledum.

"You think you cute now?" I towered over Nikki, and she stopped laughing abruptly.

"As a matter of fact, I do!" She stood. "Now, what are you going to do about it?"

"Actually, I just came over here to thank you for the gesture. However, since I know you can't really afford such an expensive bottle, I wanted to share it." Just like that, I poured the whole bottle of red wine over the top of her head and watched it spill all over her outfit.

"Bitch!" She wiped the wine out of her eyes just in time to see my hand as it slid across her face. I grabbed her hair and pulled her into a chokehold. The tramp bit my leg, so I let her go.

"Gucci!" Mario called out, which distracted me long enough to receive a blow to the face.

Within seconds, we were enmeshed in an all-out girl fight. I was determined not to lose, and so was she. I slammed her up against the table, and she kicked me off of her, right into the wall.

"That's enough!" Mario grabbed me, and Anjela pulled Nikki. Neither of us wanted to stop.

"Another time and another place, bitch!" Nikki laughed.

"Fuck that! Right here is good for me." I removed my Chanel earrings, prepared for war.

"Ain't nothing between us but air and opportunity." Nikki removed her shoes just like she had at the hair battle and held them in her hands to be used as weapons.

"Shut the fuck up!" I smacked my lips. "You ain't hood, so quit trying to pretend you about this life!"

"Bitch, I'm more hood than I get credit for. Don't forget I was hood enough to whip your trick ass."

"Come on, Nikki, you don't need to go to jail again. That bitch ain't worth it." Anjela grabbed Nikki's phone and purse from the table, then ushered her toward the front door.

"Next time, Nikki!" I yelled over Mario's shoulder.

"Gucci, I told you I would spank that ass every time I saw you."

"You didn't spank shit!" I spat.

"G, put your earrings on and let's go!" Mario actually acted as though he had an attitude with me.

"I'm sorry." He apologized to our waitress, who was standing there looking like a deer caught in headlights. "This should cover the damages to your establishment and your tip." He handed a stack of bills to the frazzled young girl and left me inside the restaurant to retrieve my things.

Chapter 96

Mina

Sam and I had been inseparable for the past few days, and I was in hog heaven. The night before, I had finally told him about Mario and Gucci's predicament, and he suggested that I take him to their house. I was leery, to say the least, because I didn't know if this meeting was a good idea, especially since we were just popping up unannounced.

As we pulled up to the gate, I pressed the call button and held my breath. My last visit to this house didn't end on a good note.

"Yeah!" Mario's voice boomed through the speaker.

"Mario, it's Mina. Is Gucci home?" When there was no response, I looked at Sam, who looked straight ahead. After we waited almost a minute, the iron gate finally opened.

I pulled up into the wide driveway and turned off my car. I could see Gucci waiting in the doorway with Maria on her hip.

"Hey, girl," she called out and placed her hand over her eyes to block the sun. Just as she spotted Sam, whose appearance was unchanged, I could see her posture change. "Well, what do we have here?" She shifted the baby to her other hip and reached up to hug Sam.

"What's up, Gucci." He smiled and rubbed Maria's curly hair.

"Girl, what happened to you?" She had new scratches and fresh bruises.

"Long story short, it was round two with Nikki. Now, come on in. Mario is in the living room playing the Xbox."

As we walked into the living room, Gucci pinched my arm but didn't say anything. "Mario, you have a visitor," she called over the sofa.

"That's your friend. She didn't come to see me." He never looked up.

"What's up, big homie?" Sam said, and immediately, the game paused. Mario stood up and mugged Sam.

"Nigga, I don't know who invited you over here, but it's time to leave." He pointed at the door.

"So, it's like that?" Sam asked.

"It was like that the minute your bitch was identified as a narc and you skipped town."

"I swear on my mother's grave that I didn't know Chloe was a rat." Sam raised his right hand.

"Yeah, whatever!" Mario smirked. "I groomed you from a pup to take over the family business. I broke bread with you, and then you go and do me dirty."

"Mario, I know what you did for me, and I'm forever grateful," Sam explained.

"You were so grateful that you skipped town and left my organization hanging?" Mario sat on the arm of the couch and appeared ready to pounce on Sam.

"Some shit went down, and I had to leave."

"Tell me what was so important that you just up and left with no explanation." Mario folded his arms.

I looked at Gucci. Up until this point, I had never told anyone why Sam left in the first place. There were some things that needed to go to the grave, and this was one of them. Sam looked at me, actually impressed that I hadn't uttered a word about what he'd done for me.

"I left town because I killed Mina's husband. He beat her and raped her, so I did what I had to for my girl."

"You did what?" Mario asked for clarification.

"Not that it matters, but Mina can vouch for me."

Gucci looked at me, and I nodded.

Mario stared in disbelief, but he wasn't at a loss for words for too long. "Now, you wanna hear some funny shit?" He looked at me and Sam. "Chloe sent a letter to Nikki, confessing about killing Tre'."

"What?" Sam looked puzzled.

"She said she did it to save me from going to jail." Mario laughed. "This shit is comical."

"Mario, I shot Tre'. Chloe followed me to Mina's old house because she thought I was creeping out on her. After I did what I did, I went out to the whip to conceal my gun and went back inside to clean up the mess. While I was inside, someone must've called the police to report the gunshots. I heard the sirens and dipped back outside only to find my whip was gone. The crazy bitch had stolen my truck. She took the rap because she had no other choice. All the evidence pointed toward her because she was spotted speeding away from the property, and the gun was in her possession. I thought she would try to rat me out. That's why I left with no explanation." As Sam talked, Mario's face softened. "I only came back for Mina. When she told me what was going on with you, I knew you needed my help, so I'm here."

At the sound of business, Gucci and I left them alone to talk. I exhaled because we could finally put the beef with Mario behind us.

Chapter 97

Lovely

"What's up, girl?" Tiny sat beside me at the lunch table. Today's meal was Spam, apple sauce, and string beans.

"Hey," I replied with no enthusiasm. I just stared at the odd food combination.

"You look upset." She noticed.

"I think Maine is cheating on me," I murmured.

"Lovely, stop it." She laughed, but I was serious. Since his last visit, shit had been different between us.

"On the phone, he always sounds preoccupied, like his mind is on something else," I admitted.

"Bitch, his mind is on something else, and that something is getting you out of this god-forsaken place. Don't let the devil get the best of you. Maine loves you and is out there pounding the pavement, trying to get you out," my friend declared, and I knew she was right. My mind was definitely playing tricks on me.

"I get out of here soon, and if it makes you feel better, I'll do some snooping and send word back to you."

"Thanks, Tiny." Knowing that I would have an ally on the outside put my mind at rest. If anybody could get the job done, it would be Tiny.

"No need for saying thank you, because if I find out he slippin', I'm going to be right back in this bitch for having your man executed." She laughed.

"Don't do that, because my baby won't have anywhere to go," I joked.

"Well, maybe I'll just cut his dick off instead."

"Yeah, that's a good idea. He has no need for it while I'm in here anyway." We both laughed.

Chapter 98

Nikki

Maine was just what I needed to bring me out of my funk. We'd been in contact several times that week, and it was refreshing. I felt the pep come back to my step and hadn't thought twice about Mario or my fight with his mutt, Gucci. I was ready to put the old Nikki to bed.

"I can't believe you want to cut your hair off!" Coco, my hairdresser, played with my hair while staring at me through her mirror.

"You act like I have long hair." I laughed. That morning, I had awoken with a new attitude and wanted a refreshed look. Therefore, I decided on a new haircut, so here I was.

"No, it's not down your back long, but it's long enough to be missed." She fingered my hair while shaking her head. "Tell me why you're doing this?" She placed her hand on her hip.

"If you must know, I have a new boo thang." I smiled, and she spun me around to face her.

"What's his name?" she pried.

"I'm not telling you until it's official."

"You better tell me!" she demanded playfully.

"His name is Jermaine. I met him at WVC while visiting Chloe. He was there visiting his sister. Now, are you going to keep questioning me or do my hair?" I laughed, but she looked upset about something.

"No, I'll do it." She frowned.

"I don't need you cutting my hair with an attitude. Do I need to pull an Angela Bassett and do it myself, or should I get in someone else's chair?"

"No, I got you, Nikki. I'm just shocked that you moved on, that's all." She pulled a pair of scissors from her drawer.

Silently, I prayed I was making the right decision, but I didn't sweat the issue too hard, because I could always purchase new hair and have Coco sew it in.

After a few easy snips, I was sent to the shampoo sink for a deep conditioning. Being practically bald made the wash go a lot faster, and before I knew it, I was back in the styling chair.

As Coco styled my hair, the hairdresser stationed next to us leaned in. "Girl, I heard you gave Gucci something awful." She reached for a high-five, and I reluctantly obliged. "Word around the way is that you sent ol' girl to the emergency room."

"Is that so?" I tried to conceal my smile, but it was useless.

"Just one question, Nikki," Coco whispered in my ear. "Did that shit feel good?" She laughed, and I did too.

"I'm not gon' lie. It really did."

"Girl, that homewrecker had it coming!" another stylist yelled from a few stations down.

"You got that right! Had that been my man, I would've burned that bitch!" some other stylist said while waving her hot iron in the air.

"Don't nobody want that broke nigga except your ass," a customer said on her way to the bathroom. The whole salon erupted into laughter.

"Whatever! I better not see your ass on Fenkell then," the stylist tossed over her shoulder. I laughed to myself because the mention of the popular street named Fenkell let me know that these women were arguing over some damn male dancer.

Almost exactly an hour later, I was paying the receptionist and throwing everyone the deuces. My new cut matched my new attitude, and I was feeling myself big time.

On my way out of the salon, I stopped to retrieve my cell and damn near lost my breath. Standing less than ten feet away from me was Gucci, all wrapped up in the arms of a man. The kicker was that the man with his hands all over her ass was not her husband. Thinking fast, I hit record on my cell phone and walked past the loving couple.

"Smile! You're on Candid Camera!" I said just as their embrace was broken.

"You bitch! I'm going to fuck you up!" she screamed as I crossed the street.

Stopping at my car door, I turned and smiled. "That's exactly what your husband will be saying to your trifling ass after I send him this video."

Chapter 99

Gucci

"Shit!" I stomped my foot as Nikki pulled off, wagging her finger.

"I take it that wasn't your bestie." Cartier laughed.

"I told you not to be touching on me and shit. Now that bitch is going to go run and tell that shit to Mario." I don't know who I was more upset with: Nikki, Cartier, or Mario.

If my husband would've answered the phone when I called him earlier, I never would've needed a ride from Cartier in the first place. I'd gone downtown to put money on the books of our soldiers who were locked up and came out to find that my whip had been towed.

"Will I see you later?" He winked, and I tossed him the middle finger. "I love you too, boo." He laughed and ran around to the driver side of his ash grey Hummer with chrome features.

I stepped into Salon 3K, and all eyes were on me.

"Hey, Gucci, you know your girl just left," Wanda, my hairdresser, hollered as I walked to her station.

"Yeah, that bitch was up in here talking about she sent you to the emergency room," some chick added. "I was like, 'Oh, hell no, Gucci ain't some chump bitch!'"

"That's fo'sho." I nodded my head and ignored the hand she raised for a high-five. I knew how chicken heads in the salon talked shit and came to the conclusion that this chick was probably lying. Hell, she probably had just done the same thing to Nikki, trying to gas her up.

"So, what are you getting done today?" Wanda asked.

"Braid me up. I want eight across, straight to the back."

"Huh?" Wanda asked for clarification.

"Yeah, I'm going old school. The next time I see Nikki, I'm fucking her up! I don't need anything for her to pull on."

Wanda laughed, but I was dead-ass serious. Had the incident with Cartier and her camera phone not happened, it would've been lights out for her.

My hair appointment only lasted thirty minutes, because I'd washed my own hair that morning at home. After paying and tipping Wanda, I contemplated calling Mario again for a ride but decided against it. I wasn't sure if Nikki had dropped dime on me yet, but I wasn't ready to find out.

I stepped outside, prepared to hail one of the many cabs passing by, but there was Cartier, posted out front. "Boy, what are you still doing here?" I said, approaching the passenger-side window.

"I thought you might need me." He smirked.

"Thanks, but I'm going to catch a cab."

"Girl, stop acting silly and get in. I won't bite if you don't want me to." He laughed, and I got in.

"Where are you taking me?" I asked about ten minutes into the ride. He obviously wasn't taking me home, because he didn't know where I lived.

"Just ride." He turned up the music. His car speaker was currently playing 2Chainz's "Boo Thang."

I must've dozed off, because when I opened my eyes, we were pulling into a garage.

"Where are we?" I stretched.

"This is my crib. Come on."

We stepped into a beautiful condominium off of the Detroit River, and I was amazed at the fancy space. It was the ultimate bachelor pad with red and black leather sofas, rugs, and accent pieces. A 70-inch television adorned the wall across from the sofa. There was also an oversized fish tank strategically placed in the wall between the living area and the bedroom.

"Why did you bring me here, Cartier?"

"Can't you just chill with a nigga?" He removed his Christian Lacroix studded shirt and laid it across the railing leading to an upstairs loft area. I tried not to stare at his body, but the tattoo on his chest caught my eye.

"When did you get my name tattooed on you?" He definitely didn't have that back when we were together.

"I got this while doing my bid." He placed his hand over it. "I told you that you were the only girl to ever have my heart."

"That's sweet, Cartier." I smiled at the gesture. "My own husband doesn't even have my name on him."

"Why are you with him anyway?" he asked while walking over to the sound system.

"I love him," I answered truthfully. I could tell Cartier was uneasy with my truth, but I wasn't going to lie just to make him feel good.

"What about me, Gucci? Do you still love me?" He looked at me curiously.

"Cartier, I will always have love for you," I started, but he cut me off.

"Do you still love me?" He picked me up off the couch and pinned me up against the wall. "I want to know if you love me, because I still love you."

Cartier kissed me, and much to my own shock, I kissed him back. Right before things got *real,* my cell phone rang, and I knew by the ring tone it was Mario.

Chapter 100

Robin aka "Chloe"

I sat in my cell, reading the latest issue of *Jetset* magazine and trying to imagine myself anywhere but there. I closed the magazine and lay down on my side. Earlier I was told that I would be moving to another floor and getting a new cellmate. I didn't ask any questions, just followed the C.O. to my new home. I silently wished my new cellmate was decent. At this stage in my pregnancy, I couldn't be fighting or worrying about getting shanked. The pregnancy made me an easy target. My belly was now rounder and poking out, which made it impossible to appear vicious.

Rubbing my hand across my belly, I thought about my baby and wondered what type of life it would have without me. I shook my head at the thought and turned my attention to wondering why I hadn't heard from the bitch Nikki since her last visit a few weeks ago. It unnerved me that she hadn't even had the decency to at least write.

"What's wrong with you? Why is your face all twisted up?" my new roommate asked as she entered the cell.

I looked up to see the other black pregnant woman from when I first got to this facility.

"Girl, it's these stomach pains," I lied and rubbed my belly.

"I know what you mean." She rubbed her stomach too.

"Are you my new cellie?" I smiled.

"For now, I guess." She smiled too.

"How far are you?" I looked at her belly, which appeared way bigger than mine.

"I'm almost eight months. How far along are you?"

"I just turned six months yesterday." I stood from the bunk and removed my bedroll. "Here, you can take the bottom."

"No, you don't have to give up your spot." She shook her head.

"It's okay. You can't be climbing up there."

"Thank you." She smiled

My new associate and I talked all night, and I actually liked her. We found out that since the facility didn't have a maternity unit, they decided to put us in a cell together on the level one side. That's where the non-violent inmates were stationed. It was a funny thing, because we were both in there for murder. The only difference between us was that she was awaiting trial, and I had already been sentenced. She swore on her dead mother that she had never killed anyone, but those cries fell on my deaf ears. The woman looked innocent enough, but I too looked innocent and lied well, so I didn't put shit past nobody. In my opinion, everyone was capable of murder when placed in the right situation or circumstance. The fact that her father was known as Lucifer on the streets in his heyday told me the apple didn't fall too far from the tree. I slept with one eye open but treated her as a friend all the same.

Chapter 101

Nikki

"I'm glad you chose to take me up on my dinner invitation." Jermaine spoke over the soft music.

"I'm glad I did too." I played with my cheesecake.

"Quite honestly, I'm shocked that you actually chose the Cheesecake Factory for dinner. I would've liked to have taken you somewhere more swank and upscale." He leaned back in his seat.

"There is nothing wrong with this. Truthfully, I prefer the simple things in life." I bit into my pineapple up-side-down cheesecake.

"Why is that, Nikki?" He leaned up and reached for my hand. "A woman like you should have every luxury life has to offer."

"Maine, I've been there, and I've done that." I looked away. "I'm ashamed to say this, but my ex-husband was a drug lord." Although I knew Mario was still hustling, I replaced the word *is* with *was* because I didn't want to incriminate him. "I've had every luxury afforded to me that came with that lifestyle," I reassured him.

"Well, I'm curious . . . why did you leave?"

"I left because my husband cheated and made a baby with his mistress." I looked away again.

"Wow!" Maine exclaimed. "That's tough."

"You have no idea." I pretended to laugh. "So, why hasn't somebody swooped you up yet?" I wanted to change the subject.

"I just haven't found the right one." He sighed.

"Tell me about your last relationship." I pried and watched Maine gaze off into space.

"I loved her unconditionally, and I'm sure the feeling was mutual, but our timing was off, I guess." He shrugged. "Now she's gone, and it's too late."

"They say if you love something, let it go. If it comes back to you, it's yours, but if it doesn't, then you know."

"It would take a miracle and divine intervention to bring her back to me." He wiped the corners of his mouth with the black linen napkin. "Anyway, it's bad luck to mix old business with new business, so enough about that. Let's go."

As we pulled into my driveway, Maine cut off the engine and came around to open my door. "Nikkita, tonight the pleasure was all mine. It felt good to converse and let loose, ya know. In my line of work, I don't get to relax a lot."

"Yeah, I understand. Same here." I leaned up against the door and took in the night air. "I haven't been on a date in a very long time, and this was amazing. Thank you, Maine. Good night." I stepped away from him, and he pulled me back.

"Did I tell you that I love this new hair?" he asked while holding my waist.

"Yeah, you did, but I don't mind hearing it again." I giggled.

"Would it be rude if I kissed you?" he asked, and my heart raced.

"It would be rude if you didn't kiss me," I whispered and leaned in to lay one on him.

After a few minutes of kissing like high school kids, I stepped out on a line and offered myself to him. "Maine, I want you bad."

"Baby, I want you too." He reached under my dress and played with my panties.

"Take me right here," I moaned.

"Outside?"

"Yeah, it's dark. No one will see us." I giggled.

"Are you sure?" He scanned the quiet street.

"Are you scared?" I laughed and removed my underwear. Back in the day, both Mario and I were spontaneous. I guess old habits die hard.

"Girl, I ain't ever scared." He reached into his car and removed a Magnum condom from the glove compartment. In one swift motion, Maine lifted me onto the hood of the car and entered me. The warmth from the engine was no match for the warmth I was experiencing inside my body.

"Oh, Maine," I moaned loud enough for him to hear but not the neighbors.

"Nikki, you're so wet." He plunged deeper into me as I grinded on him.

I closed my eyes while he sucked my nipples through my dress and bit down gently. We had sex on the hood of that car for about forty minutes. I came multiple times, but he only came once.

When Maine pulled out of me, I noticed something in his face that made me uncomfortable. "What's wrong?" I slid off the car and fixed my dress.

"The condom broke."

"What?" I damn near shouted.

"I'm so sorry, Nikki," he said while fastening his pants.

"That's okay." I smiled. "Let me get in the house to clean up this mess."

"Can I walk you up?"

"No, go ahead. I'll be okay." I waved bye as he pulled out of the driveway. I needed to get to the bathroom to remove his sperm ASAP.

"For real?" I heard Mario say from the shadows, and I pissed on myself a little.

"Rio, what the fuck are you doing here?" I fumbled with my key.

He approached me from a dark corner. I made a mental note to get my porch light fixed in the morning.

"Who was that nigga?" Mario followed me into the house as I disarmed the alarm.

"Why does it matter, and what are you even doing here?" I removed my shoes and set them neatly by the door along with my purse. Just as I tried to make a mad dash upstairs, Rio grabbed my arm.

"Answer my fuckin' question!"

"You answer mine!" I yelled over him.

"I came to see my son."

"At midnight?" I smacked my lips. "Let me go." I snatched my arm away and ran upstairs into the bathroom to clean myself up.

"So, you fuckin' strangers outside on the car now?" He followed behind me and stood in the doorway of the bathroom. When he saw the white slime oozing from my vagina, he really hit the roof. "And you let dude hit it raw!"

"First of all, the condom broke! Second of all, you don't need to concern yourself with whom I'm sleeping with." I washed my hands, placed my towel on the towel rack, and went back downstairs. Once again, he followed behind me, flopping down on my couch and putting his leg up.

"Get your feet off my couch." I dialed Anjela on my cell phone. "Hey, cuz, thank you for watching Junior. You can bring him home now. I'm back." I went into the kitchen to retrieve a bottle of water. "Yeah . . . right . . . yeah." I one-worded her because Mario was all up in my conversation. "Okay, bye."

I tossed my phone on the couch and stared at Mario, who looked pissed off. I didn't care that he was mad. It served him right to show up at my house unannounced.

"Your son will be here in thirty minutes." I walked toward the stairs.

"So, are you dating already?" He looked bewildered.

"Yeah, I guess I am." I laughed and skipped back up the stairs with glee. I could still feel Jermaine's juices, so I decided to wash up again.

"Who is he? I need to check him out," he called up the banister.

"He's legit." I stepped into the shower and was out in ten minutes. On my way into my bedroom, I called out to see if Mario was still here.

"I'll be down in a minute," I yelled over the banister.

"Yeah, a'ight." He sounded muffled.

After dressing in an orange Detroit Tigers T-shirt and white stretch pants, I made my way downstairs. Once again, I was caught off guard by Mario, who was standing there like a goon.

"What the fuck is this shit?" he screamed, waving my Android around.

I stared at the video of Gucci from earlier but remained silent. I really wasn't going to send the video to Rio. I had only threatened her for leverage.

"Nikki, you heard me."

"Why were you going through my shit anyway?" I snatched my phone back.

"Because I can!" he responded.

"I don't know why you are getting hostile with me." I smacked my lips. "Instead of checking my phone, you need to go home and check your wife's."

"Look, tell my son I came by."

"Leaving so soon?" I giggled.

"Whatever, Nikki." Rio started down the steps and toward the door. "Oh yeah, your girl Chloe is full of shit. She didn't kill Tre'."

"Well, who did?" I asked.

"You don't need to know all of that. Just know I have the real facts, so you can tell that bogus bitch to kick rocks." Mario stormed out the front door and let it slam behind him.

Chapter 102

Lovely

"I swear on my life, I'm ready to kill somebody." I paced the small cell.

"What's the matter?" Chloe asked.

"It's Maine and some bitch, I know it!" I had tried to let Tiny calm me down, but my mind was back at it again.

"What?" she asked for clarification.

"Maine hasn't been to visit me in two weeks. I call the house, and he always sound preoccupied. I asked him why hasn't he come down here, and it's always this excuse or that. I know he is fucking somebody else."

"Girl, calm down."

"How can you tell me to calm down when you're in the same damn boat as me?" I looked at her like she was stupid. "I need to get out of here." I slapped the concrete wall.

"Now, that's the shit I want to talk about right there. Instead of harping on these men, we need to be planning our escape."

"You've been watching too many movies. Can't nobody break out of here." I smacked my lips and walked out of the cell.

"Where are you going?"

"I need to call Maine before lockdown," I said and headed for the phone.

On my way down the hall, I tried to calm my nerves, but it didn't work. The minute Maine accepted my collect call, I went off.

"Who the fuck is she?"

"Who is who, Lovely?" He sighed.

"The bitch that's keeping you from being here," I yelled.

"I keep telling you I'm out here trying to get you back home. Yeah, I missed a few visits. So what! Look at the bigger picture!" he yelled back.

"The bigger picture is that I'm in this stale, stinking, disease-infested place, and you're on the outside, living life without me."

"What do you want me to do?"

"I want you to be a man and tell me who got your attention," I snapped.

"Everything I'm doing out here on these streets is for you. Why can't you understand that?" He was getting tired of me.

"Tell me what exactly are you doing for me, Maine? Every time I see my lawyer, nothing has changed. I still have court next month, and Meechie is still going to testify." I was fed up.

"Lovely, calm down," Maine spoke softly.

"Fuck you and that bitch! You ain't ever got to come and see about me," I said and slammed the phone back onto the receiver. My outburst had caught the attention of a guard, and before I knew it, she was all up in my face.

"Calm down, inmate, before I pepper spray you!" she yelled.

"Pepper spray me for what? This doesn't have anything to do with you." I rolled my eyes and tried to walk away, but she reached for my shoulder, and I turned around and pushed her. We tussled for about two minutes before I was forced to the ground and detained with plastic hand ties. I knew I was out of line, but today, I had woken up on the wrong side of the cot. Nightmares of giving birth in prison will do that to you.

Chapter 103

Gucci

It had been three weeks since the video incident with Nikki, and Mario still had not said a word. Although he remained silent, I knew he knew something, because he was acting strange. Lately, he had been catching more attitudes than necessary with me, and sex was nonexistent. There was no way he knew that I spent time with Cartier at his house, because I had Satin pick me up and bring me home. I was tired of the tension between us, and I needed a way to smooth shit over, so I went into his office and invited him for dinner.

"We haven't had a date night in a minute. Would you like to go out to eat with me?" I took a seat on the arm of his leather chair.

"Where?" was all he said, not once looking up from the computer screen.

"I don't know, but I'll surprise you." I rubbed his back, and he tensed up.

"What time?"

"In about an hour if that's okay with you." I stood.

"Okay."

Just as I reached the doorway, I heard a cell phone ring. "Who is this?" Mario said and pressed speaker phone.

"Dog, you know who this is, so let's cut the small talk," the caller said.

"I'm listening."

"Like I told your girl before, Meechie need not be present at my girl's trial."

"I'm trying to figure out what it is you expect me to do. My uncle is in witness protection." Mario looked at me.

"I expect you to do what you got to do! I'm not one to keep repeating myself, so I'm going to say this one more time. If my bitch doesn't come home, neither does yours!" *Click.*

"Fuck!" Mario slammed the phone down.

"Don't stress, baby. We will work this out." I walked back over to the desk.

"I don't know what this cat wants me to do. I don't even know where Meechie is, and if I did, I'd be damned if I'd hand my mother's brother over to that nigga."

"Come on. Let's talk about it over dinner. You know we strategize best over food." I smiled because I knew this was my way out of the doghouse.

We entered Erica's food joint on Six Mile and were immediately shown to our booth.

"Damn, this place is a throwback for real." Mario took his seat at our usual spot in the back. The owner, Erica, used to sell dinners on the block back in the day, and we were her favorite customers. There was nothing like her cooking anywhere in Detroit, and Mario wanted to see her succeed, so he gave her the money to open up her restaurant. It had been open for about seven years now, and her business was thriving.

"I wonder if Erica is here." I scanned the place to see if I could spot her, and there she was, walking toward us.

"What's up, nephew?" She placed a bottle of champagne on the table and sat down beside Mario. "What's up, niece?"

"Hey, Auntie Erica," we both said on cue.

"What can I get for y'all tonight?" Erica dabbed sweat from her forehead. The place was crowded, and I imagined she'd been working hard that day.

"Auntie, let me get that chicken lasagna." I licked my lips, anticipating the delectable meal.

"Let me get the ribs, greens, dressing, and macaroni," Mario said without looking at the menu.

"All right, I'll have your food right out." She stood from the table and grabbed our menus. "Dinner is on me."

"Thanks, Auntie."

I stared at Mario as he looked out the window. My husband looked so handsome when he was deep in thought. Just as I was about to bring up the Meechie thing, I noticed a familiar face approaching, and my stomach turned.

"Girl, I thought that was you." Cartier stopped at our booth and bent down to hug me. Instantly, my body stiffened, and my heart dropped to my stomach.

"Hey, Cartier." I cleared my throat. "This is my husband, Mario. Mario, this is my good friend, Cartier." I fumbled through the introduction.

"Good friend?" Cartier looked offended.

My eyes pleaded with him not to make this worse for me, but in true Cartier fashion, he carried on.

"I'd say we're more than that." He smiled.

"Nigga, you got one muthafuckin' second to remove yourself from this table." Mario spoke through clenched teeth.

Cartier challenged Mario by pulling up a chair to the table. "Or what?"

I watched the two alpha males stare each other down for what seemed like an hour, yet in reality only lasted two seconds.

Crash! Mario took the champagne bottle off the table and smashed it up against Cartier's head, then followed up with a combo to the face. Cartier was stunned but unstoppable as he tackled Mario to the ground. *Wham! Whop!*

I took a large gulp of water and watched the show. I knew better than to throw myself in between two men. In my peripheral, I caught those flashing red and blue lights we hated so much. I grabbed my purse and yelled the word every hood nigga across America can hear in his sleep.

"Hook!"

Just like that, all the fighting ceased. In a matter of minutes, police were coming through the front door, and we were exiting the back.

"Are you fucking that nigga?" Mario spat blood to the ground as we hustled over to the Range Rover.

"No!" I shouted as Cartier zoomed past us like a nigga with warrants.

"Are you fucking that nigga, Gucci?" Mario hemmed me up against the car.

"I said no! Now, get your fuckin' hands off of me." I tried prying his hands off of my shoulder.

"I swear to God I will kill your bitch ass if you're fuckin' around on me," Mario yelled.

"I said I'm not fucking him!" I yelled and fumbled with my purse, trying to reach for my precious .22 handgun.

Mario finally let me go and went around to the driver's side of the vehicle. I stormed off down the street because I was pissed. He followed behind me for three blocks before I gave in and got into the car. If it wasn't for the pain in my feet, I would've kept going.

On the ride home, Mario said nothing, so I took the opportunity to speak. "Cartier was my first boyfriend. He went to jail before I started running with you," I explained.

"That's all fine and good, but why was the nigga hugging you like y'all just fucked last night?" Mario gripped the wheel so tight the side of his hands turned red.

"He just did that shit to get you mad."

"Kudos to that nigga, because it worked." He took his eyes off the road and faced me. "Anything else you wanna tell me?"

"Like what?" I shrugged. I didn't owe him any explanation about my life before I knew him.

"For starters, you can tell me why that nigga was palming your ass a few weeks ago." He raised an eyebrow.

"That bitch!" I spat. And to think I actually gave her credit.

"Naw, don't blame your fuck up on Nikki. She didn't even show me the video." He turned right and took the corner so hard I flew up against the door.

"Slow the fuck down!" I fastened my seatbelt.

"You better start talking," he warned.

"Look," I snapped. "I went downtown, and my whip got towed. I called you, but you didn't answer. I called Satin and Mina, and they were both unavailable."

"This is Detroit. Cabs run like buses!" Mario cut me off.

"Would you shut the fuck up and let me finish? Damn!" I smacked my lips. "As I waited for a cab to take me to my hair appointment, Cartier was leaving the court building. He offered to take me, and that was that. When we pulled up to the salon, he got out and opened my door. Just as your ex walked out, he reached for my ass, but I quickly put him in his place. He knows we're married and we have a daughter. He just wants to be hardheaded." I sighed.

"Well, a hard head makes a soft ass. You better tell that nigga not to get got!" Mario rolled down the window and hawked spit. "I'll fuck around and have that nigga come up missin'."

"Anyway, since Nikki didn't show you the video, how did you know there was a video in the first place?" I crossed my arms and watched him squirm.

Chapter 104

Chloe

Lovely had been in the hole for a few weeks now, and I was really concerned about her, but there was nothing I could do.

"Jones, you have a visitor."

I figured it was Nikki again, so I made no effort to check my appearance. The worse I looked, the guiltier she would feel. As I walked in the open room, I scanned the sea of faces and almost pissed myself when I spotted Sam. I'd put him on my visitors list when I first got there, but never imagined he would show up. Instantly, I smoothed out my hair and slid my tongue across my teeth to get any leftover residue.

"Hi, baby." I smiled nervously.

"Chloe." He nodded and gestured for me to sit down. I noticed his eyes land on my stomach, so I made a show of taking my seat with this huge belly.

"It's nice to see you again." I glanced over his tall frame and noted that he hadn't changed one bit. Still fine as ever.

"So, I heard you were looking for me." He got straight to the point as if he didn't want to be there.

"Yeah." I smiled, although my feelings were hurt. "As you see, I'm pregnant. Obviously, I can't keep the baby

in here, and I don't have any family, so I need you to take
her." Recently, a doctor in the infirmary had given me an
ultrasound and told me I was expecting a little girl.

"Is it mine?" Sam didn't even blink.

I wanted to go the hell off, but I would end up in the
hole like Lovely, so I played it cool. "Sam, you know this
baby is yours."

"I don't know shit." He flexed his jaw muscles.

"Well, I'm sure you know that I wouldn't be in here if I
told the cops it was you that pulled the trigger." I smirked.

"I bet you would've pinned the murder on me if you
could've, but my prints weren't on the gun." He smiled.

"Anyway, are you going to take custody of our daughter?" I switched the subject because he was right. If I
wouldn't have been driving that truck and my prints
weren't on the gun, I certainly would've dropped dime
on Sam.

"Sign this." He slid a document my way.

I frowned as I read the contents. It stated that after
giving him sole custody, I wouldn't have any contact
with him or my daughter.

Chapter 105

Mina

I unloaded the last box from my apartment into our new house, and I was thankful that I had never fully unpacked in the first place. Just as I carried the box into the kitchen, I heard the side door open.

"I'm in the kitchen, Sam."

"Hey, baby." He kissed my neck and grabbed a Pepsi from the fridge.

"Hey, how was the visit?" I took a seat on the stool and stared at him. The visit had been on my mind all day.

"Well, her ass is definitely pregnant." He sighed heavily.

"What does that mean for us?" I held my breath because things could've gone sideways fast. He could've gone there and rekindled his love for her, leaving me high and dry once again.

"The baby doesn't stop my feelings for you, Mina. I still want to be with you, but this does change things." He sighed again, and my stomach tightened. "Once I get custody of my daughter, she will be with me forever. I need to know that you can handle that before we move forward."

"Of course I can." I stood and went over to him. "As long as we're together, nothing else matters." I smiled.

"That's good to hear." He picked me up and placed me on the countertop. "I love you." He kissed me passionately.

"I love you more, baby."

"How much do you love a nigga?" He raised a brow while tugging on his zipper.

I got the hint and slipped down off the counter while removing my T-shirt. I dropped the shirt, my jeans, panties, bra, and socks in a trail leading to the bedroom door. I was completely naked, and Sam followed suit.

Chapter 106

Gucci

"So, have you talked to Cartier?" Satin asked over lunch at P.F. Chang's.

"Not since the scene he caused."

"Good," she said while reading her menu. "That boy ain't nothing but trouble for your marriage."

"I didn't come out with you for lectures." I rolled my eyes.

"What's new on the home front?" she asked.

"Nothing much. It's actually been pretty quiet. There has been no drama from Nikki, although I'm waiting for a rematch."

"Girl, you need to let that beef with Nikki go. Let her have that one and move on." Satin sipped water from her glass. "Anyway, have you guys heard anything on the Meechie situation?"

"Nope. Mario can't get in touch with his uncle, but he has someone looking into Maine. We need to find this nigga before he comes at us again."

"Girl, don't look now, but there goes Nikki with some fine-ass nigga. I guess she finally moved on." Satin tapped my arm.

"Ain't that a bitch!" I said aloud as I watched the nigga who threatened me leave the restaurant with Nikki.

Obviously, they were well acquainted. My mouth dropped as he leaned in for a kiss and nibbled on her neck. Just as I watched them pull off, my cell phone rang.

"Yeah."

"What's your twenty?" Mario asked.

"Out to eat with Satin. I just saw Nikki." I smirked.

"G, we ain't got time to be playing and shit! Why in the fuck you spying on her? You are supposed to be waiting on my call about Maine," Mario said.

"Well, Sherlock, it turns out I didn't need your call after all." I had to contain my laughter. "Your boy Maine just left with Nikki." There was silence on Mario's end of the phone, so I kept talking. "By the looks of it, they know each other very, very well, if you know what I mean."

"What the fuck are you talking about?" Mario was obviously bothered.

"I'm trying to tell you that old boy is probably banging your ex-wife." At that point, I began to laugh hysterically and noticed that Mario had hung up on me. I was willing to bet my life savings that he was about to blow up Nikki's phone at this very minute.

"What's that about?" Satin stared at me.

"Come on. Let's go." I grabbed my purse and headed to the door.

"I didn't even order yet." Satin pouted.

We made it outside after they pulled off. I flew to my car with Satin on my heels. Tossing my purse to the back, I revved the engine and pulled off. It took me about three lights to catch up to them.

"Mind telling me what's going?"

"Nikki is with Maine, the one that came to the house and threatened me."

"Are you sure, Gucci?" Satin buckled her seatbelt.

"I think I would know the muthafucka that pulled a gun out on me." I rolled my eyes.

"Oh, my goodness! Do you think she's in trouble?"

"She didn't appear to be in any danger, but I'm going to follow them and find out where he's taking her, then call Mario and let him handle the rest."

Chapter 107

Nikki

I smirked as Maine and I left the restaurant. Gucci and her friend were staring so hard it was funny.

"Nikki, it's been my pleasure yet again." Maine held my hand as we waited on valet.

"Maine, don't take this the wrong way, but I don't want to go to bed alone tonight." I knew I was being too forward, but my wants outweighed my need to act ladylike. Ever since our wonderful night a month ago, I'd craved his body. For a long time, it had been just me and my silver bullet. Now that I'd been exposed to penis again, my womanhood yearned for his manhood daily.

"I don't want to go to bed alone either." Maine hugged me as the car pulled up.

It was something about him that had me open and ready to enjoy what he had to offer. Things with Maine were different than things with Mario, and I enjoyed his company. Never in a million years did I believe I could find someone to restore my heart and replace my feelings for Rio.

Just as I fastened my seatbelt, my cell phone rang. Speak of the devil, it was Mario. I debated on answering the call. Eventually, I decided to send him to voicemail. He called back about four times in a row.

"You might want to answer that." Maine looked at my phone.

"It's my ex-husband." I pressed end on the phone.

"It could be important."

"I doubt it. His wife Gucci just saw us. She probably called him, and now he is calling me to cock block." I placed the phone back into my purse.

"Gucci?" Maine asked with familiarity.

"Do you know her?"

"Sounds familiar," he replied without shifting his gaze from the road.

"Well, she was a stripper at the Doll House. You might know her from there."

"Yeah, maybe that's it." Maine switched lanes.

I pulled the mirrored visor down to reapply my makeup and caught sight of the craziest shit in the world. Gucci had the nerve to be following me.

"Unbelievable."

"What's wrong?" Maine asked.

"The bitch is following us." I closed the visor and turned around in my seat.

"What?"

"That's her in the loud-ass pink Charger. She's probably trying to start shit with me again. You need to lose her," I demanded, and that's exactly what he did.

Chapter 108

Chloe

When I walked into the cell for lights out, Lovely was asleep on the bottom bunk. She must've returned from her stay in the hole while I was in the recreation room watching the Maury show. I tapped her legs lightly.

"What's up, stranger?"

"Hey, girl!" She yawned and stretched. "Did you miss me?"

"Like crazy." We both laughed. "Are you okay?" She slid over, and I sat down on her cot.

"I've seen better days, but I'll be all right." She wiped sleep from her weary green eyes.

I could tell Lovely was just as tired of this place as me. People on the outside could never fully understand the ramifications of prison life. It wasn't for the weak-hearted for sure.

"This place will get the best of you, so I understand, girl." I patted her shoulder.

"I had a meeting with my lawyer today. They said the prosecutor has offered me a plea deal." She sat up and leaned against the wall.

"What's the deal?" I sat back too.

"If I plead guilty to shooting the cop, they will drop the charge for the other man." She sighed.

"So, what's the sentence you'll get for the plea?" I asked, knowing it couldn't be much better than what she would be facing if she went to trial.

"One life sentence instead of two." She sniffed, and I noticed that she was crying.

"Lovely, we will get out of here, I swear." I tried to console her, but she wasn't hearing me.

"Face the facts. The only way I'm leaving here is in a body bag." She cried harder. "My child will never know me, and my man has moved on."

"You don't know that for sure."

"Today, when I came out of the hole, I called my best friend Coco, and she confirmed my suspicions. Maine is messing with some trick named Nikki who used to be married to a street boss named Mario," she explained.

At the sound of the familiar names, my mouth dropped. "Are you sure?"

"Yeah, I'm sure. Coco owns a popular hair salon, and all the hood gossip flows through there."

"What if I told you that I knew Nikki?" I stared at her.

"I would ask you to pretend you don't, because there is nothing I can do about it in here." She wiped her eyes.

"What if I told you that I've been devising a plan to get us out of here while you were in the hole?" I held my breath.

"I would tell you I'm game. At this point, whatever you've planned is worth a shot. What else do I have to lose?" She blinked rapidly.

Chapter 109

Lovely

I was sick as hell for days after Coco spilled the beans about Maine, and I'd been sent to the infirmary twice. The medical staff couldn't find anything wrong with me or the baby, but I knew it was because of my broken heart. There were so many questions on my mind, and I decided to call home for answers.

"What's up, Lo? How have you been holding up in there?" Do It asked.

"Is Maine cheating on me? Be straight up!" I demanded to see if my brother would lie.

"Lo . . ." He paused.

"Don't play, DeShawn." I called him by his government name.

"Look, I ain't ever lied to you before, and I'm not going to sugar coat shit now. Maine is doing what he has to do to bring you home." He sighed.

"What in the hell does that mean?" I snapped. Although I had an attitude, I spoke in hushed tones. I didn't need to alert any authorities and definitely didn't want a second trip to the hole.

"It means just be cool. This will work out. You'll see."

"DeShawn, I don't see shit but prison bars and jumpsuits! I got word from a reliable source that Maine was fucking some bitch named Nikki, and I just wanted to see if you were actually sitting by and watching that shit go down."

"Lo, you're my sister. Do you think I would sit by and let a nigga mess over you?" He sounded sincere.

"I don't know what to think anymore. All I know is that I've got people in my ear telling me my man is caked up with the next bitch." I didn't want to give Coco up, because she was only looking out for me.

"All I'm asking you to do is trust me. There is a reason behind everything, I promise."

"You sound like Maine." I rolled my eyes.

"One thing I know for sure is that he loves you and is willing to go to hell and back if it means bringing you home."

"Hopefully I'll be home sooner than you think."

I thought about Chloe's plan. She'd drilled the whole thing into my head play-by-play, and I was anxious. At this point, I had nothing to lose. I was prepared to break out of this hellhole or die trying.

Chapter 110

Gucci

"Hey, girl, what's up?" I answered Satin's call.

"You need to get down to the Doll House now!"

"Why? What happened?" I asked with panic. Although I'd been spending less time at the strip club, it was still in my heart and one of my main priorities.

"We only have three girls tonight." She spoke over the loud music. "And we have a huge party scheduled."

"We only have three girls? What happened to the rest of them hoes?" I rolled my eyes. There were only three rules at my club, and all my dancers knew them well. Rule number one: no sex; rule number two: no drugs; and rule number three stated there was to always be a minimum of eight dancers per night, especially on weekends.

"Girl, T.I. and Jeezy are doing a concert in Pontiac, so they probably went up that way." Satin smacked her lips.

"Damn!" I cursed just as Mario walked into our bedroom. I watched him as he flopped down on the bed and reached for the television remote. His mother was watching Maria so that we could spend some alone time together. However, my husband hadn't said one word to me all day. What a waste!

"Okay, I'll call Mina, and then I'll meet you there." I sighed and hung up.

"Where are you going?" Mario asked.

"Oh, now you can see me. All day I could've sworn I was invisible." I went into my closet and retrieved my dance wear.

"I asked you a question," he said after muting the TV.

I grabbed my bag and purposely waited about five minutes before responding, just to make him mad. "I'm going to the club because they're short-handed." I walked into the bathroom to freshen up.

"You ain't going to no damn strip club, Gucci," Mario hollered over the sound of the running water.

"Look, the Doll House is my club, and those are my dancers. I will not leave them hanging because you're having a sucka attack." I came out of the bathroom and slipped into a fresh pair of Victoria's Secret panties and bra.

"Ain't nobody havin' a sucka attack, but I don't think somebody's wife should be bouncing up and down on some damn poles." He stood from the bed and walked into the closet.

"Mario, chill out! You knew what my profession was when you met me at sixteen. You knew what my profession was when you married me, and you're the person that bought the club for me." I sprayed Chanel Number Five on my body after greasing up with almond oil. "Why are you acting brand new?"

"I'm not acting brand new. You just need to grow up and stop living your life like you ain't got a husband or a fucking kid to raise."

"I know what this is." I laughed. "You want me to be Nikki, right, Mario? You want me to play the damsel in distress, always waiting for you to come save me?"

"This ain't got shit to do with her!" he yelled.

"It has everything to do with that bitch, and you know it!" I snapped.

"Whatever, dog!" He stepped from the closet fully dressed. "You do what the fuck you wanna do. I'm out of this bitch!" He grabbed his cell phone.

"What the hell is that supposed to mean?" I snapped.

"It means that I'm tired of fighting with you." Mario threw up deuces and hustled down the stairs then out the door. He had been really irritated with me ever since I failed to catch up with Nikki and Maine. He tried to call her ratchet ass several times, but every call went unanswered. He even swung by her crib, but she was blowing him off, and he didn't like it.

Chapter 111

Nikki

"Mommy," Junior called from his room.

"Yes, baby?" I walked across the hallway.

"Movie." He waived *The Lion King* DVD in the air.

I took the movie and picked my son up. "Junior, are you sure you want to watch this again?" I frowned because this would be my fifth time watching this with him this week. My son didn't say anything. Instead, he bobbed his head up and down.

"All right. I guess you win." I tickled him and headed downstairs for popcorn.

Just after I sat Junior down on the couch and went into the kitchen, my doorbell rang.

"Who is it?" I called out.

"It's Rio."

"Daddy!" Junior jumped up and down. He was happy, but I was irritated. Mario might as well have had a key, because he'd been there more times than a little bit.

"What are you doing here?" I asked while swinging the door open. The look on his face told me that he was troubled.

"Hey, little man." He barged in and picked up his anxious son. "I missed you."

"I missed you too, Daddy." Junior squeezed his daddy around the neck. "Movie, Daddy." Junior pointed to the television.

"Were you and Mommy about to watch a movie?" Mario asked as I still stood holding the doorknob.

"Yup."

"Is it okay if Daddy watches the movie with you and Mommy?" Mario stared at me while asking his question.

"Yay!" Junior jumped up and down.

"Is that okay with you?" Mario put Junior down.

"I really wish you would've asked me before you put him in the middle." I folded my arms.

I guess Junior could tell my tone was unhappy, because he ran over to me and grabbed my legs. "Pleeeeeeease," he begged, and Mario joined in.

"I guess it's okay, but after the movie, you have to go to bed, and Daddy has to go home," I warned them both before they could cook up any more ideas.

Chapter 112

Mina

As a favor to my friend, I climbed out of my cozy bed with Sam and met her at the club. Luckily, my cabaret license hadn't expired yet.

"Thank you so much." She hugged me tight as I entered the dressing room.

"It's not a problem, girl. I got you." I smiled and went over to my old locker. It was still unoccupied, so I reclaimed it for the night. "It's a lot of people out there," I added.

"Yeah, Cartier is having a welcome back party." Gucci disrobed and revealed a sheer outfit.

"Cartier?" I slammed the locker and went over to her at the makeup table. "You little tramp." I laughed, and she did too.

"It's not like that. Satin didn't tell me whose party it was when she called."

"Yeah, okay." I rolled my eyes. Just then, we heard Gucci's name over the loudspeaker, asking the crowd to welcome her back to the stage.

"Wish me luck." She winked, and I followed behind her, because I had to the see the show she was about to put on for her ex.

Just as we hit the main floor, a spotlight dropped on Gucci, and the house lights dimmed. The rapper named Future blared over the speaker. *"Turn off the lights . . . I'm looking for her."*

The crowd cheered and whistled as Gucci did her thing. Once she was on stage, she stood there and yelled, "I ain't doing shit until I see the bread!" and just like that, money came from everywhere. Right on cue, the DJ played the new song "Bands Will Make Her Dance," and the crowd got even more hype. After a second or two of that rap music, the DJ turned on a slow mix, and Gucci went to work like never before on the Beyoncé song "Dance for You."

I smirked to myself, because she was putting in work for Cartier and he was enjoying every minute of it. The look on his face told it all. The two of them definitely had chemistry. As a matter of fact, they appeared to have more chemistry than she and Mario did.

Chapter 113

Chloe

Tonight was the night, and it was now or never. For several days, I had been coaching Lovely on how to execute the plan that was going to get us out of there. As soon as Sister Mary, our resident nun, and the corrections officer walked past, it was on and poppin'. As we patiently waited, my adrenaline raced, and my heartrate quickened. I swear the sound of my beating heart was loud enough to wake the dead. I needed to calm down.

Right on schedule, they reached our cell door. "Do one of you ladies need prayer tonight?" Sister Mary spoke through the open flap. On Tuesdays and Thursdays, the facility allowed nuns from a local outreach program to come and pray with inmates. I noticed this scheduled event from the moment I became a resident and immediately knew I could use it to my advantage.

"Yes, Sister Mary, I do." Lovely stood from the bed. During rehearsal, I told her to rub her swollen belly for good measure as I faced the wall and pretended to snore lightly.

"What seems to be troubling you, my dear?" Sister Mary was the first black nun I'd ever laid eyes on, except for Whoopi Goldberg in the movie *Sister Act*.

"It's the baby. I think there's something wrong, and I need you to pray for me." Lovely cried softly.

"Father God—" the sister started, but Lovely cut her off.

"Please, sister, I need you to lay hands on my stomach if you can," she pleaded. There was no way Sister Mary could fit her arms through the small flap and touch Lovely, so the only other option was for her to go inside.

"I can't let you go in there, sister," the officer said. "Brown, you're out of luck." She attempted to shut Lovely down, but my girl didn't skip a beat.

"Please!" Lovely cried harder, and I thought she was auditioning for a movie role. "All I'm asking for is a prayer for my unborn baby. Can't an inmate get that? We are all God's children, right?"

"Open this cell, please." Sister Mary spoke softly.

"Sister, I can't do that." The officer was adamant.

"This woman is in turmoil and needs my help." Sister was persistent.

"But—"

"What would our Savior do?" Sister Mary's words must've spoke volumes to the officer, because I heard the cell door open.

"You've got five minutes, Sister." The officer stood guard outside the cell. She was ready and waiting for something to go down, but right on cue, there was a call over the walkie-talkie that all hands were needed on deck down the hall. "Sister, you've got to come with me," the officer started, but by then, Sister Mary was in her prayer zone on the main line with the Lord. After the second call for assistance, the officer had no choice but to leave Sister Mary alone with us. "I'll be right back," she said and slammed the cell door locked.

Instantly, I sprang to my feet like a jack-in-the-box. "Sister, I'm going to need you to undress." I demanded while removing a makeshift shank from the spine of a novel I'd borrowed from Cupcake titled *Money Over Everything*. I'd made the weapon with a spork I'd been given for lunch. To my surprise, the sister not only didn't utter a word, but she didn't fight against us. She simply stopped praying and undressed as told.

Within minutes, I was in her clothes, and she was in mine. I taped her mouth, wrists, and ankles with the tape another inmate had stolen for me. I positioned her on my bunk and faced her toward the wall just like I had been lying. After tossing my blanket on top of her, I had not a minute to spare before the corrections officer approached the cell. I placed my hand on Lovely's belly and began to pray like my life depended on it.

"I'm sorry about that, Sister." The officer apologized, none the wiser to what had taken place.

"It's okay." I purposely disguised my voice to mimic Sister Mary's. "This woman needs to see a doctor."

Chapter 114

Nikki

"Thank you for putting him to bed." I was on the floor, picking up little fragments of crushed popcorn.

"That's my son. You don't have to thank me." Mario bent down to assist me. "You could just use the vacuum."

"And risk waking him back up?" I shook my head.

"I need to talk to you about your boy Maine." He cut to the point.

"How did find out his name?" I was curious.

"Nikki, that nigga ain't who he's pretending to be." Mario stood.

"Since you seem to know so much about him, tell me what he is exactly." I folded my arms.

"For starters, his ass is a killer," Mario announced. "His chick is doing a bid at WVC behind some shit with Uncle Meechie. He approached Gucci a while back, trying to get us to stop Meechie from testifying so his girl could walk. I told him to beat it, and he told me if his girl didn't come home, mine wouldn't either."

"You're lying." I knew Mario was telling the truth, though, because the WVC was where I'd met Maine. I just didn't want to believe it.

"I wish I were lying, Nik. Originally, I thought he would come after Gucci, so I put protection on her, but I see he got to you too."

Instantly, fear and embarrassment came over me. Not only did I feel stupid for thinking that someone other than Rio could be interested in me, but I had also slept with this man, and there was a good possibility that I could be pregnant by him. For days now, I'd been ignoring my morning sickness, acting like the symptoms didn't exist.

"What's wrong?" Mario stepped closer to me.

"I feel used," I admitted.

"Nik, I'm sorry I had to break it to you like this. I would've told you sooner if I knew that was him outside with you that night. Gucci saw you and Maine at a restaurant about two weeks ago, and I've been trying to get at you ever since."

"I knew she saw me, and I ignored you because I thought you were trying to cock block." I hung my head low because I was devastated. I'd been used by someone I thought was really into me.

"If it makes you feel better, I miss you." Mario licked his lips, and I bit mine.

I'd been fighting my true feelings, and I prayed for resistance, especially while I was vulnerable right now.

"How are things at home?" I tried to change the subject and walk away.

"Why you act like you don't miss me?" He cornered me in the kitchen.

"I do miss you," I finally admitted. "But what do you want me to do, Mario?" I shrugged my shoulders.

"You can start by telling me that you missed me too." He kissed my neck, and I damn near fainted. "Better yet, why don't you show me how much you've missed me?" Mario picked me up and pinned me against the wall.

"Stop," I barely whispered. Honestly, I wanted this, but it was wrong.

"Open your legs," he demanded, and I did as I was told, letting my nightgown rise up my thighs. The minute the heat from my bare vagina touched his jeans, he was as hard as a rock. "I want you, Nikki."

"I want you too." I kissed his lips, and my juices began to flow. There was something about Rio and me that felt right, so I went with the flow.

Within minutes, he was inside of me, laying pipe like a professional plumber. We went at each other like teenagers. We made love on the stove, the sink, and we even made love while standing up against the refrigerator. The whole event lasted an hour. I came a few times, and so did he.

Just as we were about to do it doggy style on the island in the center of the kitchen, his cell phone rang.

"Yeah," he answered, stopping mid-stroke. I was too tired to put up a fuss, so I didn't. "You sure?" He pulled out of me. "I'm on the way."

"Gucci?" I asked while readjusting my attire. At the mention of her name, I actually felt bad for sleeping with Mario.

"No, that was Sam." Mario grabbed my dish towel and wiped his unit off.

"Sam is back?"

"Yeah, he showed back up about a month ago. I got him handling some shit for me with Maine, and I need to go and check it out. I'm sorry I have to leave like this." He smiled. "But I will be back soon."

"Boy, stop." I laughed. "This was nothing more than a booty call. You just happened to be in the right place at the right time, but you won't catch me slippin' again."

"You know you missed this dick." He smirked and walked toward the front door.

"Whatever!"

"Aye, Nik, if your boy Maine calls or comes by, don't answer," he warned.

"Okay." I nodded, prepared to chain-lock my door after Mario left.

"I would die if something ever happened to you, girl." He kissed me.

"Please be careful, because I would die if something happened to you too." I closed the door behind him.

Chapter 115

Mina

Sam had just picked me up from the Doll House when he spotted someone suspicious parked near the back door of the club.

"What's wrong, baby?" I asked.

"What door does Gucci leave from?"

"She always goes out the back. Why? What's up?" I asked, none the wiser.

"Because some dude has been parked back there ever since I pulled up." He squinted, trying to get a clearer image. "I'm going over there to see what the fuck is up." He reached into the glove compartment for his revolver.

"Be careful," I whispered as Sam approach the vehicle. Honestly, I didn't think it was anyone to be concerned about. I did, however, think it was Cartier, and I feared that Gucci's spot was about to be blown up.

The passenger window rolled down, and out popped a round of fire. Instantly, Sam dove to the ground and flew behind a parked Volkswagen. I slid down onto the floor of the car as best I could and covered my head.

Within seconds, the shooting had stopped, and Sam was back in the car. He didn't wait on me to regain proper seating as he whipped off into the night.

"What's going on?" My voice was unsteady as I tried to regain a sense of composure.

"I never made it to the car before I got shot at. I think that was Maine or one of his goons." Sam fastened my seatbelt just before blowing a red light.

"I hope we're not following this maniac?"

"Baby, I can't let this nigga get away."

He never looked at me as we went speeding down Woodward Ave. Our high-speed chase lasted for about twenty minutes before we turned down a one-way street on Bethune. As we made our way to the end of the block, we noticed the car we had been chasing was in the middle of the street with the doors open. Our enemy could be anywhere right now. The right of the street was a row of houses, and the left side had an apartment building. This was a death trap, and I knew it, yet I said nothing.

Sam parked without cutting the engine off and pulled out his phone to call Mario. Twenty eerie minutes went by, and still, there was no movement. I prayed nothing popped off until backup arrived, because I was sure Sam was down to one bullet.

Finally, my prayers were answered when Mario pulled up like a mad man and stepped from his SUV in full force, accompanied by four other men. Sam jumped out of the car and told me to get into the driver's seat.

"If anything happens, you better pull off," he warned, and I nodded.

Just as they set out to canvas the dark block, there was an explosion of gunfire from the house across the street. Shots rang out from everywhere, and it was hard to see anything. All I could hear was gunshots and men hollering. Someone had been hit, but I didn't know who because the area was covered in smoke.

Fearing the worst, I went against my better judgment and stepped from the car. I knew Sam told me to leave, but I would be damned if I left my man dying on the sidewalk. As soon as I closed the door and dropped to my knees, I heard a crash. A bullet had just burst the driver-side window. Immediately, I froze! For a second, I sat stunned, because had I not moved when I did, that bullet would've pierced my head for sure.

"Sam," I called, but I heard nothing from him. I fanned smoke from my face and gasped when I saw a pair of legs lying out in the middle of the street.

"Oh my God!" I cried and crawled over to the body. Upon further inspection, I noticed the Gucci sneakers did not belong to Sam. I was relieved, but saddened nonetheless, because the face of the shoe owner was familiar. It was Mario! He had been shot and was bleeding profusely. There was no movement, so I frantically searched for a pulse.

"Grab him and let's go!" I heard Sam direct the other men.

They slid Mario over to the waiting SUV, and Sam picked me up off the ground. I was a ball of nerves and crying hysterically. Beside television, I had never seen death so close.

"Is he dead?" I screamed as Sam placed me back into his car. My hands were covered in Mario's blood and trembling uncontrollably.

"Did you feel a pulse?" He was sweating bullets as we pulled off behind the truck like a bat out of hell.

"I don't know. Those men took him before I could tell."

"Fuck!" Sam punched the dashboard.

Without a word, I stared down at my blood-stained hands and pondered how in the world I would be able to tell my friend that her husband may be dead. Mario had been shot in the head, and pieces of his flesh were no longer intact.

To be continued . . .

The Real Hoodwives of Detroit 2

Coming in June 2021

Dear Readers,

*Thank you again for taking this ride with me. It's my prayer, these stories are especially entertaining and leave you wanting more. I know most of you guys were anticipating more of Lovely, Maine, and Do It, from Dope, Death, and Deception. However, while I have your attention, I wanted to introduce you to some additional characters. It's my desire to demonstrate versatility by writing from the personal perspective of several characters. I know there is a little bit of Nikki, Gucci, Chloe, Tonya, and Mina in all of us, or at the very least, someone we know. **Nikki** just wants to be down for her man but when she realizes that this lifestyle isn't perfect and doesn't just affect her husband, but herself as well as her son, it was almost too late. **Gucci** is just yearning to love and be loved. However, she looks for love in all the wrong places. She was content with being the other woman until she finally got what she thought she wanted, but it wasn't at all what she imagined it to be. **Chloe** is a sneaky bitch who wanted to play by her rules in a game that she thought she'd created. Instead, she got played. **Tonya** made a bunch of mistakes, and unfortunately, it* *was her time to go. She'll never get a second chance to right her wrongs. It's sad because her kids are the ones that suffered by losing their mom, long before she actually died. Ladies, it's okay to party, have a good time, and live the good life, but always make sure that home is taken care of first!* **Mina** *was just a woman that needed to renew her lease on life. It's unfortunate that her husband lost his life in the process. She's now free to start her life over - without abuse. No one deserves to be beaten!*

Now that you've finished The Real Hoodwives of Detroit, I look forward to reading all of your emails, tweets, Instaposts, and posts on facebook. Again, I humbly thank you for all the support.

Until Next Time,
India